WE EAT OUR OWN

A NOVEL

Kea Wilson

WITHDRAWN

SCRIBNER

New York   London   Toronto   Sydney   New Delhi

SCRIBNER
An Imprint of Simon & Schuster, Inc.
1230 Avenue of the Americas
New York, NY 10020

First Scribner hardcover edition September 2016

For information about special discounts for bulk purchases,
please contact Simon & Schuster Special Sales at 1-866-506-1949
or business@simonandschuster.com.

The Simon & Schuster Speakers Bureau can bring authors to
your live event. For more information or to book an event,
contact the Simon & Schuster Speakers Bureau at 1-866-248-3049
or visit our website at www.simonspeakers.com.

Interior design by Kyle Kabel

Manufactured in the United States of America

1 3 5 7 9 10 8 6 4 2

Library of Congress Cataloging-in-Publication Data is available.
ISBN 978-1-5011-2831-8
ISBN 978-1-5011-2833-2 (ebook)

For Herbert and James

WE EAT
OUR OWN

RICHARD

New York

You get the call during a rainstorm. It is 1979.

Your agent doesn't have offers like this for you often—six weeks at two hundred and seventeen dollars a week to fill in for a guy who has just quit the production of an Italian art film with American characters that's shooting right now in the Amazon rain forest somewhere in, I don't know, Brazil or Colombia or Peru, but don't worry about that. We're talking good odds on European and American distribution here, we're talking international exposure here, and we're not even talking supporting cast here, guy: this is the lead role. Plus the script's in English. Plus they've already seen your 8 x 10. And did I mention it's an art film? Because God knows I've heard enough already about how much you need to be doing *art* films, even if that commercial I got for you would have paid SAG union rates—but you know what, never mind now, it's water under the bridge, it's water under the fucking bridge because we have *got* this. We have *already got this* if you would just get yourself up and out that door and onto the train and make it down to this address for a screen test right now, I mean it, kid, right goddamned now or not at all.

1

Yes, I said the Amazon rain forest. Colombia. That's it, I remember now.

No, I don't know anything else about the part.

Yes, I said two hundred and seventeen dollars a week. Six weeks. Do the math on the goddamned train.

Pack a suitcase. You may not have time to go back to your apartment.

The plane to Bogotá leaves in six hours.

· · ·

Let's repeat some things:

You get the call during a rainstorm. It is 1979.

You live in a studio apartment in Queens with your girl-friend, Kay. She won't find out that you've left until she gets home from the architecture firm where she works, half an hour later. Even then, she won't have any idea where you've gone. She'll tug the lightbulb chain in the entryway, her wrists still stiff from the drafting table, a long stripe of charcoal streaked through her blond hair. The bulb will buzz on, hum. She'll call out your name into the single empty room.

You'll have written her a note: four hastily scrawled sentences on a scrap of drafting paper, tossed on the coffee table, where you're sure she'll see it. Three minutes after you leave for the casting agent's office, the radiator will rush on and blow the note into a cobwebbed corner just behind the couch. Kay won't find it for two days. She'll set down the broom. She'll kneel, exhaling hard as she turns the paper over and reads.

Agent called, last minute out of town job. Big deal. I'll call when I know more. I love you.

Even before she finds the note, Kay will know you've left her. She'll know it because you've left her before: fill-ins for

commercial jobs, student productions, all the times you got cast as a last-minute swing on a Midwest musical tour that paid next to nothing. She can recognize it by all the new space that's suddenly opened in the apartment. The hangers swaying on the closet rod. The clean square on the desk where you've dashed aside her pyramid of neatly rolled blueprints in search of a stray résumé. On the floor, there will be a single trail of dustless hardwood, wiped clean by your shirtfront as you belly-crawled to where the suitcases were kept under the bed.

Kay will lie down there, too. She will try to understand what she sees there: crumbs and dust and glittering change, the wide parabola of the bedsprings as they sag under the weight of nothing.

·   ·   ·

Here is something you will never know:

The name of the Italian casting director who regards you as you sprint into that glass-walled Manhattan office. You slough rainwater off your shoulders. You grin as you stammer your apologies, wipe your wet palm on your pants pocket, and thrust it out to him. You do it just like you've always practiced in your audition classes: you enunciate every syllable of your name.

But the casting director keeps his eyes on his lap. He is staring at a 8 x 10 photograph of you, printed in glossy gray-scale. You are grinning in three-quarter profile. You've always been proud of that head shot: it has a Mona Lisa quality to it, the eyes sad and coy in equal measure, a mouth that could double as a smile or a frown. The casting director tosses it to the side table with a hushed sigh. With his other hand, he draws a cigarette to his lips.

You offer him the soaked résumé.

Non importa, the man says.

A second man's voice behind you clucks: Eh. Va' là.

A piece of white butcher paper has been taped to the wall. You don't understand what the men are saying, but you know you are supposed to stand in front of it and you do. The casting director's assistant tugs at all the lamp cords in the room, snaps portrait lights on, fiddles with the tripod. You glance quickly around the room, rushing to get a look at them before the room goes dark: two emaciated men in gray suits, thin lips and pronounced temples, expressionless eyes. The casting director smokes a cigarillo, filling the room with a smell like burned cloth. The assistant curses in Italian, adjusting the portrait lights so they blind you more directly.

You've never done a movie before, not really. Student films and commercial screeners that went nowhere. Nothing like this. The assistant touches the lights more than he touches the camera, angling the bulbs to highlight your bone structure, your posture, your eyes. You make yourself stare straight into the lens. You try to project your thoughts silently through the air, to issue telepathic promises.

You turn left to three-quarters and think:

I will learn Italian if you need me to.

I will sleep for weeks under lean-tos in the jungle with whatever poisonous reptiles you've got.

I will do whatever you need. Just please. Please. Give me this.

You turn full forward. You don't blink. The casting director smokes and murmurs, his fingertips moving on the rim of his ashtray like marsh grasses drifting around the mouth of a sinkhole. The assistant holds a tea saucer behind the bulb and angles it to create a halo of shadow around your head.

Basta, the casting director says. Then, in English: That's enough.

The assistant snaps off the light and shuffles his camera into an equipment case. For a moment, the darkness is total: no one moves to turn the lights back on. There are zips and clatters, the smell of rising smoke. You stay in front of the square of butcher paper, and you could swear you feel it: the casting director still staring, his gaze landing like a throwing knife along your shoulder seam.

Here is something you will never see:

The contact sheet filled with twenty-eight frames of your face, none of them smiling. In some, you are a reverse jack-o'-lantern: the flash flattens the bridge of your nose and shadows clot in the line of your mouth and the hollows of your eyes. But in others, the lighting is straight on. Your dark hair falls to your cheekbones, which your modeling agent back in LA used to call "boyish." Your eyebrows angle toward the fluttering pulse point between your eyes. Your mouth is tensed in that expert Mona Lisa nonsmile, the one that could lean toward agony or laughter with a millimeter's motion of the lips. You trained yourself to smile this way, to look mysterious and indecipherable, to make the casting agent hungry to hear the photograph speak. You located all the minuscule muscles around your mouth and eyes and learned how to use them.

The casting director speaks slowly, his words crowded by an accent like a thick liquid. No, he doesn't have a script. No, he has no more information. He says, You will go here—a vague gesture to a map on the side table—the rain forest. Today.

Thrill is beating in your chest and down your arms, but you try to keep your voice calm. I really don't mean to bother you. I'm sorry. I'm so grateful for the opportunity, it's just—

He stubs the cigarette out and exhales. His smile stuns you. It is full of angular gray teeth.

You tell me now, he says. What is the size of your shoe?

. . .

Here is what you do not know:

The name of the film (*Jungle Bloodbath*).

What the film is about.

What the name of your character is (Richard Trent).

Who the director is.

Anything about the script. (You haven't seen a copy.)

What is out there in the rain forest.

The name of the actor whose place you're taking. (You will never be told.)

Why he quit.

Where he is now.

And, most important, that he was your exact height and within five pounds of your weight. That he *had* seen the script, because this same casting director was the one who gave him a ride to the airport, and the actor had begged it off him on the drive. The actor read the whole thing in the miles between Manhattan and JFK, the pages jolting as the town car swerved onto the shoulder to pass slow traffic. The actor kept reading anyway, a heaviness gathering in his throat.

You don't know anything. No one tells you anything.

No one tells you that the first actor didn't even get on the plane. That he hung back as the rest of the crew handed over their tickets and lined up on the jet bridge, the script clenched in his hands, the last page facing up. When everyone else was through the gate, he grabbed the casting director by the elbow,

steered him over to the long sweep of window. He said, simply, shaking, Man, you've got to drive me home. I can't do this.

You weren't there.

You couldn't have seen the director at that moment. He was six paces past the ticket collector and through the door, leaning against the jet bridge wall and studying his watch. Even if you'd been there, you wouldn't have realized who he was. He is shorter than a director should be, his nails too clean, his clear-frame aviators too cheap. When he turned and looked over his shoulder, his expression was inscrutable; you wouldn't have been able to tell that he was listening.

His name is Ugo Velluto.

You did not see the careful way Ugo set his suitcase down, or the suitcase, hard-shelled, dark green. No one in line noticed as Ugo turned and started to make his way back up toward the gate, though a few crew members leaned out from their desks and stared. The gate agent chirped, Sir, you're not allowed! The director kept walking. Beyond the window, a plane tore through the cloud cover with a sound that shook the air.

The actor braced himself, stammered. I'm sorry, sir, I just—

Ugo walked right past him.

Ugo didn't have to tell the casting director to follow him. He didn't have to raise his voice for the actor, for everyone, to overhear. They stood in front of a newsstand, silhouetted by the frantic colors of a dozen magazine covers. He did not murmur when he spoke.

He told the casting director to find someone who wants this: someone who will take anything that's offered to him, no questions asked.

I want young.

I want unknown.

Check the acting schools.

Avoid anyone unionized.

And don't show him the script, he said. We need someone who is desperate.

The casting director nodded, his gaze avoiding the twitch in the center of the director's left cheek. The actor stared at the balding whorl of hair on the back of the director's head, until he turned around, and then he struggled to find anyplace else to look. The gate agent picked up her blue telephone and murmured something hesitant about a suitcase left on the jet bridge, but when Ugo turned back toward the line, she set the receiver back down.

And make sure he wears a size ten and a half, Ugo added, walking away. We're over budget as is, and I'll be damned if I pay for another pair of boots.

· · ·

Here is how the film begins:

A black screen, white text: *What you are about to see is real.*

A frizz of pink static. Then: a silent blond anchorwoman in a shoulder-padded suit jacket, pressing her third finger to her earpiece.

The footage is pixelated, a recording of a recording. You can hear the faint echo of a PA in the background yelling dead air, dead air, and the anchor shushes him. We have new reports incoming from Colombia, the anchor pronounces. Government officials have recovered evidence that our own reporter, Richard Trent, is—

But then she pauses again.

The ticker tape at the bottom of the screen unspools. No, the

woman says, I'm sorry—we've received evidence that missing journalist Richard Trent *may have* died. Just—hold on—

The ticker capitalizes: CHANNEL 8 JOURNALIST RICHARD TRENT AND TWO CREWMEN HAVE BEEN MISSING FOR SEVEN MONTHS IN THE AMAZON RAIN FOREST PRESUMED—

The anchor leans forward, her eyes still jogging offscreen. Wait, wait, she says. She enunciates: While Trent remains missing, it seems his *footage* has been located. We will warn the viewers that this may be disturbing and young children are not advised to watch. Let's go to it now.

A smash cut to black.

And then we are in the jungle, and we are with you. We are with Richard, the man you will play, and he is full-screen and full-definition.

He is running as fast as he can.

It could be night or it could be day. The leaves around him are so dense. He is ducking under the overhang, razor-edged palm leaves and webs of vines, looking over his shoulder every third step. An animal screams from the canopy. The audio is full of these sounds, the rustle of running thighs, the suck of the mud on the ground, breathing. Richard's pants leg snags and he falls, facedown, palms down. He pushes himself back up and keeps running. He looks over his shoulder again, at whoever is filming him, this person who is getting so close.

There's blood in his eyes, blood running down his neck. The camera is close enough to see that now. The way it's filmed makes the wound look so real. Whoever is holding the camera sprints close, cranks the zoom, gets a tight shot of his face. The nick is on the left eyelid, no place to hide a squib, no way the actor could have struck the blood balloon right there and made a gash that looked like that, no. This is his blood. When the

people who love you watch this film, they will gasp. They will whisper to each other—Jesus, he's really bleeding.

Please! Richard yells, Please, don't—

But halfway through the next word, whoever is holding the camera catches up.

.   .   .

When you are gone, Kay will sort through the closet. She'll find the lumberjack shirt with the threadbare elbows, balled in a corner behind the laundry basket; she'll find the picture in the tin frame.

There's nothing else. You didn't know what to pack, so you took everything you could grab.

The frame is dented at one corner. The picture is of Kay herself: you took it, and your index finger is a pink flare along the upper edge of the shot.

She will lie down in your bed and listen to the radiator rush. The rain will turn to sleet and cling to the windows. You will not be there to see it, and you will never wonder how she must have felt: if this was the moment when she realized that you weren't coming back. The last time you left, you took this picture with you. She will wonder what it means, that this time you left it behind.

She will look at herself, standing on a shoal.

GIUDICE A LATERE: Signor Velluto, you stand accused before the Corte d'Assise of three counts of murder in the second degree, criminal negligence, obscenity, incitements to violence, and conspiracy to commit violence. Do you understand that you will be tried by a panel of eight giudici—

VELLUTO: Yes, yes.

GIUDICE A LATERE:—two of whom have been selected from the primary judiciary and six from amongst the popolari in order to deliver an unbiased judgment—

VELLUTO: Well, if it were unbiased, you'd throw the popolari out.

[Whereupon the procuratore capo whispers to his supporting counsel.]

PROCURATORE CAPO: Is he drunk?

GIUDICE A LATERE: Avvocato, please instruct your client to remain respectful of this court.

AVVOCATO: I will, signore.

VELLUTO: He will try, signore. I can't guarantee he'll succeed.

GIUDICE A LATERE: That's enough. How does your client plead?

AVVOCATO: We believe there is insufficient evidence to support these charges and request an immediate mistrial.

GIUDICE A LATERE: The Pubblico Ministero has already issued his decree, signore.

AVVOCATO: But there are no bodies.

GIUDICE A LATERE: We have a list of three actors who are presumed dead.

VELLUTO: Presumed.

GIUDICE A LATERE: Teo Avati, actor and known associate of the accused.

VELLUTO: "Known associate." Like I'm a mafioso.

PROCURATORE CAPO: Swiss national Irena Brizzolari, actress and—

VELLUTO: You can't confirm this. The film has no credits. You can't confirm.

PROCURATORE CAPO: We have numerous testimonies from relatives, friends, crewmen on the film—

VELLUTO: But no *bodies.*

GIUDICE A LATERE: I understand that these three actors die on tape.

AVVOCATO: A feature film, sir, a simple—

[Wherein Signor Velluto laughs loudly.]

VELLUTO: Listen to the man. There's tape!

AVVOCATO: What my client means is—

VELLUTO: That's beautiful. Who needs bodies when there's *tape?*

GIUDICE A LATERE: Signor Velluto, are you done, or may we proceed?

VELLUTO: Of course. I'm sorry. I'm sorry, just let me . . . Let's watch the tape! Come on, Giudice, let's see where those bodies are!

TEO

Ovidio

Three days after he arrived in Colombia, Teo Avati saw his first anaconda.

He wasn't sure what it was at first. His skin was hot with rage and he was walking fast down the riverbank, but then he glimpsed it. Ten meters off into the shallows. Something twisting. Brown scales and muscle. A shining knot, wide as a sidewalk and moving almost too slowly to see.

He made himself stop. He made his breath still. The snake was half underwater and coiled like a stacked rope pushed over in a rush. Every twist of its body was as thick as a man's waist and squeezing.

In the center of it, something was still alive, one black eye staring out from the center of the coils.

He stared into it, fascinated. He realized why: it reminded him of Anahi.

.   .   .

He finds Anahi later that night, like he has every night since he came here. He tells the woman at the front desk that something

13

in his room needs fixing. He requests that Anahi be the one who comes. But what he really wants is to ask her about the snake.

Are you sure it was brown? Like that? She nods toward the band of his wristwatch. She says it in Spanish: Teo studied it in school and can puzzle out cognates for the words he doesn't know.

She is standing on a chair, rigging mosquito netting over the door to his room. He wanted her to put it back up over his bed, but she refused. It is night. The darkness over the clearing they use as a parking lot is its own deep blue. She holds her breath to keep her balance, raises an arm over her head. He watches the knot of muscles move in each of her shoulder sockets.

He shrugs. Close to it. The water made it look darker.

And very long?

I don't know. It was muddy.

But thick as your waist? You're sure.

It was coiled. He takes a pull from his San Tomás and sets it down on the wood chips they've got carpeting the lot, leans his head back against the wall. I think so, but I'm not sure.

Anahi slips a nail out of the pocket of her jean shorts and holds it against the wall, taps lightly with the hammer so she won't wake the other guests. The hotel walls are tissue-thin, plywood, no insulation. Teo can hear the voices of the rest of the crew murmuring in Italian, quiet televisions, toothbrushes moving in mouths.

The humidity beads over the bridge of his nose. He drinks again.

But if it's the snake you're thinking of, he asks, what is it called?

Anahi searches for the name. In my family we call it mata toro, but we aren't from here. I think for most of the people here, it is anaconda.

How long are they, usually?

Sir, I don't really—

You know. Come on. I know you know.

She lowers her hammer to her side. She squints, deciding what she can say to him.

Why were you out there alone, anyway?

.   .   .

He could tell her the truth:

Because the director told him to shove the Indian as hard as he could into the tree, to jam his shotgun into the triangle of skin under the Indian's jaw and put as much pressure on it as he could stand. Because Teo did it, and the Indian yelped and screamed something in frantic Ticuna, and Teo pressed the gun harder into his jaw to close the man's mouth. The Indian writhed under the pressure, the grass skirt slipping open over his hip. Teo could see the bit of wriggling pink in his mouth where the man was biting the edge of his tongue. He sneered and laughed, let the full heat of his breath push into the Indian's face.

Teo could tell Anahi that he liked this part. But he doesn't want to scare her away; not yet.

The director nodded. Okay. Okay. That's enough.

Teo pushed the sweaty hair out of his eyes and let the gun fall to his side. He knew it was only a rehearsal, but still, his breath wouldn't slow, his nerves wouldn't relax. The cameramen were still clustered in the lunch tent, just visible through the trees. He watched one ladle a mound of what looked like meat onto a plate and laugh at something. The Indian put his hands on his knees and spat a pink rope of saliva onto the ground.

In his periphery, the director said: Di nuovo. Again.

It was the eighth time they'd done it. Teo had worked with

Ugo on a dozen films before, but they'd never rehearsed like this—and of course, Teo had never rehearsed with Ugo at all, not as an actor. In Italy, he'd worked as a grip, hoisting cameras up ladders and onto tripods and taken them down again as Ugo's mood dictated. They'd shot on soundstages that rented by the hour, wheeled wax palms in on dollies and knocked out every frame on a schedule drawn up to the minute. Ugo fed his actors their lines, and Teo had watched these men and women arrange their faces into expressions of horror or exhaustion or lust and pronounce the words straight to camera. And that was it; cut to print, no second takes. Getting out of character was as easy as shrugging off a thin coat, or at least it looked that way from the top of the crane. They'd make another one in six months, basically the same film but a different title, *Jungle Something, Something Massacre, Revenge of the Whatever the Fucks.*

But then Ugo had called Teo two weeks ago, at a weird mid-morning hour: I want to do another jungle film, fifteen thousand lire a week, are you in? His voice had sounded strange, muted, like the volume had been turned down on the receiver somehow. He was offering three times what he'd ever paid Teo in the past. When Teo asked why, Ugo had said he wanted Teo to act in the film. When Teo asked him what the hell he was talking about, Ugo had hung up.

Eight days later, a plane ticket arrived in the mail, Bogotá, one-way. No address on the envelope. No script, no mention of the role.

Teo called Ugo's flat and listened to the phone peal thirty-two times.

He hadn't gotten a gig for three months, not since the union had gone on strike. He'd spent the time smoking in his apartment and watching the news reports on the Red Brigades station bombings, waiting for something better to do. He had

never really asked Ugo questions about what they were filming, not even when he was on set—never What do we shoot next, or Why is that character supposed to be killing that extra, or What's on the green screen now? He had the script. He knew how to mount a camera and dismantle a backing and break down a lighting setup. Ugo had the entire production planned to the minute; what more did Teo need to know? And acting, he suspected, was probably the same way. The actors Ugo hired in Italy were runners-up in rural beauty pageants or last year's conservatory grads or old-timers who survived off bit parts on cop dramas and shlock films like this. The women always brought their own wigs. The men were always ten centimeters shorter than their résumés said and needed apple boxes to stand on during kissing scenes. To Teo, the work they did seemed to take as much insight as being a plumber, and maybe half the skill. And anyway, he'd be kicked out of his apartment soon when he didn't make rent, and where else would he go?

But it was different to puzzle out passport restrictions and vaccinations, to show up at the airport at five in the morning with no idea why you were there. It was different to sit next to the director on the plane: thirteen hours of pressurized silence, Ugo stirring his cocktail straw, occasionally tilting his chin up to sleep.

The director had been mostly silent on set, too, besides those two words that had become a mantra over these last days: Di nuovo. Again. For the last week, they'd spent every day running through chase scenes in the mud, over and over, until Teo's quadriceps burned and the skin on his knees was raw from falling, yelling the same lines until the words morphed and lost all sense. Right away, he could tell: this was different from the soundstages. The point of all this wasn't to block the scene or frame the shot. Some days, they didn't shoot at all.

Ugo just stood on the sidelines with his arms folded, a crease in the center of his forehead and his eyes scanning behind his aviator-frame glasses. The best Teo could tell, Ugo wanted to exhaust him: wanted Teo to hear the direction so many times that it became a voice in his own head, a nerve impulse in the fibers of his wrist.

He would let the cameras roll only then—when Teo was tired and furious.

He was tired and furious. Ugo said, Marks.

The Indian's shoulder landed too hard on the bark. The scrape it left was faint pink and looked too complicated to be random, like a rune. Teo shoved his face close to the man's ear and said, in Italian, I'm going to kill you.

Too early, Ugo called. Wait for my signal.

The man murmured something at a high pitch; it could have been a prayer.

Di nuovo, the director said. You know what, fuck it. This time with film.

Teo could smell something leafy on the man's skin, the sour breath the man was holding inside his mouth. He leaned back and smiled, lowered the gun. He adjusted his grip.

But before the cameras were set to roll, something happened: the Indian shoved Teo back, both hands hard and flat against his ribs. The air left Teo's lungs in one rush. The Indian pivoted and ran, stumbled in the mud, his bare heels carving deep pits into the earth and his knees bowing out in a way that looked painful.

And then Teo's body was moving, too, without signal or warning from his brain, chasing after the Indian, the gun swinging in his fist. The Indian's head craned over his shoulder and that was when the butt of the gun hit him, hard, the pain sudden between his shoulder blades. Teo felt like he was

watching himself from above. A man with a gun, dark-haired and lunging; a quick grunt, and the Indian was down.

The cameramen barked something from the lunch tent and started to run. Behind Teo's back, the voices came closer.

Basta! Hey!

But Teo kept his gaze down on the Indian. Kept hitting. The butt of the gun, the barrel, and when the gun wasn't fast enough, his fists. The bone at the back of the Indian's neck looked painful and strange. It wasn't broken, but it was one of those bones in the body that looks fractured even when it's not. It bulged and shifted as the Indian curled into himself, as the Indian covered his skull with his hands.

Then the voices were right behind them, telling Teo to stop.

Then Teo made himself stand, made himself watch the way the Indian winced and drew one shaking hand forward and crawled, just an inch. His knuckles were white, gripping at slick earth.

Then Teo picked up the gun. Before the cameramen reached him, he bit his tongue to still the itch in his trigger finger and strode straight east, into the trees.

· · ·

He doesn't tell Anahi any of this, of course. He doesn't want to scare her off.

Instead he pulls on his beer, squint-smiles at her, and says, You didn't answer *my* question. How long are those snakes?

She winces at the innuendo. I can't—

Come on. Answer mine and I'll answer yours.

The girl is sitting on the chair now. The mosquito net is hung up behind her, breathing in the breeze from the fan inside the room. A lightbulb is on in there, too, 15 watts under

a heavy lampshade. The net filters the glow down to a strange dim wash.

Why did you do it? she says. Today, when you hurt the Indian?

His beer pauses in its arc to his lips, How the fuck does she know? She wasn't there.

If you're acting, she says softly, couldn't you fake it?

Stop changing the subject, Teo says, his voice still bristling. He hasn't told Anahi that he isn't really an actor yet, and he decides instantly that he never will.

I'm sorry.

How did you even hear about that?

The maids gossip.

And here is where Teo recovers, softens his face and his voice back into a tone she can trust. Well, then, he says, tilting his head so his hair falls away from his eyes. The maids shouldn't gossip.

She hesitates. I know.

He narrows his eyes and takes in the size of her: smaller, now, than she seemed when she was standing on the chair. The span of her hips is probably no wider than the width of his hand if he spread his fingers out. He puts a laugh in his voice when he talks, to relax her: I was supposed to stay in character.

Anahi is biting the edge of her thumbnail, her posture rigid against the back of the chair. When she speaks, it's slow and careful: I don't think the Indians understand this.

Understand what?

What the movie is about.

I don't really know, either.

She looks at him. You don't?

Teo pulls the beer off his lips, makes a blah-blah motion with his hands. I think it's a play on an exploitation film, blood-

thirsty savages, all that. You know. A teenage girl gets captured by the filthy natives. A journalist comes down to look for her, slaughters about a hundred of them. Blood and guts and grass skirts, all that bullshit.

From the way she's looking at him, he can tell she hasn't understood half the words he said. Her lips move so carefully when she talks: What happens to the girl?

Teo grins at her. I have no idea. We don't even have an actress to play her yet.

But you could ask the director, at least. You and the director at least understand each other.

He drinks, tries not to let on how much he's bullshitting. That's still not how it works.

You said he was your friend.

That's not exactly true. We work together.

But you speak the same language, at least. At least you can say no.

Immediately, Anahi looks like she regrets the words.

Teo stares at the side of her face, a feeling like hunger growing in his stomach. He smiles, glances up at the mosquito net: I don't think that net will stay up.

It will.

Check it.

I don't—

Stand on the chair and check it again for me.

She does. As she steps up onto the seat, he watches the sinews in her ankles move. The wood creaks as she shifts her weight onto it. He can hear her holding her breath, trying not to fall.

There's no script, Teo says.

What?

That's why I don't know what happens in the movie. There's no script.

She takes out the hammer, holds it as close to the claw as she can so it won't make much noise.

He doesn't usually work this way, he says. Ugo. Usually we shoot on soundstages. They have every frame of the thing on a schedule and we just knock it out, bam, bam, bam. We shoot the whole film in a weekend. Can you believe that?

Anahi rises onto her toes. He stares at the muscles above her knees, bracing.

That's how we shot *Vacation in Hell,* he says. *Psycho Venom, Four Hundred Teeth,* all of them. They rent out a trained monkey and spritz all the actors down with water so they look malarial and add some jungle sounds in post. That's how we always worked. Hell, that's how all of these jungle exploitation movies are made. It's a genre.

She taps. Teo can't see her face from where he's sitting, but he can see it in the rest of her body: she is trying so hard not to look at him.

But something happened, he says.

She doesn't respond.

Something happened to Ugo, and now he's got this whole vision, wants to make this *new* kind of film.

He wants her to ask—what kind of film? He wants her to say anything, but then the hammer stops sounding, and Anahi starts to climb down, careful, like she's stepping down onto ice.

She does it so quietly. Teo can't help himself.

He leans over and rattles the legs of the chair.

She stumbles, yips. He laughs and shouts, Boogeyman! but she doesn't laugh back. The chair clatters and settles, and she finds her footing on the ground, takes a step back into the parking lot, covers her face with her hands. She catches her breath while Teo laughs himself breathless.

Why did you do that? she says, meek.

I was just kidding! Come on.

I could have broken a leg.

You're fine, he says, the first time joking, easy, pushing himself to a stand and tossing the bottle on the ground, ambling into the lot. But when he says it again, he is right next to her. His hand is on her waist and his words are a command.

You're fine.

Anahi stares at the ground. The lot is so dark, but Teo's close enough to see the fine creases at the inner corners of her eyes, her short eyelashes, and the little blood vessels in the white.

Now tell me about the snake, he says. You promised.

She looks up at him once, long enough to take in the curl of a smile at the corner of his mouth. Then she strides out into the lot, finds a branch, drags it through the wood chips they've put down over the mud. He listens to them clatter. The line she makes must be six meters and curves like a tilde. He cocks his head as he watches her do it, her body moving in the orange light of the mosquito coils that are burning all along the perimeter of the lot.

It's this long, she says, when it's stretched out.

She stares at the line. She stays on the other side of it, away from him.

In the dark, Teo looks straight over the line at Anahi and thinks of the mata toro, the way he looked at the animal in the mata toro's grasp and thought instantly of her. He's not sure why they evoke each other, except that there is a thrill to this kind of looking that he hasn't found elsewhere. Even when she walks away from him, she can't stop him from looking: he can still see the tiny globe of her jaw joint shifting as she grinds her teeth just a bit, the way the skin darkens over the bone when she does it. He knows how her skin works. He saw how the snake's skin worked: the way its lower jaw unhinged when

it had corkscrewed all the air out of its prey and was ready to swallow, how the scales drifted apart as the skin stretched around the body of the animal. When he looks at Anahi, he thinks of that new flesh between scales: that shocking pink, petal-delicate. The whole continent of the jaw joint moved and then separated, unhinging into its composite bones, drifting farther apart until the skin at the corners of its mouth stretched white. The snake put its lips around the head of the animal and pulled itself over, over, slow, a sleeve.

He had the shotgun in his lap, the barrel hot from the sun, a bar of pure heat. It was the exact thickness of a light pole shaft, and something about this made Teo feel powerful, like he was capable, like he knew exactly how to use this thing, though he'd never held a gun before in his life. He liked the feeling of holding it, of knowing what he could do and not yet be doing it. He liked how it felt to wait up above on the bank.

Teo looks at Anahi and thinks of how easy it is: he is looking at her, so she can't move at all.

She says, now: Who is your character in the movie?

Her feet are rooted, her posture rigid. Teo leans against the wall again, tries to sharpen his gaze so he can see her in the dark.

I don't know anymore, he says.

How can you not know?

Like I said, we don't have scripts. The director feeds us our lines, a shot at a time. He changes things around.

But your character has a name.

Well yeah, it *used* to be Mike, Teo says. Now it's Joe, I think. But then an actor quit, so everything might change again.

Who was it that quit?

You didn't meet him, Teo says. The American. He didn't even get on the plane.

The American?

We need at least one American in the cast. It makes international distribution cheaper. We've got a new one coming to replace him in a few days.

What part will he play, the American? When he gets here?

Probably Richard, but who knows? He could be anyone. Teo laughs. Who knows what part I'll play, hell.

But how can you shoot a movie like that?

Fuck if I know.

Why do you *want* to shoot a movie like that?

He hesitates. Directors recast all the time, it's not—

That's not what I mean, she says.

When did her voice get so bold? It's too dark for Teo to see her face. Her little hammer is clutched in both hands in front her, dangling like a golf club. He takes a step into the lot, grinning.

What do you mean, then?

I mean the violence, she says, bracing. I mean the blood and the killing and the guns. Hurting that Indian.

What about it?

She bites her lip. Never mind.

No, tell me. He walks a little closer.

Anahi looks off to the side. What I meant was . . . Doesn't it bother you? To even pretend to do things like that?

Teo is close enough, now, that he can hear the simmer of the mosquito coils. There is less than an arm's length between him and her and he can see the glint of her silly little hammer, the way her hands are trembling.

Look at you. He smiles. So worried about me.

The first time Teo called for maintenance, Anahi told him that she couldn't go inside his room when he was in it. The

owner would get angry if she did, she said; Teo would have to rehang the rest of the netting over his mattress himself. She offered to call one of the male employees, but Teo said no: he wanted her. Even if she could only hang the netting over the door, he wanted her.

He had said he wanted her the next night: a smashed light-bulb. And the next: he torqued his room faucet until water leaked out of the base. As far as he could tell, she wasn't allowed to say no.

Teo smiles once at her, then turns around, ambles through the curtain of netting and back into his room. He kneels and rifles under the bed for another warm beer, cursing as his elbow strains. His vision is blurred from the alcohol, but he can see the shape of an empty T-shirt under there, an untied shoe.

He hears her voice, hesitant behind him and far away.

You should be careful. Sometimes there are animals underneath.

· · ·

Here is something else Teo does not tell Anahi:

It took him an hour to get back to set after he left the snake in the river, a half-kilometer walk with elephant grass thrashing at his ankles. He beamed himself in the forehead on low branches. The heat dropped and the humidity rose, every trunk he steadied himself against slick with mist like the trees were sweating, too. For the last half kilometer, Teo lost the trail he'd made going in and had to follow the sound of voices through the black. He could hear the cameramen best, loading in the equipment, planning a joke they wanted to play on the lead actress, a twenty-year-old girl from southern Switzerland

who they all thought was sexy and took every opportunity to tease. They'd stolen a fake skull from props, and they were going to bury it in the mud near the makeup tent, ask her to come take a look. They mimicked it: Irena, Irena, what's that over there? They said it in exaggerated accents, mocking her inflected Italian. Teo couldn't see them, but he could imagine them pantomiming the face they thought she'd make when she saw it, laughing in whispers. They'd unhinge the jaw of the skull and make it laugh, too.

Teo focused on the laughter as he lunged over something wet and soft and wide on the ground, maybe a soaked sheet of bark or a body. The voices were so close, but he had to keep his eyes on his feet. It was so dark he couldn't have seen the silhouettes of the cameramen, even if he'd searched.

So then how did the director see *him*, pushing through an unexpected gap in the tree line and onto the black mud of the beach? Ugo didn't have a flashlight. His cigarette was lit and that's what Teo saw: a fleck of orange, moving from his mouth down to his side.

He winced when he heard Ugo say his name. He braced for the director's curt, quiet anger: Where the fuck were you, where have you been all this time?

Instead, Ugo issued one emotionless laugh into the dark. You smell like shit.

Teo murmured, I went for a walk.

It was like the director's gaze had its own magnetic resonance, the kind of look that could vibrate a cell at fifty meters. Ugo had always been intense but this was different: that look felt different here, in this country that smelled like mud and sweat and iodine, the river plashing out there somewhere in the dark.

I upset you today, Ugo said, a statement of fact.

We're fine.

You don't like this new process I'm trying.

He didn't ask Teo whether he liked acting, period.

Teo said nothing. He heard Ugo swallow, saw the vague shape of him folding his arms in front of his chest as he spoke.

What happened today—maybe it's a sign.

Teo flattened it from a question into a statement: A sign of what.

That maybe you're not right for the part of Richard, Ugo says. I was considering you for it, you know. For the lead.

I—

When the American quit, I thought, why not, let's try Teo in the lead? But I think now, I need someone more—what's the word.

Teo could feel sweat creeping through his scalp like insects, nosing under individual strands of his hair.

Someone more raw, Ugo said. More naïve.

Teo laughed. I've never acted a day in my life. I'm not sure how much more raw you can get.

That's not what I mean.

Then what do you mean?

I mean I want to take the script in a different direction.

What script?

Ugo coughed. The story, then.

Teo wanted to ask: Why no script? Teo wanted to ask what happened, why he was in this fucking country at all?

But something about the rough edge to Ugo's voice told him not to. Instead he clenched his back teeth, tried to find Ugo's face in the dark.

I can try to play innocent if you want me to. If that's the question. I'm new at this, but I can try.

Come on, Ugo said. We've done, what, eleven films together?

Teo paused, surprised Ugo remembered. Twelve.

And that last one in Milan, with the teenage girl, what was her name, the one who worked craft services?

All the muscles in Teo's face went slack.

And all that bullshit you put us through? All that hush-hush business, paying off the parents so we wouldn't have to stop production? You didn't think my production manager wouldn't tell me all about that, did you?

I—

You cost me money on that, Teo, Ugo smiled. Come on, don't tell me you don't remember.

Teo looked at a point on Ugo's cheek, above his mouth and below his left eye, and said nothing.

You can play innocent. The director laughed. Huh. Come on, Teo. We may not know each other well, but trust me, I know *you* better than that. And besides—

Teo will not tell Anahi what the director said next:

The way we're going to shoot this film—I need someone who's not just playing.

·   ·   ·

Teo doesn't flinch when Anahi mentions the animals under the bed. He pushes himself off the hotel room floor and stands, the beer warm in his fist. He puts a laugh in his voice, looks straight through the mosquito netting when he speaks: And what big scary things are under my bed?

Anahi is so still. He can't make out the particularities of her features through the netting, her nostrils or her eyes. Her eyebrows are thick and perfect. Her shirt is white and he thinks

it says HOTEL OVIDIO on it in black block capitals, but he can't be sure. She is crossing her arms over her chest.

Insects, she says. Rodents. They get under the beds.

Not snakes?

Not this far from the trees, no.

Teo puts his beer on the corner of the bedpost and slams the bottle cap off with the heel of his hand. Are you sure?

Anahi doesn't say anything.

He smiles. I don't know. I think I hear something in here. I think it's hissing.

Her arms fall to her sides.

I'm scared, Teo teases. I think you better get in here.

She says, I don't get paid more if I work late.

Save me, Anahi.

I need to go.

But I need your help.

I can't—

He shhs her. He hisses. Sssss. Listen. Did you hear that?

Teo cups a hand around his ear.

Hey, hey. I think it's coming for me.

He stares at her through the net. He keeps hissing. He will keep doing it until she breaks down and moves beyond the curtain, until he can see every part of her up close. There is a part of Teo that hopes it will take hours to wear her down. There is a part of him that loves this part best, that wants for it to take all night.

· · ·

Anahi stands as still as she can in the dark of the parking lot, looking at the actor, waiting for her behind the curtain. The humidity whirs against the nape of her neck. For a reason she

can't name, she thinks of her father. She thinks of the last time she saw a mata toro.

It was on the table in the middle of her father's kitchen, carved into hunks of wet, black steak. Her father and three of his friends were picking out the bones, drinking cachaça and laughing over a joke. Two were from the cartel: they'd brought back crates of liquor and clean shirts from the capital, cases of them layered over the kilos of coca paste in the speedboat. Half the liquor would be a gift to her father for putting them up on the trip north. The third man was an Indian named Unay who had been expelled from his village a year ago; her father was trying to teach him Spanish.

Unay dug his hands wrist-deep into the body of the snake and squealed at the sensation. He was laughing so hard he was weeping. The tears drew dark rivulets into the filth on his skin, and his mouth kept moving in an aimless way. She could tell he was already too drunk to talk.

Anahi stared into the pile of meat. It had so many parts inside: black tissues that came off in long strands, a yellow fluid that got under the men's fingernails. She saw a blue something that looked like lung fiber. She could not see anything like a heart.

How did you kill it? she asked her father.

One of the men from the cartel looked up. You're not afraid of the big snake, are you, girl?

She swallowed. No.

I think you are. You need us to protect you?

Anahi held her breath. The man walked closer. He was very fat and, she knew, more powerful than the other men. Maybe even the boss. She could tell by his watch, silver and leather flecked in snake blood, and by how close he got to her, and because when he did it, her father said nothing.

I used a great big gun, he said. It's out in the truck. Thing is this long, and the kickback is crazy.

When he laughed, she could see the grains of raw meat in his molars. She could smell the carcass steaming all over him.

Just say the word, baby. He licked one of his back teeth. I'll protect you.

Her father glanced up, but he kept slipping pieces of rib out of the meat like sewing pins, didn't tell the man to stop. The man was breathing into her face, her mouth. There was a wet, blue-black smear on the floor, some organ that had been dropped or thrown, and she focused as hard as she could on that.

Finally, her father put down the snake. It was already dead, he said. These assholes just found it out in the road.

Unay let out a sudden laugh. He shouted something in mixed Spanish and Ticuna that Anahi couldn't understand. She heard the Spanish words for *afraid* and *girl*. She heard her father tell him to shut up.

In the lot, Anahi looks through the mosquito netting at Teo. She wets her lips to make her mouth work.

You know, snakes aren't what you should be afraid of, she said.

She is thinking of the men in her father's house. She is thinking of the mosquitoes clinging to the mesh, working their way under the gaps at the doorframe. She is thinking of the larvae that clot in the mosquito's belly, the parasites that travel along the proboscis and into the blood. She is thinking of how they must look as they unspool in the glands, microscopic ribbons, pure white and silent. She is thinking of Unay's leg under the table, mottled with dark blood, swollen huge with elephantitis.

She can see Teo's shape edging closer to the net, closer to

her. He says, Why? Is there something bigger than an anaconda out there?

Anahi thinks of a tiny worm in the center of Teo's heart,
working.

No, she says. There isn't. You're safe in there.

RICHARD

Bogotá

You fly to Bogotá, and as instructed, you wait.

The casting director told you the set was a charter flight away from the capital, but he didn't tell you how long it would take for someone to come put you on the next plane. To be fair, you didn't ask. You grinned and nodded when he pressed the envelope into your palm, leaned close to listen as he murmured, Hotel Ignacio. Here is money for the bill and for your meals, he said. Arrangements will be made to take you to the set.

The casting director smelled like Royal Copenhagen Ultra and match sulfur. A square gold pendant hung in the deep V of his neckline, nested in his pale brown chest hair, and you were embarrassed to notice it as you nodded yes, yes, you understood.

You had thought you'd have to wait two nights, tops. You thought they must be on *some* kind of a schedule. You knew, at least, that they'd need you soon, if the part was as big as they said. On the flight, you ordered a gin fizz and reread your copy of *Respect for Acting*, the corners of the pages shivering with the motion of the engine. You were too excited to sleep. As the sun set and the lights in the cabin went down, you eavesdropped on a conversation between a Scottish woman and her young

son: Look, love. Look. Can you tell where the sky ends? That's the water.

. . .

You had thought two nights, tops. Two nights and three days, and then they would come. But then the newspaper slides under the door, the date stamped in black ink above the masthead, unrefutable. Four days have passed.

The Hotel Ignacio is seven blocks from the statehouse, four from an open-air market that sells headless calves strung up by their anklebones. The city is surrounded by black mountains to the east and north and south. On the first day, you walk as far as you can, through the crowded streets and south to what you think must be the city center, but in no less than twenty minutes you see jungle. Even the foothills are covered in it. Forty-foot trees lean over a highway overpass and cast blue shadows across the road. Leaves push at the diamonds of space in a wire fence, branches hacked off at a disturbingly neat perpendicular a foot above the rail. The whole city has that sense of something barely contained, an epidemic or a state secret. When you swipe at the sweat along the side of your neck, you find an insect sitting on your collar like a tracking device, its domed eyes steady as little cameras.

You turn back. You wander to a movie theater, but everything they're showing you've already seen. *Jaws*; *Salò*; *Picnic at Hanging Rock*. Their titles are handwritten in Spanish on a piece of paper and taped to the window, and the marquee is blank. A blind man with a missionary pamphlet stands outside the empty box office and tries to stuff his leaflet into your shirt pocket, weeping and gasping, tears darkening the fabric above his name tag.

Some violence is happening in the capital, that's clear to

you. Every morning, a police jeep with a roof-mounted machine gun trawls the dusty thoroughfare, five stories down, matte army gray. Heat pushes at the hotel window and makes it steam. You can't believe how many people are still in the streets, walking two feet behind the slow wheels of the jeep like it's simply not there, bear-hugging briefcases as they jog toward a departing bus. The machine gun roves, side to side, then up toward the water stain of daytime moon. Why isn't anyone on the street afraid? How do they live this way?

Or do they? Maybe the jeep is your own personal and daily hallucination. Maybe the newspapers that you find slipped under your door are a joke someone is playing on you; you never see the person who puts them there, never even hear their footsteps coming or going down the hall. You almost don't believe the articles are real: these photographs of men kneeling, hands knotted behind backs with twine, flour sacks pulled over their heads so they can't see what's coming. These headlines: Administración Turbay Ha Capturado Enclave Guerrillero. Under the fold, a 3 x 5 of the president, unsmiling in a striped bow tie.

You don't speak Spanish. The flour sacks are stamped with red stars and arching wheat and the word *Harina,* creased deeply at the vowels. You study the word like a cipher.

Why don't you call Kay, like you told yourself you would?

You should have done it the first day you got there. Why didn't you? You couldn't have known how long it would take for someone to come for you, that past the third day, the telephone would clang you awake every morning and a man on the other end would scream at you in Spanish, probably for payment on the room. But that is what has happened. The money in the envelope that the casting director gave you won't come close to covering it all. Almost all of your own cash that you managed to bring is gone, spent on the room, soggy takeout meals, the

dozen toiletries you forgot to pack, and one souvenir: a figurine of a flamingo in a yellow, blue and red bikini. It is a present for your mother. You leave it on the nightstand. You stare at it as the phone clangs again, anxiety streaking through your limbs, the flamingo grinning openmouthed at her tiny maracas.

The Hotel Ignacio has brass mail slots on every hallway, pale green baseboards, thin walls. On the fifth day, you drop a peso down the mail slot and listen to it clang against sixty feet of sheet metal, waiting for the sound of it landing against the floor of the basement. It doesn't come. You put your ear to the slot and think you hear someone murmur something—Qué coño?—but you can't be sure. You remember the word *coño* from your days in LA, hurled between car windows across lanes of traffic. You never asked anyone what it meant. You don't know how to respond.

·   ·   ·

After six days of waiting, you decide you can't stay in another night.

The phone book in the nightstand looks like it's been spun in an industrial dryer, but you manage to find the name of a club in its pages, an address that you circle in pencil on a map. A speck of a place, two kilometers away. The fourth entry under the heading labeled BAR.

If you were a woman, you'd squeeze the hotel key between your second and third knuckles as you walk, try to remember the spot beneath a person's eye that will dislodge his cornea if you gouge at the right angle. But you are a man, so you keep the key in your pocket, fingering the little red ribbon it's tied to, trying to keep your gaze forward. The back of your throat tastes briny and dry. The streets are empty at this hour and loud with voices from inside buildings, televisions, music, women screaming at children.

When you get to where you're going, you don't realize, at first, that you've arrived. The nightclub is in a former storefront with black house paint rollered over the windows. Uncertain, you hand a man three pesos at the door, and he hands you a stout green bottle without a label, full of carbonated liquid that smells vaguely industrial, like some sort of solvent.

You drink. They're playing a song in English that you don't recognize, projecting a black-and-white porno from the 1930s onto each of the three walls. The stereo sings: *Watch new blood on the eighteen-inch screen; the corpse is a new personality.* The guitars pluck, the rhythm too slow for dancing. Teenage girls dance anyway, in clusters, in front of men slouching in red chairs. The light from the projector turns their bodies white, then black, then marbled. You realize you've been wearing the same dirty shirt for three days.

If Kay were here, she could understand what the girls are saying. And here is something you do not even consider: that if Kay were here, she would tell you that you need to leave, right now. That this place is for guerilla sympathizers plotting a socialist revolution to take down the administration of President Turbay. That she overhead a conversation. That you wrote the address in the phone book down wrong, and you're not safe here. She would whisper it quick into your ear, Let's go, but she wouldn't drop her smile until you were out on the street, three blocks away. Only then would she exhale, all the tension leaving her body in one awful rush.

But you don't know anything, and now the music is getting louder, and Kay is in New York, sitting alone on a roof with no view.

A sweet sort of guilt sits in you as you think about her. Her Spanish, quiet but steady, accented perfectly. The straight lines of her body, the pale wall of her hair. After your career bot-

tomed out in LA a year after college, you'd pronounced to Kay that the theater scene in California wasn't the right fit for you, that you needed to be in New York, and she'd surprised you by asking, simply, when the two of you would leave. She had contacts from architecture school in Manhattan who could get her a job. You were her boyfriend; what was the question? You didn't know how to say no, and so she took the long drive with you through Arizona and New Mexico and Texas, ordering at all the restaurants and asking for all the directions.

That's the thing about Kay: she is so weirdly sure about you, a cool shadow that follows you patiently, even when you sprint. From the moment you met her she's been that way, sitting alone in a turtleneck at a pool party in central LA that a friend had dragged her to and then abandoned her to smoke peyote. Within five minutes of offering her a drink, it was over; it was like she'd decided you were the one person at that party who was meant to be her friend. She told you that night how she grew up an only child outside of Sonora, and how her best friend as a kid was a Peruvian acupuncturist named Elka who worked at her parents' ashram and spoke about five words of English. You didn't know what an ashram was, and it all sounded a little ridiculous. But there was something vivid and weird about Kay that you liked, even if it was the exact thing, later, that would make it so hard to break it off: the way she held her margarita glass with both hands around the stem like she was reading tea leaves in a chalice, how out of place she looked on that pool deck at that party with all those tanned, laughing girls. It took an hour of conversation for you to get her to smile, though she never stopped looking you straight in the eyes. When she did, it was like a white bird had finally opened and showed you itself, the trailing edge of its wing yellow as a sunburst.

In the club, the girls are whispering. They have skinny

chains looped around their abdomens, little shiny scars on their bellies, tiny girlish teeth. The dark crowds over them like a thunderhead and flees as they nudge each other into the beam of the projector. One of them points to you and yells, Venga, and another lunges at this girl, still grinning, and covers her friend's mouth with both her hands.

Cállate, zorra!

They giggle and screech. A girl with black hair is shoved out into the light.

Él te puede oir! Vaya!

The girl is so small and dark. She makes herself exhale, relaxes her shoulders down her back, minces forward across the dance floor. Her friends titter. She is coming straight for you.

On the road trip from California to New York, passing through the western states, you had to goad Kay into the gas stations. Your Spanish is amazing, you said, and she swatted you, shrieked, That's not the point! You watched her from the car, across the parking lot and through the spattered glass of the gas station window. She was awkward in jeans and a white button-down that were both too thick for the weather. She looked rigid and formal and bizarre next to the display of Technicolor Jaritos and plantain chip bags, but the man behind the counter grinned at her with his whole face.

You think: Is this when it started? The jealousy, rising just an inch in you, like floodwater.

The girl in the club says something in Spanish—Quieres bailar?—and you say yes.

When Kay came back to the car, her whole body had relaxed. The Juárez wind hauled over the border and mussed up her hair, made her skin pinken and go bright. He was really nice, she said. He gave me a pack of cigarettes for free.

What did he say about the hotel?

42 · Kea Wilson

It's six miles north. She chewed her lower lip. But there's someplace he said we should go first.

When you hold the girl in the club, you can feel her lower ribs move under your hands. It feels less like breathing than like a boat tilting in a wave, and when you glance at her face, you see this, too: something queasy and weightless about her expression, the music moving her to an imperfect rhythm, like water. The piercings in her ears look new, a little fringe of blood around the stud. What's your name? you say, in English, but she just leans into you, puts her chin against your shoulder, and mouths something to her friends across the room, thinking you can't see, that you can't feel her jaw moving on your shoulder.

The place the gas station attendant directed you to, the Lightning Field, didn't look like much when you pulled up: a low sweep of land, dusk. Rain shimmered over the windshield. Kay leaned back on the headrest and closed her eyes, murmured, The air here tastes—*different,* somehow. Then, after a thoughtful squint, she said: Pale green.

It *tastes* pale green?

What? It does.

You smiled, loved her again. You're so fucking pretentious.

No, Kay said. I'm a synesthete. I'm exact.

Beyond the windshield, the sun dodged a fistful of clouds, and you finally saw what was in front of you: an outdoor art installation of lightning rods, a square mile of them glinting in the new light.

Her voice was full of thrill and wonder. Do you think it will storm?

It didn't.

The men in the club watch the girls drink. When you look them directly in the face, a sudden loneliness strikes at you, bruising a tender place deep in your chest that you didn't know

was there. Their hands look too big for their beer bottles. Their coats are all shiny fake leather, all look like they've just been bought new for tonight. The music is too slow, and they are not like you: none of them are dancing.

· · ·

Here is something you do not know:

The name of the girl who puts her tongue in the hollow of your ear as you dance. (Luz.)

Why her breath is so quick. (She has never danced with a man before.)

Why she limps as you spin her slowly to the music, her hips pressed tight against yours and held there, immobile, her hands clasped together behind your neck. You don't notice, as you turn, that she looks at her friends over your shoulder and mouths the word *Dios*, and later, Ayúdame, laughing. Even if you saw it, you couldn't decipher what she means. You're gripping her waist too hard. You're staring at the porno women projected on the wall, running their hands over each other's corsets, their expressions so bored. You're trying too hard not to let what you're feeling show.

You're not drunk. You don't kiss Luz, but you don't stop her from kissing you, either. The lightning never came at *The Lightning Field*, and you have that feeling now, that feeling of waiting for something. A low red field, dusk. A charge in the air that makes you nauseous, all your skin alert to something you can't see but know is coming.

The women on the wall tie each other up in leather ropes.

The music is in English, but you still can't understand it.

You said to Kay, This is bullshit. How long are we supposed to wait for something to happen?

Kay looked confused. But waiting for it is the best part.

Here is something you don't know:

Luz and her friends had followed her brother Andres to the club that night, waited outside until he left again ten minutes later with six teeners of coke sweating in the waistband of his underpants. Of course Luz didn't know about the cocaine. She doesn't know, still, about the copy of *Das Kapital* wedged in the space between his bed and the wall, or that he's going to sell the cocaine to a man down the block from this club for a handshake and four grenades in a shoe box. Just like you, she doesn't know about the revolution, but that is because she is thirteen and her mother hides the newspapers, won't let her go downtown without someone to watch her.

A few years from now, the minister of justice will be shot by a teenager riding a moped with an Uzi in his fist, and that teenager will be Luz's boyfriend.

But for now, Luz is dancing. For now, Luz doesn't know about the car bombs, or what the M-19s are, or that her brother Andres is one of them. She doesn't know how to kiss, and that is why her heart flips over as she puts her tongue into your ear, whispers something in Spanish that you can't understand, that she is far too young to understand herself.

· · ·

The next morning, you sit down to write Kay a letter.

The pen doesn't work. You try to carve her name into the paper with the inkless tip, but the paper is thin and keeps breaking. You are so tired. You are tired because you never went to bed.

Then the pen is on the floor across the room where you've just hurled it, and hot tears are clotted up in the corners of your eyes,

the telephone in your hand. You're spinning the dial without thinking, missing the country code, yelling Shit and pounding the hang-up button and swiping furiously through the numbers again. Your thoughts are so loud—Fuck the hotel bill, I don't care if it costs seven bucks a minute—that when you hear the sound of Kay's phone ringing, it barely registers. Your blood is pumping hard in your ears. When you hear Kay's voice, it punctures you.

Hello?

The air-conditioning whirs. You swallow salt. It's me, you manage. It's me, I'm here.

There is static on the line. She says your name and hangs a question mark on it.

I'm in Colombia, you say. I got a movie. I'm sorry I couldn't talk about it, I—it was a sudden thing.

There is a silence. When her voice comes back, it is striped by static.

You have to talk—I can't hear—tell me where—

Kay, you're breaking up.

Static. Please—

You shout every syllable: I'm in Co-lo-mbia!

A terrible electronic sound scribbles out of the phone.

Kay?

Static.

Kay!

Your face is wet and your palms are wet and the phone is wet in your hand. The static changes pitch and squeals for a full minute before you give yourself permission to hang up.

As soon as you do it, the phone rings again, so loud it makes the nightstand tremble. You pick it up quick and shout her name.

On the other end, someone is speaking English with an Italian accent. A man.

Who is Kay? he says.

You can't remember your own language. The plastic blinds slap in the breeze from the air conditioner. Your suitcase is already packed and zipped, lying at a diagonal across the brown carpet. You will never feel a quiet again like you have in this room: humid, incomplete.

My girlfriend, you say, as slow as you can. Kay is my girlfriend, I was just talking to her. I'm sorry. Who is this?

The voice is aggravated, speaking too fast. He tells you he is an associate of the producer, and that he's left the meter running in the taxi. That we are very late and need to leave for the airport. Please to get down here, now?

A surreal heat spreads through your face and down the veins of your neck. Your mouth moves by some mechanism you're not controlling. Now? We're leaving now?

The associate sighs loudly and hangs up the phone.

Before you leave, you stand in the door with your suitcase, the teeth of the key biting into your palm. If you stay right here, facing into the hotel room, you can feel the churning cold of the air-conditioning on your front and the laundry-room heat of the hallway behind you, each in equal measure, dividing your body into two exact halves.

.   .   .

In the final cut of *Jungle Bloodbath*, there are no shots of your character on a plane, no mention of how he got to the jungle. Just smash cut from the opening sequence, and there he is: Richard, sitting on the bench of a canoe. He is slipping off a lens cover, filming the center buttons of his own shirt as he struggles with the focus. Then he picks the camera up and holds it high above his head to block the sun out of his eyes.

Richard in safari khaki, in a green boat floating over khaki-

colored water. He squints straight into the lens and says, Ve-ronica Perez went missing six weeks ago.

The delivery is uncertain. By this point in filming, you won't even know who plays Veronica—if anyone will play Veronica, or if, by the time you find her, Veronica will be reduced to a couple of prop limbs and a gallon jug of corn-syrup blood splashed across a sacrificial altar. You'll shoot this scene at high noon, a weird midday wind loud over the camera's built-in mic, water flashing at the edges of the frame. Two other actors will be in the boat behind you, rowing at the stern and the midship thwart, but the camera's angled so you can't see them yet. The director will be offscreen, watching from the shore.

Richard speaks: From what we've gathered, ah, Veronica and her parents, famed anthropologists Amanda and Esteban Perez of Houst—*Abilene*, Texas . . .

(You'll make up all the names, of course. With the director staring at you, you'll be too nervous to come up with better ones.)

—they came down here to study the Yanomamö people's cannibal rites, and um—unfortunately, it seems, were . . . *abducted* themselves.

(The director will have fed you the premise but not the specifics, told you to ad-lib the lines. You will tell him you're no good at improv. He won't respond to that. He'll be the one who rolls up his pant legs and walks into the mud, pushes your boat out onto the water.)

The deaths of Amanda and Esteban seem all but confirmed, unfortunately. Richard says: But Veronica, we still have hope for her. She was last seen by a traveling—um—*fisherman*, north of a Yakuma settlement, after an intertribal fertility ceremony. We're headed there now.

And here Richard pauses. His brow lowers to a squint and

his gaze spans out over the water, in a way you must think looks thoughtful, unaffected, a genius aiming his vision at the future of his medium. The oars lap and lap. Someone in the background murmurs Avvicinati, get closer—Ugo to the sound guy, floating in a nearby boat—but it's quiet enough that the sound editor will mistake it for a whisper of water and leave it in the final cut.

This isn't a rescue mission, Richard says, finally. I'm a journalist. I'm not equipped to be a hero. But if what we find out here leads us to Veronica—if we don't have time to signal to the capital, to wait for the heroes to arrive—well . . .

He lowers the camera. If you look closely, you can make out the actors behind him: a woman at the stern, a man sitting wet-assed in the middle of the boat, rowing and looking annoyed.

The heroes have failed, Richard says. So far. If a journalist has to be the one—

This is when the boat pitches.

The frame tilts. The woman in the back of the boat yips, flashes into the center of the frame: brown hair, a white shirt over a skinny rib cage, her oar flailing. There's a loud thump in the built-in mic and a ray of sun flares as you hoist the camera higher. It happens in the space of a second: the whole boat turns over.

The water will be hotter than river water should be. There will be an animal circling at your ankles, you'll be sure, a crocodile or a river dolphin, or maybe just long ropes of kelp. You will keep the camera high, somehow. It will keep recording as you dog-paddle, filming the sun, the cloudless blank of the sky, trees and trees and trees, and finally, when you've adjusted your grip, the underseam of the boat, flipped and bobbing, gleaming wet in the light.

Your chin will be craned high. You'll be terrified of the water, of the parasites in it sloshing into your mouth.

The actress will be laughing, pushing sheets of hair back from her face.

The other actor, Teo, will be stern-faced and crawl-stroking, righting the boat.

This should be an outtake, but it won't be. Postproduction will tone down the background noise, the producers' voices shouting, Get back in the boat, madre di Dio! They'll salvage the film, in an airtight box full of kitty litter to leach out the moisture, a month after all of you are gone.

This should be an outtake, in any other film it would be, but this—this is exactly the kind of footage the director wants. The negatives scraped raw by silt. The unpredictable, rising like a creature out of the water, bucking the shot. The director on the beach, out of frame, nodding and nodding.

.   .   .

The lobby of the Hotel Ignacio is painted teal and beige and has only one lightbulb, hung two steps in front of the desk. That is where the driver stands: directly underneath it, in an amber circle of light. He is hunched over a road map, squinting. He is one of the shortest men you've ever seen, his shoulders narrow like a twelve-year-old's, the muscles in his arms wiry and dense. When he looks up at you, you see a tattoo on his neck: an upside-down tree, rooted at the jawbone and bursting into a snarl of leafless branches just under the shirt collar.

You will never learn the driver's name, or what the tattoo means. His car won't have a license plate and the roads to the airport will all be eight-lane highways, roundabouts, the lanes inclined toward a background of skyscrapers and black

mountains. You will think of the tattoo again and again, the red parrot in the branches hung by its feet and peering sideways across the hollow of the driver's neck. It is impossible and it is insane and you know it, but in the next weeks, you will think that all this was part of the movie, somehow. The director, he wanted it this way.

PROCURATORE CAPO: And you were aware, Signor Velluto, of the precarious political situation in the area at this time?

VELLUTO: No more precarious than here.

PROCURATORE CAPO: More than seventeen nations have issued travel warnings due to threats of domestic terrorism and cartel violence in Colombia, correct? Ovidio sits at a largely unpoliced region between these two nations, correct? This was the state of things during the time you were scouting for production? I'll refer the jury to subexhibit 5C, producer Baldo Palaggio's production notes.

VELLUTO: Have you read *La Repubblica* today?

PROCURATORE CAPO: Let me ask the questions.

VELLUTO: The Red Brigades bombed six trash cans outside the Defense Department this morning. Seven blocks from here.

PROCURATORE CAPO: We are not discussing Italy.

VELLUTO: We should.

PROCURATORE CAPO: Well, then, pardon me. But bombing trash cans isn't quite the same thing as kidnapping international dignitaries.

VELLUTO: You'd forget the murder of Prime Minister Aldo Moro?

PROCURATORE CAPO: I would never forget, but our state police have worked tirelessly to neutralize—

VELLUTO: They are not neutralized. Terror is never neutralized. Not in Italy, not anywhere.

PROCURATORE CAPO: Sir, *you* are the one on trial here.

VELLUTO: And what about the student revolutionaries, the neofascists, who else—

GIUDICE PRESIDENT: Signor Avvocato, please instruct your client to comply.

PROCURATORE CAPO: I believe our giudici are aware that our

country has its own issues with guerilla insurrection at the moment, signore. Please answer my question.

VELLUTO: Answer mine. You say all of those—the Red Brigades, the neofascists, the students, all those together are not as bad the M-19s?

PROCURATORE CAPO: Please answer my question.

VELLUTO: Setting aside that Colombia has about twice as many guerilla and paramilitary fuckheads as Italy—the FARC, the ELN, the AUC, I could go on—setting all that aside, you think the fucking teenagers in the M-19 were the kings and queens of this prom?

PROCURATORE CAPO: They're not all teenagers.

VELLUTO: But you *concede* that—

PROCURATORE CAPO: Signor Velluto, let's get to the point. Were you aware of the political climate in Colombia when you selected your location?

AVVOCATO: Objection, relevance.

VELLUTO: Oh, nice of you to finally join us, friend!

PROCURATORE CAPO: This goes toward establishing Signor Velluto's disregard for his actors' safety.

VELLUTO: And I'm saying that doesn't matter. They were just as endangered in Colombia as they are here in Italy. No more.

PROCURATORE CAPO: And the American? What about him? *His* home country is not in a state of domestic war.

[Whereupon Signor Velluto laughs loudly, and Giudice Palermo calls counsel to the bar.]

ANDRES, EL PUÑO

Bogotá

There were four of them on the second floor of the house, and between them, they had twelve names.

Outside the walls, in the world beyond, he was Andres: seventeen and clean-shirted. It was the name his mother called him. It was the name that would be printed on the arrest record, if they found out—when they found out—where he went each day when he left his mother's house.

In the Patient's room, though, he was El Puño: a voice through the floorboards, the smell of garlic and ammunition and metal. The Patient had another name, too, and a life and a family and a post as the cultural attaché from Venezuela, but not while he was there—in the room they had built for him, under the bed, and the trapdoor, and the half meter of perfect darkness.

. . .

On nights when the Patient was brave, he asked El Puño for Bach. He stood as tall as the room allowed him to and raised his arm up over his head, knocked on the underside of the trapdoor as lightly as he could, just like they showed him. Three

times and a lull. His voice was a hesitant falsetto: Señor, are you up there?

It was a quiet sound, but still, Andres could feel it in the floor beneath him, hammering through the bone at the center of each heel. He put the butt of the rifle down on the ground and braced himself against it as he kneeled, tucked the edge of the hood under his chin to arrange the eyeholes better. There was a single bright crack between floorboards, and that light was the Patient. He aimed his whisper there.

Quiet.

But—

Andres hesitated, but El Puño stiffened his jaw. Don't make me tell you again.

The Patient paused, long enough that Andres had time to picture the man down there. The Patient would be on his feet, not quite standing, his neck craned at a painful angle, eyes up and studying the stripe of dark room between the boards. The room they kept him in was long and squat, two and a half meters by one and a half, not quite tall enough to stand upright. There was a shuffling and a hushed grunt; the Patient gave up, lowered to his knees. He listened as the Patient coughed an apology, addressed to no one, and Andres had to stifle the urge to say It is all right before the little light went out.

For ten full minutes, Andres knelt in silence in the dark.

This was how he always felt when it was time to leave the Patient's room: like a child who'd just watched his mother walk silently into a bedroom and turn the lock. He couldn't leave the room until the feeling went away, until it wouldn't show in his face anymore.

He couldn't let the compañeros see it on him.

Because if they did, they would ask him what was wrong. And what would he say? It was because of the Patient's silence.

It was because the Patient never asked where he was; where he had been taken by them. He never screamed or called them bastards, even the time Andres watched El Clavo push his rifle into the back of the Patient's soft palate and force him to bite down with all his teeth.

El Clavo had another name, too—Juan Carlos—but the Patient had never tried to ferret it out. The Patient thanked them for the food they brought him. He asked for Bach. He turned off the light when they told him to, and he lay down to wait for the hours to pass.

Andres wiped his nose with his sleeve and tried to focus on his breathing. In the next room, the compañeros were playing Toruro, yelling that the deck was stacked, there were too many fucking swords.

He summoned the strength to stand, crossed to the bedroom door and closed it quietly behind him. He yanked off the mask in one motion, sucking at the air, blinking at the light. He waited for the room to come back into focus and for a voice to start in his throat that was not exactly his own.

· · ·

He wants the symphony again, El Puño said to the others.

Two of the compañeros were arguing, El Clavo and Matón. They gestured wildly with their cigarettes, curtains of smoke thrashing through the air. La Araña, though, was just ignoring him. She leaned way back in her chair and sucked hard on the neck of her beer bottle, her cheeks caving under the last pinch of baby fat.

El Puño swallowed. I said he wants the symphony, he pronounced, forcing his voice louder. We haven't given it to him in a week. What should I do?

You should sit down, asshole. La Araña glanced once toward the empty chair next to her and let her gaze settle on the pot again. It's your deal.

But he's going to get restless, Andres said, turning the deadbolt. We need to give him something.

The rules say if you're leading to the first trick, and you have the three *and* the king of trumps—

That's not true! El Clavo slammed his beer bottle down hard. You're playing with those fucking Santander rules, Matón.

So what if I am?

Maybe that's how you goat farmers run it, but here in the city—

Can we just play? La Araña leaned her head way back and pinched the bridge of her nose with two fingers. Between you two fighting and El Puño playing babysitter in there, it'll take us all night to finish the game.

What did the Patient want this time? El Clavo asked.

Andres coughed. Symphony.

Fuck him, Matón groaned. Puño, write down your lulo from the last round. I'm not letting you forget.

The pot had seventeen pesos and an American revolver in it. Puño penciled a shaky three on the scratch pad and picked up his cards. I just worry about him going crazy in there, he said. What if he starts to think there isn't hope?

Matón laughed. So?

So what if he starts thinking there's nothing to lose, tries to get someone's attention?

Clavo flicked at the dog-eared corner of a card; it made a sound like Chinese water torture. So, fine, whatever, we'll play it for him again. Now deal.

Puño tossed a card in, sighed as he spoke: But it's still suspicious.

Why? What?

The symphony. What if someone hears it?

So?

The same symphony twenty times in a week? Won't they think—

Trump! Matón slapped the table. He looped the pot in with both his arms and kissed the revolver, his lips gushing over the barrel. Oh. Ohhhh. Get over here, gorgeous.

Araña tossed her hand back in the middle and clenched her teeth. Andres, she says, it's fucking classical music. No one can tell that shit apart but you.

Puño, he whispered, correcting her.

Pussy, she whispered, grabbing her beer, stomping into the bathroom and slamming the door.

Puño listened to the sound as the toilet lid closed, imagined Araña sitting down on it and raking her hair back from her face with both hands. He focused his eyes on the revolver on the table: it looked like an animal that had crawled out of an oil slick and died.

Can we play three-handed? Matón said. Puño, deal it out.

·   ·   ·

La Araña's real name was Marina.

Andres wasn't supposed to know it, just like she wasn't meant to know his real name was Andres and not El Puño. They had sex every day in the bedroom over the Patient's cell, on their shared guard shift, on the bed or against the wall, the ammunition on her belt tocking against the wainscoting. Andres never wanted to do it there, but she said they had to. She said, the Patient needs to hear this. To know who's in control.

And anyway, better the Patient hear than those horny com-

pañero assholes out there, playing round out after round of Truco in the living room, jacking off to photos of that actress from *Los Ricos También Lloran* in the bathroom all quiet, like no one knows why they brought the magazine in there.

That day, she put on the Bach record to cover their noise. That day, she asked him to whisper her alias, over and over, as he pressed the side of his face to her sternum.

Afterward, they lay together on the bed, the bed pushed over the trapdoor, both of them staring into the pupil of the ceiling fan. Marina had taken off her mask as soon as they got in the room, and it hung limp over the bedpost now, breathing in the wind. Andres had told her to keep it on—what if the Patient managed to pick the lock somehow? What if he saw their faces?—but she told him to shut up. She kissed the fabric over his mouth until it was wet, ran her hands under the mask and fingered the trickles of sweat at the corners of his lips. The trapdoor locks from the outside, she said. She told him it would all be fine, kissed him with force and shoved him into the mattress.

Twenty minutes later, she lay on the other side of the bed, waiting for the heat to pass from her body so she could go. Twenty minutes: that's all it took. For a while now, Andres knew, Marina had been getting bored with him. He'd started to suspect that she only let him fuck her because she knew he'd never tell the other compañeros about it. And the bigger reason: unlike her, Andres' assignment wasn't stationary. Marina hadn't been allowed to leave the safe house in four months, while Andres went home every day, to his mother and his seven sisters and the outside world. He brought the world back in with him, too, the smell of street food and asphalt on his clothes, and Andres knew that Marina was this type of girl: a scent hound. She wanted to inhale this part of him, to feel it stick in her lungs and discard the rest.

Lately, though, something was different about her.

He reached out across the bed. He twisted the end of her braid around his knuckles and decided on how much he could say.

I went to Club Simón last night, he whispered to her.

It was just the flicker of a smile, but it betrayed her. I remember that stupid place, she said. The pornos on the walls?

It's disgusting but the drinks are cheap.

It's the only place I could *get* drinks for years.

You're a pretty girl. Come on. You never had that problem. She snorted.

And anyway, you'll be eighteen when you get out of here.

Nineteen! She laughed, punched him in the ribs. I'm eighteen already! Hey, I earned that year, hijueputa. Don't take it away.

You did. Andres pulled her in to him, put his cheek on the top of her head. You did, big girl, I'm sorry.

That's what it was: those little silences that slipped into their conversations like splinters, his need reaching out through the air and finding her, cold. That's what had changed between them.

Marina rolled over onto her back, tried to laugh it off. Hey, tell Jul he's a pervert for me, she said. Hesitated; remembered. Just tell him he's a pervert.

The fucked-up thing is, I saw my *sister* there. Andres picked up her braid again and chewed the ragged ends, faked a grin to show he was still relaxed. The thirteen-year-old, he said. Luz. She must have followed me there with all her little friends. She saw me talking to Alexander.

Another silence cleaved the air.

He wasn't supposed to say any names in this room, not loud like that. He remembered as soon as the words left his mouth. The Patient could overhear and use it to identify them later, when he was nestled under a medical blanket in a police interrogation room, when he'd had time for his ribs to heal and

his memory to sharpen. Andres felt Marina stiffen, a change surging through the whole electric field of her body. He braced himself for the quick push out of bed, the crazed eyes and the furious whisper.

But she stayed, leaning on the crook of his outstretched elbow. But when she spoke, her voice was thin and eager.

You mean Alexander the dealer?

Yeah.

Were you doing a drop?

No, he said, stroked her neck. I gave him something. To trade.

What?

Andres sniffed deeply, rubbed the place on the mask just beneath where his nose jutted up. Oh, you know. Just a little something.

She bit her lip to fence in a laugh. She crawled on top of him.

An eight ball?

Maybe.

Tell me you saved some.

No, but I could next time.

What did you get for it?

Andres smiled even though he knew she couldn't see it. He pantomimed holding a grenade to his mouth, pulled the invisible pin out with his teeth and hurled it over her shoulder. She cackled as he pulled her into a barrel roll, whisper-screaming, *Blaow! Blaow! Soldiers! Take cover!*

· · ·

It was not like acting: pretending to be El Puño, pretending he would not care if Marina left him.

It was not like acting, because acting was about taking some-

thing true and small and secret inside you and carving it out, working it like canvas until it was as wide as your entire skin.

What he was doing was lying.

Andres left Marina and La Araña together in the bed, two women napping under a ceiling fan, in one body. He threw his mask on the card table and went to wash up. A clean shirt was hung over the shower rod to steam out the wrinkles; he kept it there so when he went downstairs and out of the house, he wouldn't smell like the compañero's hashish or Marina's sweet, strange filth. They all had to take turns showering, so the water bill wouldn't look suspicious. Marina tasted like a papaya slice that had fallen in the dirt.

As he did the last buttons under his neck, Andres tilted his chin up and caught his own reflection in the mirror. He looked skinny and handsome and weak. He looked like a boy who had never held a gun, and Andres couldn't decide if he liked this boy in the mirror better. The shirt was a light-gathering green that rhymed with the hazel in his eyes. He swallowed once, ran a comb through his hair until it was soft.

Andres had just picked the last flake of tobacco out of his teeth when he heard it: a thump and a jingle, a door opening and the wind chime on the porch beyond it. A woman's singing Hello, hello. Alguien está en casa?

The voice was coming from downstairs.

Andres pivoted through the bathroom door frame and charged across the outer room, grabbed the messenger bag full of textbooks on the way and threw the door to the stairwell back. He closed it, paused to check the lock, rushed on. The stairs were dark but he tripped down them expertly, two at a time. It was the first Sunday of the month, the day the landlady always came to collect the rent. But today she was an hour early.

El Clavo wouldn't be dressed. Shit. Clavo wouldn't be *showered*.

Andres would cover. He had to. He straightened the lapels on the shirt, shook the fabric to get the smells out, because downstairs, the shirt was a costume. Downstairs was acting. Downstairs he had another name.

. . .

El Clavo was the one who told Andres about the difference between an alias and a pseudonym.

It happened a month after he'd joined the movement, eleven months before he was posted in this house. Andres had been following the M-19 for years by then: the breathless coverage when they stole the sword of Simón Bolívar from that stuffy museum north of the park to symbolize the new populist revolt, the buzz in the neighborhood that half the block was with them, that so-and-so had picked the lock on the display case himself. El Clavo lived in the neighborhood then, too, and he was the one who told Andres he was finally old enough to join. He was the one who whispered: Meet me Monday, and I'll give you a new name.

They met in the back row of the lecture hall at the university. Andres was hot as shit under a polyester shirt that he'd paid half his savings for and worn to blend in with the college kids, too young for the university by two years, then, and it all showed in his face. El Clavo, on the other hand, looked five years too old for the Physiology 101 class he was in, a sophomore with a full beard and voice like a TV announcer, dressed in clean shirts and tailored pants his mother had bought him by mail.

Of course, he wasn't called El Clavo then. He was Juan

Carlos, Andres' friend from the neighborhood, who'd been like an older brother to him since they were kids. And that was his first lesson, Juan Carlos said, whispering over the little desk in Andres' lap: When you start calling me by my alias, I'm not your friend anymore. I'm your compañero.

At the front of the lecture hall, the professor drew a diagram: two circles and two arrows, labeled FLUIDO and FLUIDO. This is all the human body is, the professor challenged. Two fluid sacks that need to remain in balance.

My alias is El Clavo, Juan Carlos whispered, and from the way he jabbed his index finger into the fleshy center of his own palm, Andres knew this was important. Because the alias, from now on, would be Juan Carlos' *real* name, his truth, who he would be until the day he died. He'd probably have a pseudonym, too, once he got assigned, but the pseudonym was the lie: that was the name he'd give the police when they held him down under the water and told him to admit it all. Never the alias. You don't give that away, Juan Carlos said, not even if the water fills your lungs, not even if they put the long blade in.

Andres paused. But what about your *real* name?

What do you mean?

I mean Juan Carlos. Andres shifted against the orange plastic of the seat. I mean the name I've called you since we were kids, cabrón. Come on.

Juan Carlos stared through the center of Andres' Adam's apple, thinking. Settled on: That's a stupid question.

The professor lectured. The fluid density of the human body is 985 kilograms per cubic meter, he said. That's significantly less than seawater.

Andres' mouth was dry. He forced his voice to lower, so he would sound less eager. I want to help, he said. I want to help take back Colombia.

Juan Carlos leaned over across the desk again. We have a new operation starting in a week. If you have any more stupid questions, El Puño, ask them now.

And there it was: his alias, a gift.

. . .

His pseudonym, though, that didn't come until later.

His pseudonym was the name the landlady called Andres when he jogged down the stairs and through the parlor door: Jhon! Jhonito! What a treat! I would have expected your uncle!

The landlady was past eighty. She had blue veins in her hands and blue rings on her fingers, hair dyed the color and crispness of burnt toast. You've done something different today, dulzura, he says, kissing the hinge of her wrist. You've never looked more beautiful.

This was Andres' big assignment, how he would help the armed resistance take back the nation: flirting with a geriatric. He wore green shirts that matched his eyes and carried a backpack full of books he'd never read and convinced her, somehow, that he was the nephew of her renter, Vicente Mosa, a thirty-one-year-old wunderkind shipping magnate who, of course, did not exist.

Did not exist, but there he came, tripping down the dark stairs; there he was, Juan Carlos, transformed by a button-down shirt, apologizing about a call from Kyoto, so sorry, it had made him so late.

It's no trouble, Vicente, the landlady said, Jhon was keeping me company.

She squeezed Jhon's kneecap with one blue-veined hand. It felt like the last lurch of a heart.

Maybe if Jhon spent less time with you, he'd keep up with

his work for me, eh? Vicente winked at his nephew, hiked his slacks to his ankles so he could cross his legs as he sat. I noticed you didn't finish painting the trim upstairs. Is this a summer job, or did you think it was a dating service?

There was no trim to be painted, but Jhon didn't say anything. They visited with her for an hour, Jhon chattering about the night classes he was taking in the university this summer, Vicente ribbing Jhon for how little help he'd been with the renovation on the upstairs apartment. The landlady squinted back and forth between them with an unflagging grin. Every time her gaze turned from nephew to uncle, Andres thought: Has she noticed? Juan Carlos was twenty, only three years older than Andres, and full beard or no, simple nearsightedness couldn't overlook that.

But then, miraculously, the visit was over. Vicente glanced at the clock and cursed a conference call he'd forgotten to reschedule. Vicente helped the landlady up off the couch, and Andres stood too, waited quietly for the old woman's knees to straighten and for Vicente to kiss his goodbyes. He studied his own hands as he waited, the fingernails he had to remind himself to keep short and very clean. Because Jhon wouldn't touch his expensive books with hands like Andres had; Jhon didn't live the type of life that puts a stripe of grime around each cuticle every day, or makes dark calluses roughen over the heels of your hands. It might have been crazy, but Andres was superstitious. He was sure that when he took the landlady's hand in his and kissed her soft, pale knuckles goodbye, that somehow she would notice these small things. Somehow, these things would give them all away.

She would call the police and stammer an address.

They would find the compañeros upstairs, gnawing toothpicks, all unmasked.

He could imagine it too easily: Marina, La Araña, still lying naked on the bedspread under the curling breeze. Marina's eyes lighting up with fear; Marina's wrist bending, the Kalashnikov sunk like the head of a sleeping husband into the pillow beside her.

Andres could see it: the barrels of the police rifles, rising to meet her.

· · ·

He was surer of it every day, every time he went into the house: they were so close to being caught.

This is why Andres cooked the Patient steaks, well done, the meat firm as a tensed muscle. He roasted plantains and froze the peels so that the fruit fly eggs hidden in their skins would die, so Jhon Mosa could put them in the compost heap to fertilize the tomatoes. The tomatoes ripened in a week. He sliced them over a green salad and put them in a bowl for the Patient.

He did these things to protect them, in his way: if the Patient lost hope, it would not be because of El Puño. If the Patient heard the landlady come and beat his fists against the floor until she noticed, it would not be because the M-19s were simply thugs.

When Andres opened the door under the bed—the first time in three days—the Patient was sitting upright on his mattress, staring at the clock with a kind of furious thirst. He'd taken it off the plantain crate they gave him for a nightstand. He gripped it in both his hands, holding the thing at eye level like a shelled fruit that would split and leak if he threw it down hard enough.

How many days has it been? the Patient said.

You aren't counting them anymore?

The pen dried up.

When?

I forget how long.

You should have told me.

I should have. The Patient laughed strangely, repeated, I should have. But maybe I didn't really want to know.

The Patient hadn't asked for the clock. Andres was the one who convinced the compañeros that he should have it, that the man needed some kind of dignity. Marina told Andres it was a fucking terrible idea, and fought him over it for hours, and then finally grabbed a knife, pried the clock open, tossed the alarm mechanism down onto the card table as hard as she could. It flashed under the ceiling bulb like a tooth punched out. If you're so worried about being humane, she said, maybe you should find another line of work, Puñito. Marina was still sleeping with him, every day and sometimes twice. But when she did it, now, she left her cigarette burning on the window ledge, her eyes roaming to the corners of the room.

Andres tried not to think of her as he extended his arm and lowered the bowl into the Patient's room. He kept the barrel of his rifle fisted in his other hand, the tip of it wagging over the edge of the trapdoor. He felt the Patient's gaze turn up to regard him, two satellite dishes finding a thread of signal. Thank you, he said. The food you bring is always better.

I brought you something else, Andres said. Hold on.

Maybe it was too much: checking out library books for the Patient, giving him clocks and pens, treating him like a human being. Andres told himself he did it because the revolution was about the people, not just kids in a safe house playing with grenades, and the Patient, prisoner or no, was a person, too. He told himself that, but when Andres retrieved the record from the depths of his rucksack, the feeling that tugged through him was not righteousness; it was guilt. He slid the record out of the sleeve and the vinyl flashed in the light from below.

How did you find it? the Patient wondered.

There's a classical music shop on Avenida Colón. It was in the phone book.

And you're sure it's No. 3?

Yes.

The 1936 Weingartner?

Andres squinted at the cover of the record. The script curled over a water-stained photograph of a man's back in suit and tails.

It has to be the Weingartner, the Patient pronounced. Only the Weingartner understood the overture.

Andres heard the quaver in the man's voice, felt an itch at the back of his neck, that he knew signaled an impulse to apologize. He resisited it. He coughed a quick Hey, forced his wrist to reangle the gun.

The Patient stared back. He pursed his lips and let the silence stretch between them, full of questions. Then his eyes dropped to the salad. It is good, he said. The music, the food. Thank you.

Andres eased up on his grip. The Patient raked his fork once through the lettuce and took a resigned bite. When they first kidnapped him, Andres was struck by how slowly the man ate and drank: like a connoisseur with a brandy snifter, chewing the water out of the canteen like it was bread. It never occurred to Andres until he tried the water himself: the old pipes tinged everything with a flavor like roots and copper wiring, like blood. The Patient must have been terrified of poisons.

The Patient's voice still astonished him, its strange soprano turns.

Do you have to take it back with you?

What?

The record player. The record. I'd like to play it when you're gone.

You can't.

Please. You're the only decent one. The Patient set the bowl down and sat up straighter. You're the only one of them I can ask these things.

No, Andres said, too firmly, overcompensating. The compañeros think—I think—It's not allowed.

It was horrible: the way the Patient's eye sockets filled with shadow as he looked up through the door.

I won't play it too loud, he said, I promise. Gum up the dial. Put it on the lowest volume. I promise I won't try to fix it. I won't try to alert anyone.

Andres adjusted his grip on the rifle. Pass me up your waste.

It will help me sleep. I haven't been sleeping.

You'll figure it out.

How many days has it been?

I gave you a pen to keep track.

I told you. It stopped working.

Fifty-one.

The Patient sat up on his heels, empty-handed. Let me ask you. Do you know what it feels like not to sleep well for fifty-one nights?

The barrel tapped on the ledge. Andres' wrist did it. Andres' teeth were clenched tight together and his eyes were full of tears.

Andres' voice spoke without his consent: Prisoner, it said. Pass up your waste now.

The Patient exhaled. The bucket was in the one corner of the room that you couldn't see from the little door above, as far from the books and the clock as he could get it. Andres could hear him struggling with the lid, making sure the edges were all sealed. He wondered why the Patient never tried to throw it in his face.

Thank you, Andres said.

Thank you. The patient laughed. Well, sir, you're very, very welcome.

Andres closed the trapdoor, fastened the locks, pulled the rug and the bed back over. He dragged out the record player and slipped the Beethoven out of its sleeve and onto the tray. The needle hovered and sank.

·   ·   ·

A five-part chord, repeated twice. A quarter note each. Two guillotines falling.

He tried to explain it to the compañeros. He hauled the record player out of the Patient's room and yelled at them to shut up, unwound the long cord and played those two notes again, again. Listen, he said. The violins are so sharp. Do you know what that's supposed to symbolize?

Juan Carlos picked up another dart and whetted it between his teeth.

It's the sound of heads falling in the basket, Andres said. Traitors to the cause. Do you get it?

Matón narrowed his eyes in thought. Beethoven. Beethoven. That's, like, Belgian, right?

Marina shoved her chair back and stormed into the bathroom again.

Andres watched her out of the corner of his eye, tried hard not to flinch. He focused on the little diamond at the tip of the record player needle, sparking as the record turned. He closed his ears against the sound of the shower running, closed his mind against the image of Marina furiously shucking off her jeans. Beethoven was German, he said, but it's not about Germany, exactly. It's about the French Revolution and the conquest after.

The fuck do you know about the French? Fingering the dart in his right hand, Juan Carlos leaned farther back, finding his throwing stance. He was still in his Vicente Mosa costume, the business shirt unbuttoned to the sternum and sweat haloing his underarms.

Their kings were executed by revolutionaries, Andres said. They did exactly what we're trying to do and they won.

Juan Carlos hurled a dart at the wall and laughed. Andres noticed that they'd drawn a target there, in faint pencil so they could erase it later: President Turbay, unmistakable in thin-framed glasses and a bow tie. Juan Carlos threw his dart, said, I don't think that's exactly how shit with the French ended, Puño.

Well, the symphony's about the years before they lost. During Napoleon. The good times.

What do you know about Napoleon?

It's the *Eroica* Symphony. It's one of the most famous pieces of music in the world.

I went to college and I haven't heard of it, Juan Carlos said.

Matón snorted. Two and a half years of college.

It's one of the most famous chord progressions in the world, Andres said, Listen. He restarted the record and played the opening again.

Matón passed Juan Carlos another dart, said, Aim for the keyhole. I dare you.

Juan Carlos stood. Give me your dinner if I make it.

Yeah, yeah. Matón scooped up his whittling from the table and started hacking.

Napoleon was like Bolívar for Europe.

Juan Carlos narrowed his eyes. No one was like Bolívar.

Matón spat.

Bolívar freed us from the Spanish kings, Andres said, winc-

ing at the sound of Matón's knife. Napoleon freed the French from their kings.

You're missing part of the story there, tío, Juan Carlos murmured.

Come on, listen anyway. Andres nudged the voume dial. When the horn comes in, the violins follow. Right there. Napoleon is the horn. The violins are the armies. Do you get it?

Matón glanced up. So we're like Napoleon?

And Turbay is like Louis XVI—right here, the timpani, that's him. Andres turned the volume up more, shouted. But Louis XVI was worse.

Turbay is a fucking murderer of the proletariat. Juan Carlos did not raise his voice as he aimed. And Borrero was a murderer before him. They have murdered our rights and they have murdered the diginity of the poor and they have murdered our country, a little more every time they let an American through customs to surveil our fields, every time they rig an election—

Andres muttered, I know.

Bolívar was a messiah. Juan Carlos bent his elbow, raised the dart slowly. There's never been a man like Bolívar in the history of the world, before or since.

Andres said it without thinking: Is that why we're losing?

For a moment, Juan Carlos glanced at Andres. The dart followed his gaze; his elbow didn't fall. What did you say?

Because we don't have a Bolívar.

We stole Bolívar's *sword*. If you don't understand the symbolism—

Andres' temples ached but he kept talking. But we're not one movement, not like the one Bolívar led. Not when there are M-19s and the FARC and the communists and the ELN—

We're not the ELN, Juan Carlos said. We don't fucking

burn civilians to death because the city hiked the bus fares. We have strategies.

But how many other groups are out there? Andres said. How is this a people's army if it's split a hundred ways?

Careful, Matón said to them both.

We're all fighting for different things and no one's telling us how to win the fucking war. Andres laughed. If it even is a war.

Straighten your foot, cabrón. Matón yelled, pulled on the rum again. You have to point your foot in the direction you want the dart to go. You're playing like an asshole.

Matón was the only one whose real name Andres didn't know, and he found it hard to look straight at him.

There's no war, Juan Carlos said. Not yet. The war is later. We're still raising funds. We're still making our cause known.

If we're taking war prisoners, it's a war.

Juan Carlos threw.

Foot! Watch the fucking foot!

Is that it? Did the Patient tell you this shit? Juan Carlos said, staring right into Andres. About the war? The music? The *French?*

No, Andres half-lied.

We're not losing, Juan Carlos said. We just haven't attacked yet. He threw. What does a Venezuelan bourgeois fuck like him know about the M-19 losing?

Angle your body! Matón yelled.

He's not a member of the bourgeoisie, Andres murmured. He's a cultural attaché. It's an important job.

What did you just say?

Andres bit the side of his tongue and sighed.

Forget it.

I'm starting to question your commitment—

I said forget it.

No, listen, Juan Carlos said. You need to understand this. The M-19 is not losing. There are compañeros everywhere, chico. Juan Carlos threw. I hate to break it to you, but we're just a little piece. They're in every barrio, secret houses. There are a thousand Patients, a thousand operations. He threw. And there are thousands in the jungle, right now, training for the next thing.

The horn rose like a groundswell from the bottom of the melody.

What damage can we do from the jungle? Andres felt furious and bizarre. Whose idea was that?

Don't question your comandantes.

Who are the comandantes? Andres said. Where are they? You?

Puño—

All I see is a bunch of fucking teenagers who don't know what they're doing.

There was a rush of air, a thunk. The dart was wedged exactly in the keyhole of the bathroom.

Juan Carlos looked Andres in the eye and said nothing. Somewhere in the air behind him, Matón clapped his hands and howled. On the record player, the violins began to gallop.

·   ·   ·

He couldn't have stopped it, what happened next, what had happened so many times before. There was nothing Andres could do, when Juan Carlos threw one last dart at the keyhole and missed; when he cursed and yanked the record player's cord out of the wall and stomped into the bedroom with the revolver. It was silent, then, for a moment, but Andres could still hear the chord. It was in the terrible rhythm Juan Carlos beat into the Patient's body. It was in the pause between the

two words the Patient said before the blows started: Please and Don't.

Andres heard it in each twang of his quadriceps as he pedaled his bike home, hot wind slapping at his cheeks. Again that night, as he closed his eyes in bed, and heard his sister Luz tapping a message to him through the wall.

Andres' sisters slept in seven single beds in the living room, him in the coat closet, underneath the copper rod. It was only big enough for a camper pallet, but at least he could close the door. Luz was the youngest, and their father's favorite, so she got the bed in the corner, underneath the little window with the yellow-flowering senna in it. Her mattress was pressed against the closet wall. Ever since she was a kid, she'd tapped a message to Andres before she slept, one knock for each syllable: Good and Night.

Luz and his mother and the rest of his sisters and his father all thought Andres worked in a bakery on Avenida Carrera 15, and that he left his apron at the shop for washing. Luz and the rest had yet another name for him, the name they cooed as they ran their fingers through his hair: Dresa. They made fun of his long brown eyelashes, called him Cerrito, sweet baby piglet, our only boy!

Luz, when she was small, used to sleep in tube socks when it was cold, and they went all the way up to her knees. But now Luz was thirteen. Now, when Andres tiptoed into the closet at night, Luz's ankles stuck out from under the blanket, toenails painted silver and sparkling in the light. Andres saw the strange bend in her anklebone where she twisted it in a pothole on their street last summer and it broke. Andres saw her at Club Simón two days ago, her tongue in the ear of a man twice her age.

No: Jhon saw her at Club Simón, turning in a circle to music that was too fast to dance like that.

No, Dresa saw her at Club Simón, her small forehead bright every time she passed under the disco ball.

El Puño saw her, and he went crazy. El Puño wanted to drag her off the dance floor by her waist and tell her never, ever to come back there, you stupid little girl.

None of his sisters were ever awake when Andres got home. Their clothes were heaped or folded next to each of their beds, worn synthetics, so many colors. Their eyelids were balmy and twitched; they were probably having nightmares. He paused in the breeze from the window and listened to them breathe. He closed the closet door before he could do anything to wake them.

He lay down and waited to adjust to the dark, to how little air there was. He tried not to hear the chord, repeating and repeating in his head. He tried not to think the obvious thought: that his room was just as dark, and not much bigger than the Patient's.

He tried not to think of Marina: fucking Juan Carlos in the parlor last night, when they both thought Andres had gone.

The couch in the safe house was so white: her teeth were white, and she clenched them to stay quiet. The streetlight through the window was dark blue and cast a rhomboid shape over their bodies. He heard the faint wet slap of him on her, and over it, Juan Carlos' whispering about the jungle.

There were whole villages of guerillas, he told her, shacks on stilts.

She moaned.

They read Marx to the children and teach them to clean weapons.

Andres could hear her breathing change. He saw her shift on top of him.

Juan Carlos kept talking about the weapons. God, there were thousands of them, anything they needed, in boxes shipped up

the river from Brazil, under packs of white T-shirts and sacks of sugar.

Andres wanted to leave then, but he was hypnotized, too. There is no such thing as customs on the Amazon, Juan Carlos said, no such thing as government, no danger. They could train on grenade launchers and Uzis, never worry about being heard.

I could be as loud as I want? Marina laughed.

Let me take you, Juan Carlos said. Please. It's paradise.

Andres stood behind the door. He watched Marina's hands as she grazed her fingernails along Juan Carlos' chest, scratching a white oval into the dry skin. She growled into his ear: I'd love to smell the trees.

The memory was like a splinter. He tried to push it out, and it worked itself in deeper.

Andres lay in his bed, in his closet dark as a cell, and tried to think.

He could put the grenades in the upstairs oven and turn the gas dial and run.

He could call the police and secure his amnesty, try to explain. I am a compañero in the M-19 clandestine unit, stationed in the capital. I and three other guerilleros are safeguarding a kidnapped Venezuelan attaché, Julio Barriqua Caldez, for five hundred million pesetas to fund our paramilitary operations. We are planning an attack. We will strike within the year. Get me a plan of the house, and I will give them all up.

He could say what was true: I don't know why I'm doing this anymore, and I'm too scared to go on.

Or: he could take the banana peels from the freezer to the compost pile, like he did every day. Andres could watch the peels thaw. Marina could not go as far as the garden, but Andres, he could stand there all day if he wanted, in the sun and the air. He could watch them soften into the dirt.

By the next morning, Andres had made a decision.

He biked slowly to the safe house, put on his mask, and fed the Patient breakfast.

He took the mask off in the bathroom and stared into the mirror for a long, still minute.

He said his alias three times out loud: Jhon, Jhon, Jhon.

Jhon went downstairs.

It was a defensive tactic, Juan Carlos said: a luncheon with the landlady. Two hours, three courses. He made the meal himself. Before they ate, they'd show her the completed renovation on the upstairs apartment, let her see just how far her trust in them had gone. If they showed her every corner of the house, how could they be hiding something?

It was Juan Carlos' idea, but Matón was the one who volunteered to stand guard inside the Patient's room. I think he's getting restless, Matón said, scraping his knife against his whittling block. Over the last few months, the wood had turned from a rectangle to an ovoid to something vaguely animal, or at least something with teeth. Let's see if spending some quality time with me helps him with that, he said.

Andres helped Matón lower himself into the chamber. Juan Carlos jogged downstairs and slid out the secret panel in the pantry that hid the part of the room that didn't fit between the floors. Marina hid there, directly underneath the Patient's room, stooped and uncomfortable, probably hugging her rifle like a teddy bear. Andres closed the trapdoor and tapped it once with the flat of his palm to signal they were ready. He became Jhon. Juan Carlos became Vicente. The Patient and Matón and Marina became no one, a part of the walls themselves.

The landlady arrived. She let Jhon guide her by the elbow up the dark and narrow stairs. She oohed over the four-poster bed they'd bought for the spare room, the gleaming stovetop, the

new paint on the walls. She ran her hand over the card table where they played Toruro every night, breathed deeply and asked if she smelled lavender. *We had to cover the cigarettes somehow,* Andres thought, but Vicente thumped the doorframe, smiled proudly. It's almost ready to sublease. A few more picture holes to fill, and then we'll advertise.

Jhonito could move in, the landlady said, tickling the skin inside Andres' elbow. I'd love to see more of him.

Jhon faked a smile. I doubt Uncle Vicente would want that.

Vicente smiled, too, leaned against the bedframe; he was not two meters from the trapdoor now. Come on, nephew, he said. How do you know what Uncle Vicente would want?

Jhon ladled cold soup into white bowls while Vicente chatted with the landlady about last autumn's rains. He arranged bocadillos in a little arc on the top of the platter, placed blue flowers between each of the crusts. The pantry was off the kitchen, and he knew Marina was watching him from there, from behind the secret panel and the shelves of cans, a knot in the wood gouged out strategically with the whittling knife. Jhon could feel this: her brown eye behind the hole, staring. He couldn't hear her, but he could imagine the small movement of her chest behind the wall. When he thought of it, his cock stirred, and he was guilty.

· · ·

Guilty, too, because he knew that Matón would be dead by then, or dying, thrashes muffled by the soundproofing. Matón, who had no real name and no life outside the house, just fleshy hands like an enormous child and a voice too loud for his assignment and a poorly whittled sculpture of what might have been a jaguar. Andres had studied it earlier that day, before

he went to see the Patient: little spots for eyes carved out like pockmarks, the teeth a row of uneven triangles. He'd stared at the sculpture and faltered. A voice inside his head whispered, I won't do this. No. I can't.

But an hour later, he went in to serve his guard shift anyway, the garrote in his rucksack. He unfurled it before the Patient and showed him how to use it: the piano wire around the throat, the stick through the two loops at the back to give him leverage.

The Patient stared. I can't do that.

I know, Andres, said, but you will. He'll come in to guard you in a hour.

I'll mess it up. He'll get free. He'll kill me.

You want to get out of here? Andres said. Then hide the weapon and wait.

. . .

Andres made himself look away from the hole where Marina was, made himself remember. Your name is Jhon, Jhonito, Jhon. You are not yourself.

Jhon picked up the platter, yelled Buen provecho as he swung through the kitchen door. He poured out the Bellinis. A glitter of light came through the window, the sun dodging the fronds of a wax palm in the alley and glancing off his bike mirror and then into the house. The peaches positively sparkled. The landlady murmured, Qué linda.

Upstairs, the trapdoor thumped and thumped and the Patient said I'm sorry.

Downstairs, Vicente Mosa heard nothing. He raised his glass. To the most beautiful woman in Bogotá.

In the pantry, Marina heard the scramble of feet over her

head, and then a whispered Sorry, and then silence. Then the sound of an opening door. Then the grunt of a man hoisting himself up and over a ledge.

In the parlor, Jhon toasted to the lovely afternoon, but Andres said nothing. He was waiting for the Patient to speak for him. He was waiting for footsteps on the stairs, and then the starved shape in the parlor room door, for the smell of him to fill the room, for the landlady to stand and scream. That was the plan. That was why he'd left the trapdoor unlocked.

In the pantry, Marina held her rifle in two hands and tapped the barrel to the ceiling above her, gently. She waited for Matón in the chamber to tap the signal back.

Downstairs, the landlady put down her cup and smiled. And will you be renewing your lease, too, señores?

Upstairs, the Patient sprinted to the bedroom door and found it locked.

This wasn't the plan. The Patient stood in the dark. Cold water filled his chest, his head.

He turned back to the room slowly and studied all the furniture. The bed was still in place. The trapdoor he'd locked, in case. The man he'd killed was still under there, curled up like a comma inside the room between the floors, but that was a thought the Patient had no time to think, not when he had to decide, right now, what to do.

That was when he saw the record player on the nightstand.

·   ·   ·

E-flat major, another, a rest. Allegro con brio into adagio assai, scherzo, finale. The highest the volume could go.

By the end of the first movement, Vicente will have charged up the stairs, thrown the bedroom door open, and shoved the

screaming Patient back into the room under the bed. The Patient will thrash and beat his fists as loud as he can, so Juan Carlos will leave the record going. He will explain to the landlady that he is sorry—it will not turn off—and before the landlady can put together that this makes no sense, he will hustle her into a cab and tell the driver her home address. Then he will go back upstairs, to shut the player down, to try to make the Patient shut up.

Recapitulation. The horns find the melody in the tonic. The violins stroke out the dominant chord again and again, the sound sawing at the eardrums.

When the second movement begins and she is sure that it is safe, Marina will push out the false wall in the pantry, gasping. Cereal boxes and tin cans and sacks of root vegtables will explode away and across the floor. She will step over it, out of it, into the yellow light of the kitchen. The gun she took in with her will be gripped in both her hands.

The second movement is a funeral march, C minor. Andres will have sprinted to the alley and then stopped, his hands on his bicycle's handlebars. He will not be able to decide: whether to run away now or stay and play dumb.

But when the trio comes in, modulation to C major, he will go back inside the house.

Marina will hear the front door ease open, and she will not hide like she's supposed to. She will look at a sweet potato on the linoleum, smashed with her boot heel. She will think of Matón, feet scuttling in the ceiling over her head, and she will wait.

The landlady gone, Juan Carlos will open the trapdoor again and stare into Matón's eyes, until he's sure his friend is dead. The Patient will have scuttled to the back of the cell, as far as he can get from the body, clutching the piano wire with both hands like he's presenting a bouquet of flowers.

Modulation back to C minor, and Andres will step into the kitchen.

A yank to the record player's cord. The music staggers and stops.

They will not reach the scherzo. Marina will not notice. By then she will be going through what she's seen, putting it all together. She will step over a spill of dried black beans, her eyes full of something hard and changed. She will shoot Andres in the gut, once, again. She will step over his body and go slowly up the silent stairs.

· · ·

That will be later.

But for now, there was just E-flat major, blasting, twice: sudden violins in the walls, as loud as thirty-nine kilos of sharpened steel falling.

Every one of them heard it: Andres and Jhon and Vicente and Juan Carlos and the landlady and the Patient and Marina and Marina and Marina.

Andres had no idea that Juan Carlos would lock the bedroom door, as a precaution, his key slipped into his palm as the landlady turned the corner into the upstairs kitchen. Andres had no idea how any of this would go, not really, not if he was honest. It wasn't a good plan.

But there is a moment between those two chords, a full-count rest. There is an instant of total knowing: that the chord will come again, that there are things we can be sure of. Andres stayed there as long as he could. He didn't want the second chord to vibrate in his chest, but it would. It would shake as deep in him as if he'd made the sound with his own mouth. He would feel it surge through him like catharsis, so loud his

own throat would go raw with it, and after that, every single thing he'd planned would go all wrong, but not yet. Not yet.

For now, there was a rest. For now, he held his teacup high, finishing the toast. He was so happy and so sure: the music did it. It did this to all of them. It was not him, no: Andres was not the one who did this terrible thing.

RICHARD

Ovidio

You take a connecting flight to Ecuador and sleep two nights in the airport floor with your suitcase as pillow and a bored gate agent with an eyelid sty who speaks English but won't tell you anything, but finally, after you've reread five times the one book you brought, goddammit: they let you on the plane.

It's a puddle jumper that leaves at two in the morning, but you don't let yourself sleep. You probably couldn't if you wanted to, anyway. Your nerves feel stripped. The jet you're on seems minuscule in comparison to the colossal sound of its engine. You stare out the window and try to equate that grinding rush with how the blades look to you, a tinny blur, fast as humming-bird wings in the dark. You finish a plastic cup of water and feel your mouth go slowly dry. You have never been on a plane as small as this before.

But you know what—this is a good thing. Your acting teacher in New York always said that one of the first steps to understanding a character is to isolate and confront his greatest fear. As the plane descends, you feel the last week in Bogotá draining from your memory, shaken out of you by the motion of the engine.

Through your window, you watch the rain forest creep up on the fields, until there is nothing but rain forest under you, a landscape with no edges. It is exactly what you expected: a carpet of endless black-green, the shine of brown rivers curling through. Your heart trills as you descend, the fuselage skimming upper leaves. You close your eyes and study this new terror, the exact shape it makes as it spreads in your chest.

· · ·

From here, it happens like a film slowed down to half speed: you can see all the black splits between the frames, and none of it feels real.

The plane descends, and you look out your window.

There is no airport below you.

An elbow of blond dust arcs around a surge of trees, hacked abruptly back. There are only two floodlights on the runway and they throw parallel lines across that space, stretching from nowhere to nowhere. You squint. You can't see a hangar, no terminal, no silvery windows stuffed with staring children. As you get closer, you can see a shack hoisted up near the edge of the clearing, tethered to the end of one of the floodlight beams, but otherwise, there's nothing. The whole land is black and empty. The trees are a single surface, a freeze frame of a boiling sea.

The shapes of four shirtless men with flashlights amble out of the shack, laughing about something as the plane lowers its wheels. You are close enough to the ground, now, that you can see them clearly through the shuddering window, striding into the floodlights. You could yell to them, Duck or No or You're going to die, and you want to. Their sandals drag in the dirt, and you are almost close enough to see the trails they leave in

their flashlight beams. One of the men bends over at the waist, laughing, and his teeth are so white that it stuns you.

The plane finds the earth, bangs down into it.

The windows cloud in an upsurge of dust, darkening everything inside the cabin. The speed of the jet pulls straight through you.

. . .

You stand on the runway, new sweat crowding on your hairline and upper lip, and watch the unharmed men wheel the luggage out of the hull.

The other passengers mutter in tired Spanish to the workers, pass them palmfuls of folded pesos. The money is russet-brown with a silver insignia on each bill that glints under light, bigger denominations than the casting director sent you with. When the man passes you your suitcase, you take it and smile like an idiot. You don't have anything left to give him, and you don't know the Spanish for *sorry*.

You don't know where the road comes from either, how it grows so suddenly out of the distant edge of the clearing as the fleet of cars suddenly pulls up. You can't see where the jungle ends and the lot begins, and how these dozen Fiats and Renaults come growling out of the black horizon itself. It happens so fast: the passengers hoist their luggage into trunks and leave. New passengers spill out of the cars and fill the hull up again.

You stand there alone, your little brown suitcase a thousand pounds in your hand.

The cars clunk away, one by one. The plane roars and narrows to a speck of light between two dim blue stars, and is gone.

Count your breaths: one, two, three, four. A meditation.

You lose count at five. For the first time you hear the insects, a rising drone coming from the jungle.

．　．　．

An hour later, the Volkswagen appears.

You can hear the two men inside before they even stall the car, guffawing in a strange language at some story one of them is telling. When they get out, they don't introduce themselves. They finish their cigarettes. They finish the joke. You shuffle your feet and wait for them to acknowledge you, the only other person in that black, open field.

Finally, the shorter one careens toward you, says something in Italian that might be an apology. He shakes your hand with both of his—Fabiano, però chiamami Fabi, *Fa*bi—grinning drunkenly around a gold-capped eyetooth. He motions to the taller one. This man murmurs an introduction just once, in English—Baldo, is nice to meet you—and squints over his shoulder, avoiding your eyes. Baldo wears a powder-blue shirt with a wide collar, a skinny gold necklace that he twirls around the tip of his pinky finger as he frowns into the distance, locating the road. Finally, he decides—Andiamo—and folds himself into the driver's seat, his legs six inches too long for their brown corduroys and his knees crowding the wheel.

The car rolls out of the lot, down the lightless road. Tree branches come out of nowhere and slap the windshield hard enough to make you jump. You try to ask questions, to distract yourself. Fabi doesn't seem to speak any English, and Baldo does so only begrudgingly. He keeps the windows shut to keep out the mosquitoes, ashes his cigarette into an empty Styrofoam cup between your seats as he talks. He peppers his answers with constant quips of Italian, the words aimed over his

shoulder at Fabi, slouching in the backseat. Whatever Baldo is saying is hilarious, and probably at your expense. Fabi collapses lower and lower into his seat every time he laughs, absolutely contorting himself with laughter, whacking his knees furiously with his fists. You glance up for an instant, and the seat belt is all the way up by his neck.

Hesitant, you ask another question.

We are producers, Baldo answers. Both of us. E tu sei un idiota che avrebbe dovuto leggere il suo contratto.

Fabi thumps his thighbone and roars. Bravo, bastardo! The car doesn't have a headrest, and his spittle lands on the back of your neck as he laughs.

No, I don't have the script for you. Cosa ti aspetti, che ho la sceneggiatura uscendo dal mio culo, eh?

You can tell he's not just translating. Fabi hocks a blue knuckle of chewing gum out the window, then resumes a guffaw as if uninterrupted.

Yes, we are behind schedule. The rest of the crew is already out on set. Davvero, i putti americani partono un giorno si e uno no . . .

You give up on questions. The men keep talking, smoking. The road grows smoother under the car, the dirt firmed by the weight of steadier traffic. The trees must be thinning out around you, but you still can't see them: the headlight beams don't illuminate much. They shine over things on the roadside here and there, but only at wide intervals: a tin-roofed bar called Game Over; two miles down, a brown girl in jean shorts staring stunned at a wrecked bicycle lying in the waist-high grass. No fruit stands closed for the night, no fishermen dragging the daybreak haul in. Nothing you expected. The trees arch over the road. One drops something over the windshield: a cluch of seven leaves the size and shape of machete blades.

Baldo curses and thwacks at the wiper control. In the back-seat, Fabi gives another yawp of laughter, throwing his head back toward the rear window until it arches nearly perpendicular with his neck. In the mirror, you can see the line of his teeth in his open mouth, the gold eyetooth a glinting sliver over his wet, undulating tongue.

Shadows move over the car. The car moves faster than it should on this road.

What? you ask. What's so funny?

Instead of answering you, Fabi points out the window.

It takes you a moment to realize that you're in a town. You're in it for only a moment: a handful of one-room buildings on one unpaved street, unlit signs propped up next to doorways: MÉDICO, ABARROTES, BAR. Everything is painted weird shades of salmon and tan, a sharp accent against the rotten avocado color of the trees that loom a foot behind everything. Heaps of trash fester in the alleys between buildings: broken chairs and tin cans and fruit peels that you can smell through the windows.

A loud dog sprints out of nowhere and chases you out of town. That's it. Half a minute's drive, and you've seen everything.

The trees thicken again. The road roughens under your tires. The dog disappears.

Two more minutes' drive, and Baldo kills the engine.

Ovidio, he says. This is where you stay.

This is not a part of the village you just saw. A square building, a pocked tin roof and wood walls painted a discount blue-gray. A wood-chip clearing to park cars, a thatched hut with a long table under it, covered in blue plates set out for an invisible dinner party. The air smells like citronella and bleach and mildew and the wet, dense scent of the jungle that you're just now learning.

You remember yourself. So my room—

Get out of the car, please now, Baldo mutters, slamming his own door and opening yours. Sono le quattro del mattino, cazzo.

As you tug at the stuck trunk lid, you try to remember the map the casting agent flashed at you, that sad clutch of colored paper. Where did the casting director point to, on the map? God, why didn't you ask? You remember the name *Ovidio*, you think you do, but you hadn't registered its coordinates. There was a mottled inch of green, the words *Amazon Rain Forest* etched in thin script, and a crooked Y where the country lines met. Brazil, Colombia, Peru. Which one was this town in?

You have an early shoot tomorrow, Baldo warns.

I'm sorry, I just can't get this trunk—

He thumps it once with his fist, hoists your suitcase out and shoves it into your hand. These are your keys, he says, pressing them into your other palm. We're going to bed, he says, walking away.

Fabi trips along after him, swigging from an amber-colored bottle he's produced from somewhere. You stand a minute in the lot, squinting to read the worn number etched onto the leather tag. You think you hear someone walking nearby, wandering somewhere near the perimeter of the lot, but you think you're hearing so many things: prowling cats and winding anacondas and ghosts striding slowly over brush.

You don't look over your shoulder as you walk off to find the door to your room. You don't notice the director, pacing the lot because he can't sleep, but he notices you. He pauses near the picnic table. He watches you open your door. He watches you study the room in the dark: the tatty carpet and the twin bed, the tent of mosquito netting floating beneath the ceiling, the

framed cross-stitch of a macaw. Then you find the light switch, and he turns back toward the trees.

. . .

In the morning, you wake up to someone turning a key in your door.

You startle, sit up fast in bed. Whoever's coming in hears you and gives a warning knock, three times, with what sounds like the side of their fist. You can't see the digital alarm clock through the mosquito netting so you shove the net back. The numbers are blinking 12:00, 12:00.

Good morning, pal! someone shouts from inside the glare in the doorway.

You don't register, at first, that it's an American accent. You can't see the man, either, but as he shoulders his way into the room, your eyes focus. He's wearing Bermuda shorts and a T-shirt with a spiral-tailed monkey surfing on the back of an alligator. The man's face and his arms are tanned so dark you can't tell what race he is immediately, and his voice is so loud that any accent is moot. He has no wrinkles until he smiles, and then they are everywhere. He speaks too fast for your brain to register relief, to recognize the miracle of it: the first American voice you've heard since you left New York.

Hank Vance, he says, thrusting his hand out to you with a grin. Proprietor.

What time is it? you manage, reaching for the handshake.

But then Baldo is in the room, too, pulling you up and out of bed by the collar of your undershirt. Fabi jogs in and opens your suitcase, starts rifling around. Hank laughs.

Eleven thirty. Barely dawn. Boys, boys, what's the fucking emergency?

Why didn't my alarm go off?

Generator trip in the middle of the night, Hank says. Happens all the time, no need to lose your damn mind about it.

Fabi throws you a pair of jeans and you stand up to put them on. Are we supposed to be—

Everyone's already on set, Baldo barks.

How?

They forgot you! Hank laughs. They'd been shooting for three hours before anyone thought, where's our leading man?

The shirt Fabi throws you is a white button-down, something you brought in case you had to go to a nice dinner. You button it slowly.

Hurry, Baldo says.

Hank sneers. Come on, Balso! You're not going to let me greet my guest? The thump he lands on your back makes your chest feel like an empty tin box. His smile releases a rush of new creases at the corners of his eyes; when he relaxes, you can see tan lines between them.

Baldo curses in Italian and yells something to Fabi. Fabi grabs your wallet off the nightstand and tosses it underhand to him.

I heard you're the new American! Hank cheers.

You stare at Baldo, paging through your wallet, looking for something.

I'm from Georgia, Hank says. Outside Savannah. Absolute shithole. I'm gonna bet for you . . . Nebraska! He squints and jabs his index finger into the center of an invisible map.

Ohio, you say without thinking. No, actually, New York. I've been living in New York for—

Siamo in ritardo, Baldo mumbles. Then in tourist-phrase-book English: Sir, will you please put this in the lobby safe?

He is holding out your passport to Hank.

Give me the whole thing, Hank says, snatching the passport

and your entire wallet from Baldo, striding out the door into the lot. This guy's a fellow American. My goddamned countryman! His money's no good here!

You trip after him, stunned and half-buttoned, your eyes glued to your wallet as Hank shoves it into his back pocket. Can't I keep it with me?

Merda, Baldo mumbles from inside your room. Then yells: It will be safer. We need to go.

Well, can we at least stop by the lobby before we head out? My room doesn't have a phone and I haven't really talked to my girlfriend since—

No phones in the Amazon! Hank yells, and you're about to ask what he means, when suddenly Hank wheels around to face you. His whole face is changed, painted over with a Jack Nicholson smile and his eyes jogging toward the tree line, bright with an idea.

Hey, he whispers in a new, low voice. You want to see something wild?

Baldo strides out of the room. We have to leave now.

In the sunlight, there is something about Hank's face that makes you nervous. He's handsome in a wind-chapped way, vaguely ageless. The wrinkle in his forehead should destroy his looks but it doesn't. When you don't answer right away, he chatters his teeth together exactly three times and sniffs.

I think we have to get going, you say.

Baldo yells something over his shoulder to Fabi, who sprints out of the room and goes to start the car.

Come on, it'll take twenty minutes, Hank whines. Tops. You're in South America. You always have twenty minutes in South Fucking America!

Baldo yells: Sir!

Hank yells back: Siesta! No trabajar, hombres!

His accent is so terrible it must be a joke. He turns back to you.

I've got the projector all set up for you up at the house. You can't ask me to take it down now, come on!

Projector?

This is when Baldo strides over, grabs you by the arm, and tugs you toward the car. Fabi yells from the driver's side window: Ci torniamo se possiamo! Più tardi! Avremo una festa, la prometto!

You're fucking with tradition here, guy! Hank yells back. Tradition matters! Every guest of mine has to see this movie! He yells a dozen words, this time in rapid, perfect Spanish, makes rude gestures with his arms and elbows. Don't tell me you don't speak any Spanish, wop!

Baldo shoves you into the passenger's seat and slams the door hard behind you. Fabi turns the key and the engine grinds.

Tomorrow! Hank yells through the glass. Hey, don't forget! Tomorrow!

You will never see the movie Hank wanted to show you. Hank will forget. You'll see him tomorrow, but he won't recognize you. He'll be behind the screen door of the hotel office, feet up on the desk, studying the gaps in his teeth in a hand mirror. When he sees you, he'll give you a paranoid stare, void of any recognition. The fuck are you? he'll say. The fuck do you want?

The silence inside the car, now, is heavy and porous, interrupted by the constant sounds of the road beneath the wheels, the kissy noise of the men drawing cigarettes and bottles to their lips. You watch your own reflection in the side-view mirror, shivering with the hitching of the drive line.

·   ·   ·

The canoe is waiting for you when you arrive. A short man someone's hired to row waves hard from the bank. But the Volkswagen sinks into the mud thirty yards before you reach them and it takes what feels like hours to crawl the last distance. I'll get out and push, you say, but the Italians are yelling at one another, pointing wildly, the wheels spinning loud like circular saws. I'll get out, you say, but you don't move.

By the time you make it out of the car, the Volkswagen is sunk a third of the way up the hubcaps. Baldo kicks the mud away from the tires, cursing the mud on his shoes. Fabi jogs out of the car and crouches down to climb into the boat: one foot carefully placed in front of the other, his steps moving straight down the center seam. He keeps his hands clamped to the wobbling gunwales. He keeps laughing like this is all hilarious.

There's no reason for you to be so nauseous. But as you step from mud to metal, as you find your balance over that brown seep of water, your stomach starts palpating. You taste acid and heat. There's a boy climbing in behind you, now, a boy with an oar twice the size of his body, and you realize that it wasn't a short man waving at you: it was him, a child no more than nine years old. His smell assaults you; something like burned tea leaves and the hauling wind over a salt mine. He must be native, you think. This is what the natives smell like. This is how they do things. This is where I am now.

When you look over your shoulder, you register the color of the Volkswagen for the first time: a dim powder-green that sends a shard into an interstice between your gut and heart.

Fabi clucks to the oarsman. Baldo folds himself into the tiny car like an origami trick. He presses the gas pedal, and the engine sound thrashes in the space between your skull and jaw.

The boat pushes off.

. . .

The canoe trip takes half an hour, and the whole way, you can't get your stomach to be still.

You try to comfort yourself. You try to think of your adolescence: Whiskey Island in late summer. Of your road trip with Kay, when you stopped there on the long drive east to crash with your parents for a few nights, show her where you grew up. You took her there, to Lake Erie and the ferry over to the peninsula, and the whole way she was quiet; you'd been fighting for days.

So don't think of that.

Think of an hour later, Kay standing fifteen yards down the beach from you, pulling her shirt over her head. Think of the sand pressed into the skin over the waistband of her skirt, golden, a wash of braille. A half mile off, a smell was rising off the rock pits—pork skin and clean smoke—and you and she still hadn't said a single word to each other in hours.

But then she took off the skirt, a dim powder-green thing that fluttered as she tossed it to the rocks. Even after it had landed, you watched it, gasping like a jellyfish in the wind. The fight was about money—how you'd have none of it when you got to New York and Kay would have a good job waiting at a firm in midtown—but it was hard to think about that when her bathing suit was eggshell-white and beaming at you like a searchlight in the dusk. She walked away from you, mincing toward the edge of the jump-off, gray shells sharp under her feet. She had said she would pay for you, would pay for everything until you found steady work in New York, and the insistence of her love made something calcify in your subconscious, something that had been steeping in you and gone sour over all those days locked together in the car. It made you think selfish

thoughts: that you were an *actor,* and fuck her pity, your work was just as important as hers. It made you snap at her: If I'm too broke for New York, Kay, then maybe I should just stay in Ohio.

Think of how small she looked, how sad and pale, her ribs under the loose elastic band of the bikini.

That was it: your last really good moment together. That was the moment the hard thing in you softened.

Then you were running. Then you were scooping her up under her waist and the pits of her knees, and then she was scream-laughing and you leapt, together, right off the rocks. It happened because of the water, because water, for you, had always been sex and sunlight and hungry smells, a clear-eyed, leaping feeling. It happened because you thought you loved her, still, even if this move had made you feel all messed up, and when you hit the water, it was warm and silver.

.   .   .

The river, here, is the color of coffee stirred with evaporated milk. Froth curls up from nowhere, floats past you to nowhere. The bushes on the banks sag, exhausted, wet with a sheen of rainwater that gleams like sweat. The trees are colossal: their trunks look like muscle butchered from a mammoth creature, with big dips in between sinews that collect shadows. Their branches are knitted together so tightly over the river that 11 a.m. looks like dusk. The sound and itching feeling of insects are everywhere, but you can see none of them, not until you look at your wrist and find a dozen long-legged things, inches apart and moving.

You swat. You get a dizzy feeling as you look up, as the current draws you forward. The sunlight that seeps through the leaves lands on your face in stray flecks, mottling you. You

look down again and drag your fingertips through the current alongside the boat. It feels suddenly urgent to be certain of something, to know the temperature and texture of the water.

From the bow, Fabi glances over his shoulder. When he sees you, he lunges—eh eh eh eh, porca puttana, no. No.

You haven't got a good look at Fabi, yet, not really. In the car, he'd been thrashing with laughter, his eyes closed or open into bright-black smears, the stinging smell of his alcohol somehow obscuring the image of his face. Now, though, you can see the broad shape of his nose, and that changes everything for you. His hair is curled in minute spirals close to the scalp. His mouth is childish and moist.

He puts a flat palm on top of his head, wrist to crown and fingers pointing up at the sky, and leers with his teeth bared.

It takes you a minute to get what he's trying to tell you.

Sharks? you say. In the river?

He nods. Nuotano dall'Atlantico.

He spits into the water. Sono ovunque. Attenzione.

You look back toward the slow current, and try to pay attention.

You make a count of the dead things in the river: the speckled neon inch of a dart frog, engorged leeches clinging to the furred limb of a half-sunken corpse. A rhesus monkey drifts by, no bigger than a kitten, its skull notched with a wound that drains a subtle pink into the water. Then a snarl of kelp. A cluster of drowned butterflies, their bodies pinched together at the thorax and their wings splayed out like a blossom. Your brain is saying, *seventeen. Seventeen dead things.* Then you see it: a human leg pushes through the surface and bobs.

You startle, your knees knocking the helm. The boat tilts. Fabi eyes you.

The rain starts suddenly, little stings of it on the backs of

your hands. The toes on the leg are filthy with muck. The incision is clean—no, it is perfect, *perpendicular.*

Your heart floats to your jaw but you force yourself to study it.

The wound is entirely flat. No. The wound is a bisection. A plastic shell with a hollow core, buoyed by the brown water.

The rain surges for an instant, pushes the leg downstream.

You look away, and up, nauseous. You see the cluster of bodies on the approaching shore.

You think of it again despite yourself: Kay on a Lake Erie shoal, way out in the water. You on the shore, watching the wind sift through every piece of her hair.

It is not like that.

There are natives, or what you think are natives, naked except for straw skirts and handfuls of mud smeared over their bodies. There are tall men in thin linen pants with tensed mouths, barely looking at you. One woman, in a loose white shirt. Men with cameras gripped in loose fists, eyes trained on your approaching boat.

As you're rowed closer, the rain slows, and the crowd parts to let a man through. He is surprisingly short, with bored, matte-green eyes behind thick plastic glasses. No one looks back at him as he pushes through, but he emits an energy that signals the people around him to feint. His thinning hair is mussed in the back and no one has dared to tell him. His arms are crossed in front of a filthy but finely made brown shirt.

The canoe reaches him, carves a deep wedge into the mud.

The short man watches, frowning, his eyes fixed straight at you like you've made a mess. When he offers his hand to you, he doesn't say hello.

Get out. That same venomous accent. We have work to do.

Fabi is suddenly behind you, loud and thrilled, his arms are open wide to receive no one.

Il direttore!

It shouldn't be, but this is what you'll really remember about that first day:

The wave of panic that rises in you as the director scans your body, from your ankles to your neck, squints and bites the edge of his tongue inside his mouth. The weight of the mud in the cuffs of your pant legs as you follow the director over to the makeup tent. The smell of the earth, leafy and dank. The smell of your sweat. The silence of the three men who smear more mud over your arms and your face and into your hair. The slick coolness of it. The hot mist of the air.

The costume crew gives you a green shirt with the sleeves cut off. It looks like it's already been worn by someone who was shoved down hard into wet earth, but you thank them, let them pull it over your head and sit you down in a canvas chair and take your shoes off with their thin, bony hands. They wedge your feet into heavy leather boots and delicately tie the laces. Then they walk away, blotting their fingertips on handkerchiefs that they produce from embroidered shirt pockets, muttering in Italian with elegant disgust.

The director strides over. He smokes as he sizes you up—first with his eyes, then with his hands, lipping the cigarette as he reaches into the back of your shirt to examine the tag. Up close, you learn no new information about his face: it is flat and affectless, a single worry line carved deep into the skin above his eyebrows. He pulls on the bottom hem with two pinching fingers, narrowing his eyes as the wrinkles collapse.

Bene, he says. Are you ready?

Of course you're not. You don't even know what the scene is.

Yes, you say.

But then one of the costumers jogs over, carrying a boxy black 8mm camera. He holds it out to you.

This isn't right. You want to say it out loud—I'm an actor, I'm not a cameraman. You must be mistaken. This isn't right.

But up ahead, the director is a dozen yards in front of you already, looking over his shoulder impatiently with a tendril of cigarette smoke snaking behind him. He's halfway across the beach by now, nearing an enormous tree at the outer limit of the jungle where shooting must have already started.

You run to catch up with him, the camera in your fist. I'm sorry, you say. I'm tired, I didn't realize it was a prop. Could you—

Non importa. It doesn't matter.

You're still far enough away that you can't see what's going on. It takes you a moment before you realize that your destination is a tree: a tree that you do not know is called kapok, huge with reaching limbs, the bark etched with a labyrinth of deep ridges, all the ridges edged with fluorescent moss. There are three men clustered around the base of the trunk, pointing cameras at something you can't see yet. Beyond them you can hear a whimper and a bark and a scream, all in one voice, hoarse and loudening. Then you step beyond the cameras, into the dark and leafy air of the jungle, into the scene.

Remember it: the sensation of every drop of acid in your gut suddenly roiling, the rest of your body instantly numb.

Fabi is lying on the ground, fainting into the arms of a crouching man who leans into the trunk of the towering tree. A dozen enormous and angry sores are open and weeping pus on Fabi's foot and his foot is thrust out straight in front of him. Black trails of gangrene spread up his leg and split into tributaries. His pant cuff is rolled to the knee, and the rot spreads up beyond it.

The man who's crouching behind Fabi's body has him in a steady headlock, ostensibly to help keep him still. He has an Italian profile and dark hair that skims his eyebrows. He looks directly up at you and speaks clearly, in American English.

Are you filming? Are you getting all this, Richard?

He swallows once, smiles frantically. What does he want from you?

Richard, what are you doing? Film this! We're gonna win an Oscar for this!

You think, *But my name is not Richard.* You don't know how to use the camera; you can't do what he says. You try to lift it up from where it hangs at your side, but the weight of it is suddenly too much for the thin muscles in your forearm, for the thin nerves that control the muscles and the thin electricity that lights the nerves.

A third man, now, staggers in from somewhere in your periphery, a blond man with a heavy moustache and a bandanna at his neck, and he is kneeling, too.

There is a machete in his fist.

He holds it over over that inch of skin just south of the knee joint aiming and God, God, and he is lifting it up, and then bringing it down, and down, and down—

You can't look, but you do.

Seven hacks, straight through the bone. A wet sound, then a hard sound, then the same wet sound again. The blood curls through the mud. The mud steams in the new heat.

The camera makes no sound when you drop it. Your vomit puddles in the spreading tangle of the kapok roots, and the camera man steps closer, says, Bene, bene, bene!

Here is something else you don't know:

What a frame narrative is.

You've memorized Hamlet's monologues, sure, but you've

never bothered to learn the term. You tuned out during most of the Play Structure and Analysis courses you took in acting school. It was irrelevant to you. You already knew that the best characters in *Midsummer* were the Athenians. The mini-play with the cross-dressers and the talking wall—as far as you were concerned, you could take it or leave it. Besides, you know your type: you'd be cast as a Lysander, not a Bottom or Quince. There was no reason to study the rest.

So you weren't paying attention while your acting teacher delivered her lecture on narrative interiority. She made wide gestures as her voice boomed into the auditorium, the fluted sleeves of her batik dress swinging in the air, and this—this—is what you studied. The way she moved her hands and commanded the space, gestures that would work perfectly for a Prospero or some beefy tyrant in a Racine tragedy. You know what the phrase "fourth wall" means, but missed her definition of the "fifth." Beatnik shit. Who cares? You leaned your head against the back of your auditorium seat and closed your eyes, letting her voice rush over you like a symphony.

. . .

In the final cut of *Jungle Bloodbath*, Richard's footage of the search for Veronica isn't found until the eleven-minute mark. There's a long intro first: a team of American officials journey to find whatever is left of him. They find the film canister, hacking it out from where it's nested, inside a cocoon of human bones and leaves and mud, suspended from the crooked limb of a mahogany tree in the center of the natives' village. The cannibals are bribed. The officials are rattled but triumphant. The footage is brought back to New York, wrapped in blue plastic and stuffed in the darkness of the hull.

The officials watch it: in a private screening in a darkened, red-chaired room, with mounting nausea.

On the screen, live turtles are beheaded by divers' knives. Richard stomps through bush in fatigue-print pants and a green shirt with the sleeves cut off. He orders his men to film the fascia stretching between the pried shells and the blood-dampened meat. Women from enemy tribes are raped brutally with stone obelisks and Richard films that, too. Lit torches angle toward the peaked roofs of grass huts. Brown bodies cower in the windows between the sparking flames.

For these shots, however, Richard is out of frame.

PROCURATORE CAPO: At the very least, Signor Velluto, you must have known about the extreme conditions your cast and crew would be asked to endure during filming?

VELLUTO: Define extreme conditions.

PROCURATORE CAPO: This was an undeveloped part of the Amazon rain forest, no? Complete wilderness?

VELLUTO: There was a hotel. There was running water.

PROCURATORE CAPO: Untreated water.

VELLUTO: We supplied iodine.

PROCURATORE CAPO: Mosquitoes?

VELLUTO: Well, yes.

PROCURATORE CAPO: Disease?

VELLUTO: Some.

PROCURATORE CAPO: We've heard testimony about four cases of malaria, three cases of tegumentary leishmaniasis, one man who had them *both*—

VELLUTO: He failed to take his antimalarials. The fungus rot, I don't know how he got that.

PROCURATORE CAPO: Parasites?

VELLUTO: Am I responsible for every goddamned insect in the rain forest?

PROCURATORE CAPO: If you choose to bring actors there, yes. You are.

VELLUTO: It had to be shot there. Authenticity was important to my process. On this film, it was crucial.

PROCURATORE CAPO: Predatory animals?

VELLUTO: It is the jungle. What would you have me do?

PROCURATORE CAPO: Provide safe conditions, Signor Velluto, for one. Consider the safety of your actors.

VELLUTO: They were all adults. They knew where they were going.

PROCURATORE CAPO: Numerous testimonies state that some of them did not. Some have said your male lead flew all the way from America without reading the script.

VELLUTO: That was different.

PROCURATORE CAPO: How—

VELLUTO: That was different. He needed to be kept in the dark.

PROCURATORE CAPO: And why is that?

VELLUTO: It was important to my method. He needed to be kept in the dark.

PROCURATORE CAPO: All this talk of process, method—

VELLUTO: You asked the question.

PROCURATORE CAPO: And you didn't give me an answer, signore.

VELLUTO: It is an answer. He needed to be kept in the dark. It's the answer you're getting. Next question, please.

PAOLO and AGATA

Ovidio

In Italy, it would have been simple.

In a studio, Paolo and Agata would have fabricated a mold and filled it with Spam or gelatin, seeded the whole thing through with blood capsules to make it spurt when the cannibals dug their teeth in. Under other circumstances, it could be done in three days, easy, with spares ready. What the director wanted wasn't impossible: three prosthetic bodies, fully edible, with realistic bones that would show when the knives went in deep. They had six weeks to make them, the death scenes slated comfortably late on the production schedule. They'd packed their kits. They'd had a plan. They'd had more than enough time.

But then the director had changed his mind, to four bodies, then two, and then he said: just make parts. But this morning, apparently, the new American had lost his lunch on set and Ugo was thinking of killing his character off early, so have the body ready by sunset tomorrow.

But it is different, to make a body in the jungle.

When they left the polyfoam out to harden overnight, mosquitoes swarmed the molds and died, thousands of them, speckling the form like sores. And fuck running anything in

silicone in this humidity; they'd never get it to cure. After three days of frustration, three nights in a hotel too hot to sleep in and Paolo getting angrier and angrier, Agata had surrendered. They'd just have to magic it with camerawork, plastic prosthetics, quick cutaways. The solution to this wouldn't be in materials: there were more than one thousand kilometers of rain forest between them and the nearest city, no way to ship something better in. Camera effects. Performance. If they could be flexible, they could do it.

They had tried. But the test shots looked like shit.

They filled the washtub in the river, tried to get the prosthetics clean.

We could try making them out of bread dough, Agata said.

He grunted. If we could get any flour.

Will the budget pay for transport?

Not likely. No, it's too far.

Agata chewed her lip, exhausted. She looked up through the ceiling of trees, said: Paper.

What?

Newsprint. She brightened. Or the script sides. They don't even use them anyway. Soak everything in river water, throw in some dirt. Think about it, we could fake a mâché.

But what would we form it around?

I have latex, she said.

But not enough for three goddamned bodies, he snapped. An insect shirred in his ear and he swatted at it.

Agata scrubbed. What about wood?

They couldn't eat it.

They couldn't eat it. Shit.

Around them, the jungle twinkled. Over the river, something cawed. A long silence extended between them.

We could use meat, he said.

Agata smiled.

That's an idea. We could use meat.

The foam in the water seethed at her wrists. The limbs in the washtub bobbed, and Paolo pulled one out to study it: a plastic Halloween leg, hacked off at the knee, rubber sinews trailing.

But even the meat was a hard get.

They were over budget as is. The producer wouldn't okay a flight to the capital, not for a prop. Definitely not for forty tins of shoulder meat.

Agata barely realized she was saying these things out loud, until she heard Paolo curse and turn and hurl the leg into the trees. The sound jolted her: a snap of plastic on bark. She couldn't believe how quickly his mood had shifted from focus to anger.

I'm sorry, she said. I was just thinking—

If you're still thinking it out, Agata, don't waste my time, he said. We need to have come up with a solution weeks—

Calm down.

We're supposed to be professionals.

Paolo. Breathe.

Don't tell me to breathe.

Then go get the leg.

When he didn't, she hauled the tub up with both hands, pursed her lips as she dragged it across the beach. When he stormed off, cursing her, cursing everything, she thought to herself, he'll be fine in a minute. His temper had been getting worse lately, but he always came around. She dumped the river water out on the bank and watched the mud thicken.

He would be fine if she could just figure this out.

A deep gouge appeared in the earth, and Agata watched the river sluice into it, diluting the prop blood and the soap, filling instantly with tiny silverfish.

There has to be meat somewhere, Agata thought. She studied the fish: the brightness of their bodies, the skinny tails flipping in the silt. Not near enough flesh, and it would be the wrong color.

Agata! Paolo called.

She tried to manifest it with her imagination: 200 kilos of pink meat in buckets. Cattle or hog. She thought of her father back in Italy, slicing prosciutto off a pig leg strung over a rafter, and homesickness bloomed in the center of her chest.

Agata, Paolo said, closer now, Hurry up. The canoes are leaving.

She stared into the pink water, sick: the fish were gnawing at a dead thing they'd found buried in the mud.

. . .

When the props were put away, they cut down the path through the jungle, past the permanent sets. The "path" was mostly symbolic: a stripe of wood chips sprinkled over a skinny kilometer of mud, every centimeter of it invaded by bush. They could have followed the beach, but that wasn't much better—the way would be clear, but they'd have had to walk the whole perimeter of the peninsula and it would take three times as long. Paolo had wrapped the prosthetics in the beach towel and knotted it so he could wear it like a messenger bag, one strap of terry-cloth hibiscus flowers running across his chest. He needed both hands free to use the machete, to hack down the leaves in their way. Whenever he crouched under a stalk or beat back a rush of grasses, Agata could hear it: the clatter of plastic hands and feet at his back, clambering after him like a ghost.

They didn't talk. They passed the site of the fertility ritual, the rival village, the tree of hives.

All the sets were still being assembled, the ones that wouldn't be sturdy enough to survive the rain still packed in pieces under tarps. Even the ones that were mostly done were almost invisible: it was like a Magic Eye puzzle, finding evidence of their work inside the complex tangle of the bush. A hammer hung out of the crotch of two tree limbs. A boom mike slumped in a bush full of wilted flowers. Needles of light stabbed through the gaps in the foliage. There were piles of hacked strangler vines heaped near the road, to clear the upper third of the shot, and Paolo gestured toward them, said, The park service probably isn't happy about that.

Agata mumbled. There's a park service? She focused on her feet, on not losing her footing in the mud. The first day they'd arrived, she'd thought the mud was particular to the bank, but it was everywhere. It followed them into the jungle. It clotted, black, in the eyelets of her boots. She stopped walking and leaned against a tree, rolled her ankle around to try to shake it off.

Aren't there supposed to be animals in the rain forest? she said. She raked her fingernails through the rubber maze at the bottom of each shoe, but the mud clung.

This isn't the zoo, Agata.

But I haven't seen a single one, she said. Her fingers were coated and she tried to scrape them on the bark. Just this mud. All this fucking mud.

There was an edge of annoyance in Paolo's voice, in the sound his machete made through the leaves. The animals are there. *You* just can't see them. It's a skill.

It's because everything's brown. She squinted—maybe if she took off the boot? She grunted, working the shaft of it down over the knobby anklebone.

Of course everything's brown, Paolo said.

Well, it wasn't brown on the posters in the airport. They

don't tell you how everything blends together. When you think rain forest, you don't think—

Paolo ignored her, sucked his teeth in thought. We can stay on the path if we get this branch hauled out, he said. Put your shoe back on and help me.

Do you think you can learn how to see out here? she said, stomping the boot back on. She scanned the ground for moving scales, bulges of fur, looked up at the leaves and searched for the flick of patterned birds.

The downswing of his arm made a sound unto itself. Then she heard the machete thud.

Who fucking cares, Agata? We're going to be late.

She helped him haul the pieces of branch away. They were silent for twelve minutes, and then they were on the beach again.

.   .   .

They split up at the canoes; the props they'd brought that day wouldn't all fit in one. Agata rowed as the camera guys murmured in the bow. They were starting to get anxious about the heat.

It could get inside the cameras, one said.

Through the plastic?

There are seams, said another. Little splits. It could expose everything we've shot.

When I woke up this morning all my vitamins had turned to powder.

Powder?

The script supervisor leaned from another boat and whispered: The pills had sucked up the moisture out of the air. Can you believe this goddamned place?

They had been told that the director had worked with a loca-

tion scout. He'd shown them pictures that the man had taken: yolky sunsets and a sparkling canopy of vines, the silhouettes of naked children playing in dusky water. They'd all signed on, but for what? The pictures hadn't told them shit about this humidity, these insects, this mud. The director hadn't, either.

The camera crew was supposed to be rowing, but no one was paying attention. Their oars cut vague angles in the water. They whispered over their shoulders. If we could just store the celluloid someplace airtight—but where? How can we minimize the muffle on the tape? I played it back on the DAT, the fucking flies are all you can hear—

They lost course. The nose of the boat slammed into the bank, and Agata felt the impact shudder in the center of her bones. She had an oar, too, but it was hard to steer when she was the only one trying. I can't do this by myself, scemos, she said, but her voice came out meek, and she felt like she was about to cry.

In the other boats, the actors couldn't stop laughing. Everything was funny to them: the way their canoes bucked when a fish or a crocodile nosed up under them, the way the crew looked, worrying over the equipment, yelping every time they started to tip. Paolo adjusted the grip on his oar, thought, Fucking kids. There were five of them now, two Italians and three nameless bilingual Colombians, two principals and three featured extras, one girl and a clutch of skinny boys. And now this sixth one, the American, supposedly just arrived from some inland stopover. Acting-school dropouts. Christ. They couldn't even get professionals.

One of them was in the front of Paolo's own boat. The actress; the one Ugo's casting director had sent from some random acting school in southern Switzerland, the one none of them knew anything about. She stood in her seat and threw her arms wide, heckled something in loud English, probably a line from

the script. Paolo gripped the gunwales to keep them steady as she drunk-stumbled back into her seat. There was something about the girl that made Paolo furious: her skinny legs studded with mosquito bites, the messy hair that she must have thought looked sexy when it fell over her eyes. He watched her nuzzle in too close to the guy next to her, her long brown neck swiveling so she could whisper something in his ear. He watched her arm snake behind his back and land on the seat next to his hip, her smile sending a white flash through the darkness.

Pick up your oar, Paolo thought. Then he said it out loud: Pick up your fucking oar!

The actress gave him a dirty look and kept whispering, her tongue moving close to the man's ear. He smiled, falling for it completely.

Paolo swatted a wasp out of his eyelashes. A musk rose from the water, fogging the outer edges of his glasses, coating the inside of his mouth. He could hear the prosthetics clattering in the sack behind him, still wet from the river, probably scuffing. He wanted to shove the actress into the current, to tip the whole boat over. He wanted to punish her.

Instead, Paolo shut his mouth and focused on the swirl of foam in the current ahead of him. He thought of the bodies they still had to make, of fat marbled into flesh.

· · ·

In bed that night, Agata said: I want you to know, I understand how you feel.

Paolo ran his hand over his sunburn and winced.

I hate working like this, she said. I'm afraid to ask him, too.

She meant the director, but didn't she mean Paolo, too, a little? Agata peered at the line of his profile and tried to decide.

He was sitting on the edge of the bed in his black shorts. The television was on, and it turned him white and blue.

The hotel was on the outer edge of a town built just ten years ago, a thousand square meters of jungle cleared by hand with machetes, by men who had hiked for days to get there. None of it should have been there, but there they were inside it: behind plaster walls and die-cut plastic windows, the whole building shipped down the river in flat-packed boxes and buckets and then assembled piece by piece like a dollhouse. Somehow, the hotel was at once too filthy and too clean. The walls were whitewashed, sprayed down with bleach, but the bugs and snakes and creeping plants still leaked inside. Agata listened to the diesel generator humming in the yard.

Paolo aimed the remote. You're scared of Ugo now?

I'm not, just—I'm afraid to *ask* him—

Ask him for what? The meat?

For anything.

Agata, we've done a dozen films with him.

Not like this.

What do you want me to say?

But he's *acting* differently. *Angrier.* You see it, too.

He's just focused.

He's never been—

We're in a foreign country. Of course he—

Something's different, okay? Agata said it more forcefully than she meant to; she could see it in the sharp tic in Paolo's temple. She sunk lower on the headboard, made her voice soften.

It's just that he's never asked us to work without specs before. Without materials, without a lab. If I'd known, I would have insisted we build the bodies at home and ship them down.

That's not his process.

What about *our* process? We need a vacuform. We need

life casts, alginate, clay medium, a spray booth, everything. We need a *supply* store, Paolo.

We'll make it work.

But not if he keeps revising the script. Agata can feel herself getting frantic. He doesn't even know how many of the characters will die. *How* they'll die. No director's ever asked us to work this way before, Paolo.

An actor quit and he doesn't know how the recast will go. He's revising. It can't be helped.

Then he should be adjusting faster. That's all I'm saying. He shouldn't be stringing us along while he figures it out. She twisted her wedding ring, tensed her jaw. I thought you felt the same way. Earlier. You seemed like you were frustrated, too.

I was angry today. Paolo said, softer now. But he'll tell us how many bodies to make soon. He'll settle on a number, we just have to be prepped.

She studied the vein in his temple like the needle of a fuel gauge on low, deciding whether to speak.

She decided: But what if he doesn't?

Paolo prodded the remote and didn't respond. Agata pretended it didn't bother her. She focused harder on the TV. It was thirty centimeters square with a broken contrast knob and a washed-out picture. It gave off the only light in the room: the producer had warned them that the diesel for the generators was expensive to ship, to stick to candles, don't run hair dryers, don't waste power running the electric lamps if they could avoid it. Agata didn't understand—why this hotel had a generator at all, why there was blue carpet on the floors when there were acres of mud outside, all this incongruous technology. She slumped lower in the bed and stared at the white-blue wash of static on the screen.

I'm scared of what could happen here, she said, tired.

You'll get over that, Paolo said, firmer now.

It's just that—why did he have to bring us *here*? Agata's wedding ring was stuck to her skin by sweat. She couldn't stop turning it, working the band toward her knuckle. He could have shot this movie anywhere and he chose Colombia. Did you see the papers in the airport?

No.

This is supposed to be a dangerous country right now.

Paolo jerked his wrist, prodding a button on the remote. There won't be any of that down here.

The wedding ring sucked hard at the base of her finger. Her hands went limp in her lap, sore and empty.

I know that, she said. I know. But even if there isn't—something's off about this project, Paolo. You feel it, too, I can tell.

We just have to be professionals.

How can we be?

Agata—

If he fires us, how do we get home?

Agata, Jesus.

Will he *care* how we get home? Or will he be so focused on this fucking movie that he'll leave us to rot—

I can't listen to this.

We don't have any money. That American who quit at the airport, I don't think he even gave him cab fare.

Come on, what's cab fare? And the new American's already here, you know that.

My point is that if the actors are that replaceable to him, we are, too.

No, we're not. We're specialists.

But I'm worried, Paolo. I really am.

You're worried? Paolo sparked a cigarette. *You're* worried?

Christ, Agata, if I had a partner who could keep it together for two days, maybe I'd feel a little better, too.

That was all it took: just that little rise in the volume of his voice. It hit her like a slap. Okay, she said. Okay. She rolled to face the window and pulled the sheet up to her ears. She stayed that way until she couldn't stand it, and then she threw it off.

It's too damn hot to sleep in this country.

His voice softened. I know.

Would you turn off the TV soon? I swear it makes the room warmer.

I will. Just give me a minute.

And please put the mosquito netting down.

Okay.

He sparked a cigarette. The generator droned louder. The picture on the screen changed, or at least that's what Paolo thought, when he squinted at it. He could see an object congealing in the static, its edges blurred by white. He stared until he could name it: a barn in the center of the field.

· · ·

In the morning, Agata was not in bed.

By the time Paolo got to breakfast, she was already in the mess tent with the actress. They sat on the same side of the picnic table, their forks tending toward the same plate of papaya. Agata was whispering and the actress was chattering, both of them speaking in English.

Speak Italian, Paolo said, plunking down his bowl. You know I don't understand.

She's Swiss. She doesn't speak the same Italian as us, Agata said. And besides, she needs to practice her English for the movie. Irena, tell him the idea you had. For the body problem.

Paolo ate. The mango was syrupy and meaty, bruised in transport. It was so sweet it made him pucker.

Meat is a good idea, the actress said, in theory. But I think something like beef won't look stringy enough, you know?

He extracted the words *good* and *cooked,* but nothing else. He chewed, thought, *Why is she talking to a fucking actress about the body problem?*

Agata furrowed. Why does it need to look stringy?

The actress lit up. Think about it. If you want—what's the word—*gristle?* Fat? Like, when the cannibals take a bite out, so you can really see the muscle fiber in their teeth.

The girl demonstrated, a clenched jaw and a quick jerk of the neck. It was savage and convincing, unnerving Paolo in a way he couldn't name. She ended the motion with a little laugh.

Agata nodded. Okay, I see. Maybe roots? Shredded roots?

Roots could be good.

But they wouldn't *taste* good.

I don't care about that. The actress laughed. Teo's the prissy one, he might give you trouble.

Well, *you* wouldn't eat the bodies. Agata laughed back. You would be the ones getting eaten.

You never know! The actress mock-shoved her. Ugo has some crazy ideas. He could change the whole script tomorrow.

He didn't ask, but Agata translated for him. What do you think? She smiled, joked. Should we make twenty, thirty spares? Are we up to it?

When Paolo looked at her, he felt a vein flutter beneath his left eye. When he stood, he took his plate with him.

When the actress smiled, her teeth were speckled with pulp. She spoke in loud English, aimed at Paolo's back.

Who's that guy? she said. What's his problem?

. . .

His problem was this: he respected his wife too much. Too much to see her fail like this, crying over mosquito bites and mudslicks.

No, his problem was: they had made aliens out of polyurethane and car parts. His problem was that he knew her, that she could make actors look like they'd been impaled on anything—pikes and fenceposts and the needle at the top of a skyscraper, the red light at the tip still flashing to warn off low-flying planes. On their last project, a mondo rip-off of *House of Wax*, they sculpted actresses into breathable tallow torture chambers and painted exact replicas of their faces over the masks, then melted them with a butane torch. Agata had done the sculpt. They were better than anyone else in this industry—really, *Agata* was better, incredible with an airbrush, impeccable at fabrication. She had been his student at the effects school, an instant prodigy, the best he'd ever taught. His problem was this: they were better than a few bodies, basic shapes and edible parts.

If Agata would just focus.

They were back in the jungle, Paolo slamming a matte paint cake into a rock to break it up. He did it too hard and too many times. A blue cloud extended from his fist like poison gas, staining the edges of his shirt cuff. Agata bit her lip until she could summon the courage to speak to him.

Baby, let's take a break. Go help the set dressers.

Paolo kept pounding.

You can finish it tomorrow. She ran her hand over his elbow. Ugo will be fine without us. They don't need the head till shot 19. Vanni needs help with the tree of hives.

We're not fucking set dressers, Agata.

We're fabricators, though. It's the same thing. She tried to mask the frustration in her voice. You know everyone needs to help everyone out.

I'm not a set dresser, Paolo said again, but by then he'd put the blue paint cake down, strode, already, halfway to the tree line.

Agata followed him, ten paces behind, careful not to let her gaze land too long on the stripes in his shirt. Here, at the end of two years of marriage, she'd finally begun to accept that marriage wasn't going to change Paolo: he was still the dark shadow behind her stool in the studio, squinting over her shoulder, finding the hairline rip in the cowl and tearing it the rest of the way, to force her to fix it. She'd finally learned how not to flinch when he shouted: Do it again. No, she'd learned an even better way to be around her husband; distant but there, at the outermost valance of his genius, nudging at the energy field when he wasn't looking.

She followed him into the trees. This was how she had learned to help her husband, when he was too angry to be kind to her: she followed him wherever he was going, and then she handed him tree fronds. She helped him weave them into fabric. She gave him an abstract process to complete precisely and in silence, and she waited for his blood to cool.

There were two dozen people working with them, lashing limbs together into one-legged ladders, climbing up into the lower branches of the trees. Most of them were workers from the village, or at least, they weren't Italian; they spoke a language Paolo didn't understand. The town, he knew, sat at the corners of three countries, on the Colombian side of the vertex where the borders of Brazil and Colombia and Peru all converged, and sometimes he could intuit the different slants on Spanish and Portuguese in the lunch tent, the hoofbeats of obvious cognates running through their phrases. But the

language the locals spoke was different. It had low diphthongs, long chains of glottal consonants, too many vowels in a row. Maybe it was pitched? Paolo thought it must be pitched. It reminded him of quarreling birds. It was soothing, because it was so easy to tune out as he wove.

After a while, Agata looked at him cautiously, out of the corner of her eye, and swallowed once. She swiped a swarm of buzzing specks out of the air between them and tried to make her voice bright: Vanni told me he wanted to construct the villages based on local building practices.

He didn't want to hear her, so he squinted at the leaf. He realized that its fibers ran in a set direction, like wood, following a grain.

I mean, there are exaggerations, she whispered, but this is more or less how these people actually live. In the trees. Isn't that fascinating?

Paolo interrupted her. We need more material.

It's amazing how—

Could you just get it? I'm in the middle of this. Please?

As she walked, Agata glanced at the men working. The tree of hives was only partly done, colossal, the lowest dwellings only half completed. She'd seen the set dresser's sketches: when it was done, it would be impressive, a dozen human-sized pods, each hacked in half and suspended in gridlike cells like a beehive, a rough doodle of a cannibal leering out of each one. She watched the women weave vines and brambles into enormous cups, scraping their fingers as they did it, flecking blood into the mud. None of them ever stopped working. None of them complained.

So what is wrong with me? Agata thought.

Ten meters away, a man set a nest on the ground and crawled into it, to measure. Then he scrambled out, hoisted the

thing up the ladder, and placed it in the cleavage of two limbs, lashing the edges around and around. Each of the branches was thicker than the man himself and probably weighed more than he did, too. They wouldn't break when the nests were hung, or even when the set dressers climbed inside to test them out.

Then why was Agata holding her breath?

Why was she waiting for the gunshot sound of a branch breaking?

Paolo didn't look up. He thought over, under, over.

The branch leaned and moaned. A cut of light opened in the trees and it stunned her.

The man in the nest shouted Whoa! Whoa! Easy! But neither of them understood the language he was speaking.

Neither of them heard the director, shouting their names from the beach.

Neither of them heard until he was there, in mud-drenched hip waders and smeared glasses. Neither of them saw him until he was shouting—that he needed the effects team, the prosthetic fell off, where the fuck have they even *been* all morning?

By the time Agata saw Ugo striding straight up to Paolo and shouting demands, both men were red-faced: Ugo with shouting, Paolo with shame and silent rage. By the time she'd jogged up to meet them—yelling I'm here, *we're* here, hey, what's the problem?—by then she was too late.

Paolo didn't even look at her as he spoke, his voice so much steadier than his expression.

It was my wife's idea to leave and go help the set dressers, sir.

Behind them, the nest lolled too far off the branch and someone yelled in Italian: less slack, *less*!

I won't let her make these decisions anymore, Paolo said. It will not happen again.

Agata didn't get to say what she wanted to say, then: *But we're partners.* She barely even opened her mouth.

Because the instant he heard her begin to object, Paolo wheeled around and slapped Agata, his palm clapping over the hinge of her jaw and her entire ear. Agata heard her teeth snap together in her mouth with a sound like a thick branch breaking. Her gaze landed on the ground and she left it there, too stunned to move her head.

The director looked away from Paolo and Agata, indifferent or embarrassed, wiping his lower lip like the slap had landed on him, too. A skein of tears hung over Agata's eyes; Paolo's hand had left a smear of blue paint across the corner of her lips.

The director looked up at them for one second more, and then said, Figure it out.

Paolo stared at Agata one second more, but she didn't look up to see his expression. She studied her own hands: wet bark, blue paint. Then she heard Paolo's footsteps as he moved away from her, following the director back to the beach.

· · ·

Two hours later, the crew returned to the canoes for load-out. By the time Agata reached them, there was one crowded boat left and Paolo was not on it. The sun was gone, too, and she was grateful for the darkness: she did not want anyone to see her crying.

She squeezed onto a bench with the actress Irena, let the men in the bow and the stern take the oars. Agata tried to close her eyes and pretend she was alone, but the river kept swaying, pulling the two women closer together, pulling them apart, together again. Neither of them could see the gunwales to grab onto. The water under the boat groaned. Agata stiffened her posture, to keep them from touching.

But then the actress was leaning into her, her lips close to Agata's ear. Where is your husband? Irena said, conspiratorially, a girlfriend at a slumber party. She was speaking Italian; even if she'd been speaking English, Agata had no excuse to say she had not understood.

He took an earlier boat, she murmured.

The actress smiled. He's still being a dick?

Agata didn't answer.

I heard Ugo chewed you two out today for leaving set without permission, Irena said, twisting the ends of her hair.

No, Agata lied. We're fine.

Did you figure out how you're going to make the bodies? The actress twisted the ends of her own hair between two fingers. Is that what Ugo was so mad about?

We haven't, no.

Because when he stormed off set to look for you guys, we all thought—

We're fine.

Agata bit off the words, curt. The actress stared at her and shut up. The space between them filled with the low sounds of the rain forest, night birds, water, growling. Agata kept her eyes on her own hands, blue-black and too bony in the darkness. The longer she was quiet, the more she could feel the actress' expression deflating, boredom moving swiftly through the actress' body.

Well, tell me if I can help, Irena said, studying her own fingernails. You can make a mold of me if you want. Whatever you guys need. She gazed out over the river, searching for something more interesting.

Agata tuned slowly and looked at the line of the actress' jaw. We don't need to do that, she said.

They didn't need to do that, because she knew everything

she needed to know about the actress. It wouldn't be necessary, because for weeks before they'd left, she had sketched the actress' skeleton in the back of a notebook, used the costumer's measurements to figure out the approximate diameter of her rib cage and her skull. She didn't know any of the new American's measurements yet, but she would do it somehow: she would build a body for him. She would do it in a day, an hour, however fast the director asked, and if it wasn't right, she would tear it down and build it up again. To keep Paolo happy, she had to do impossible things like this. Even if the director decided that none of his characters would die in the end, Agata had to be ready. She looked at the actress. She would approximate what this woman's organs looked like. She would make an exact copy of her heart.

The actress dragged one hand lazily through the water, humming to herself.

And suddenly Agata was angry. It came on her quickly as a heat storm and raised her body temperature until she wanted to shake. She thought of the actress' body, measured and inscribed in a tidy numbered row, in her own handwriting. She watched the actress' vague shape in the dark.

Furious thoughts surged through her mind, thoughts she had to fight not to shout into the actress' ear.

Thoughts like: You brought me here.

Thoughts like: If it weren't for you, I wouldn't be here, and none of this would have happened.

It made no sense and she knew it; what was happening between her and Paolo had gotten worse for months, film after film, and it would keep getting worse until one day it broke. It was not this film's fault. It was not this actress' fault.

But a part of Agata still wanted to push the actress off the boat and watch a swarm of silverfish devour her.

A part of Agata wanted to cry into the actress' thin shoulder

and tell her she had started to hate working with her husband, that it was ruining her marriage.

Agata stared exhausted at the bare sweep of the actress' neck in the dark and realized: she wanted to do both things. They were the same emotion.

She looked at the actress in the dark and decided. She wouldn't try to do what Paolo wanted. She wouldn't try to make him happy anymore. She wouldn't wait.

She would make the bodies herself.

· · ·

In the morning when Paolo woke, the window was shut, and Agata was not in bed with him again.

Paolo had rolled onto his back and was waiting for his head to clear when he heard the rush of static. He sat up. He'd fallen asleep with the television on. He rubbed his eyes until an image appeared in the blue glow, clearer than before, shapes bleached down to outlines. It was a woman in a long skirt, running across a field of grass.

He had been planning his apology to Agata, before he'd fallen asleep. It'd been welling up in him all day yesterday, as he jogged after the director to the beach, as he repaired the pros-thetic on the actor as he was told, as he repainted the clotted blood under the fingernails of all the extras. Steadily, just like Agata knew it would, his rage had dimmed while he worked. And then his guilt had begun to rise: an image of his wife, blue paint on the hinge of her jaw.

Paolo was not the kind of man who knew how to put words to feelings like this. All he knew was that he had to stay awake until she got home. He turned the television on. He tried to keep his eyes open. But it had gotten so late, and then he had

thought he was dreaming the sound of the door, the shift in the level of the mattress and the rustle of the sheets as she lay down.

In the morning, Paolo climbed out of bed, his headache tight like a swim cap over his skull. He opened the curtain but there was nothing outside it but the lunch tent, bustling with people.

When he turned back to the TV, the woman on the screen was gone. There was a long shot of water rushing through a narrow channel.

·   ·   ·

Agata hadn't been in bed, because she hadn't slept all night.

She paced around the parking lot, planning what she'd do. She made herself go back to the room, to sleep just a little while, but she only lay on her back and searched the ceiling. She waited until near sunrise and then she went walking in the village. She walked until the village woke up, and then she found someone who could help her.

The man had a pig on a leash, and he told her he was taking it to the river. Or at least that's what Agata thought he said, when he spoke to her; she didn't understand Spanish, but when he talked slowly, she could parse the basics. It worked the other way, too: she said, Is twenty pesos enough, and he said, Sí.

She said, The whole animal?

He said, Claro.

But when Agata said, I want it butchered, the man's brow furrowed. He picked at a scab by his ear and said back, Mascota? She didn't understand, so she said it again—Butcher, butcher, macellare—but he just held out his hand.

She put the money in it. Her mouth was dry, but she took the leash from him.

. . .

Paolo found Agata in a tiny clearing she'd made fifty meters from the lunch tent, the bush hacked back to give her space to work. He was going to ask why there, but then he saw the blood on her hands, the ground, the trees. She had already made most of the prototype.

She didn't look up at him. She worked and murmured, I tried to cut the bacon thicker. He watched her crane her wrist under the skin and dig for an intestine.

The grease will show better if the bacon is thick, she said. You want the muscle to look fresh, right?

Paolo watched his wife wind the wet meat around the tree limb, the white fat spiderwebbing as it stretched. Her hands were covered in blood and sinew and a thin, white oil he didn't know the name of.

He had planned to tell her that the director had found him in the breakfast tent, where he'd gone to look for her. He had planned to lie to her—to say that director had apologized for the day before, for getting carried away, that their jobs were safe, they were safe, that he had overacted and he was sorry.

He wanted to make her feel better, but what the director had really come to tell them was that he had some thoughts about the new actor. The American. The replacement for the idiot who hadn't even gotten on the plane.

Paolo could have said, We need to talk about what happened yesterday.

He should have insisted.

But the director had a sleepless look about him that morning, a bruisy purple at the corners of his eyes. It unsettled Paolo. He kept squinting at the light beyond the tent like it hurt him, his gaze settling too long on the middle distance.

I'm sorry we don't have the body form done, Paolo stuttered. I know you gave us a deadline.

I doesn't matter. I don't know if I'll kill him yet.

Paolo furrowed. Are you sure?

The director laughed. No, of course not.

Because if you decide you want one, Paolo said, we really need to know two weeks out. Three, ideally. I'm sorry I told you we could do it faster. Do you know when we'll shoot—

He might survive, Ugo said. He might not, I don't know yet.

Paolo paused. You mean his *character* might survive?

I've been tired, lately. Ugo had a weird, questioning lilt to his voice; he tipped a sugar shaker over his coffee and watched it stream. This production schedule, he said, it takes it out of you. Don't you think?

The sugar poured for a three count, four, five. There was something about his face. A single wrinkle running across it at a firm horizontal, like a scar. Paolo stared at it. He couldn't look the man straight in the eye.

So when the director laughed, the wrinkle deepening and spreading, it startled him like a shove.

You remember when we worked on *Savage Rites*? Ugo said. You remember that fucking—what did I ask you to do, the scene where the girl got her eyeballs gouged out with the arrowhead?

That was nothing. Glycerin and champagne grapes.

It looked so real.

It wasn't hard.

It wasn't hard! Ugo laughed. See, you had your shit together then.

He kept laughing. He kept stirring the upper centimeter of his coffee. Shame burned through Paolo and he put all his energy into hiding it. He stared at the director's cup and pictured

mounds of sugar heaped at the bottom, still as underwater mountains.

I want us to push ourselves, Ugo said. For once. All of us. I don't want this to be just another . . . fucking mondo, gory, exploitation, schlocky piece of—

That's what we do.

I know this is hard on everyone, Ugo said, and did not apologize.

By the time they got on set, Ugo would have assembled himself again, patted down his hair and thrown a steely expression up. He would be all commands, ordering the set dressers to rethatch a waterlogged roof, contorting the actors into positions they didn't understand, for scenes he hadn't yet put on paper.

This was Paolo's only chance to speak.

But Paolo didn't say: I still need the specs.

Paolo didn't say, You shouldn't have attacked my wife and me.

Paolo didn't say what he'd planned to: It was not her fault. I was wrong.

He didn't say anything. He watched Agata, her arms streaked in the pig's fluids. He looked at the pig's head where she'd thrown it off to the side, the ragged cut she'd made. He felt something inside himself shift out of its proper position.

I wonder if I whipstitch it, she said. Will the cannibals be able to tear it off?

When she looked up at him, her eyes were bright with something like love, but still uncertain.

Paolo swallowed, knelt down next to her. Said: I think that it will work.

RICHARD

Ovidio

The first time you see the body, you're eating pineapple spears in the lunch tent and playing a Colombian card game you won't remember the name of. You don't realize what you're looking at, at first. You just see the couple who does special effects staggering out of the jungle with something hoisted between them, the woman's cropped black hair mussed with sweat and something else, the man looking rattled and grim. Whatever they're carrying is red and wrapped in a clear plastic tarp. It's only when the woman stumbles and curses—Cazzo Madonna—that the tarp slips open and you catch a glimpse: a flayed red shoulder, skinless and slick.

You startle, bite down on your tongue hard and the man wraps the body back up.

Across the picnic table, Irena smiles and tilts her head behind her cards. I think that's your corpse, Richard, she whispers, and you laugh and grin back.

· · ·

By now, you're starting to tell yourself a story about Irena, about the friendship the two of you have struck up. In quiet moments, you find yourself practicing in your head how you'll explain it to Kay when you get home: Pretty much no one talked to me for six weeks solid, but my costar, Irena, she was a really cool girl. You can hear just how you'll say it, the casual intonation, the smile and the shrug. You never ask yourself why it needs rehearsing.

You met Irena in the lunch tent your first day on set, thirteen minutes after you saw an extra hack off Fabi's leg, twelve minutes after you vomited all over a kapok tree and the shoes of a nearby cameraman. Fabi himself had been the one who trundled you over there, who'd explained that he was fine, who'd shown you, with bizarrely articulate gestures, how they'd buried his real leg in mud and placed the prosthetic just under the rolled cuff of his jeans with a blood balloon strapped to the joint. He'd called over the woman from the effects crew and showed you the props: a mannequin leg just like the one you saw in the river and what looked like a latex condom filled with viscera. Fabi showed you the fake machete, too, knocking it against his forearm a few times to demonstrate that it was dull. He found a PA who spoke English to help him explain that he's a producer, yes, like he told you, but also an actor; the budget couldn't pay for both.

He'd told you to relax and have some lunch, that they'd call you back up later.

But instead you'd just sat, humiliated, on a folding chair. You watched iodine tincture mushroom and settle in your water glass, trying not to look up at the crew as they filed past you for the buffet. You closed your eyes and wished that you were home, and that was when you heard Irena's voice behind you: I know how you feel.

You looked over your shoulder. Brown hair, an unlit cigarette

behind her ear. She pulled up a chair next to yours. I know it's strange, she said, how Ugo just shoves you into a scene like that.

Then, with a half smile that killed you: And the blood, it does look real.

Here is something you'd never tell Kay:

That Irena flirted from the start. That she spoke with an American accent that you knew right away was fake, to tease you, to see how long you'd let her go on. That you'd flirted back. That she told you, of all things, that her name was Gayle, which you'd learn later was the name of her character, and though you knew she was lying about something, you kept playing along with the joke. Irena had all the easy tells of a method actor refusing to drop character between takes: her head listing to the left when you asked her a question, her gaze following a beat behind the motion. Her smile was just a millimeter too wide, her accent off only a touch on the palatal consonants. She told you how she'd gotten used to Ugo's method after the second time he'd shoved her into a scene without a script, and then she'd mixed in a story about growing up in Delaware, burst out laughing and dropped the ruse when you asked her to name literally any town in that state.

You laughed with her, so hard your stomach ached. Still, you didn't ask her real name.

Here is something else you won't tell Kay:

That it was not just that Irena was nice to you. That it was not just that she was the first person you'd met since you left New York who had treated you like a friend.

This girl-who-was-not-Gayle stayed with you for the rest of the day, through three more scene shoots and the wrap-up, catching you up on the three weeks of production that you'd missed. You walked for hours together up and down the tree line, your eyes scanning the ground to dodge the creeper vines

reaching out from the bush. You will never admit to Kay that you glanced, just as often, at the deep sandal tan lines burned into the tops of Irena's feet above the tongues of her sneakers. That the shape reminded you of a bird in flight.

You and Gayle-who-was-not-Gayle sat together on the canoe ride back from the set, the man from the props crew glaring daggers into your back whenever you forgot to row. She sat with you on the bus ride from the river mouth to the hotel, too, and told you about everything: about prop skeletons delivered in enormous wooden crates, hauled out of mounds of Styrofoam one-handed and tossed on the beach like they were weightless. Her voice was low and easy as she described the rape and murder scenes they'd already shot, how they made her heart whip against her ribs for hours. It was her first movie, just like you. She was an acting school grad, too, from a conservatory in southern Switzerland you'd never heard of but pretended you knew all about; you had no idea that people from Switzerland even spoke Italian, but you pretended you knew that, too. On the walk from the bus to the hotel, Irena kept her fingertips in the tiny pockets of her shorts, her shoulders hunched sweetly. She paused in the center of a laugh and pointed to the dimming tree line: twenty feet above the mud, in the vertex between branch and trunk, a clutch of orange birds.

Was it subconscious or overt: the tape that settled on the spool in the back of your thoughts and started murmuring? Did you consciously try to convince yourself that this actress' face was unremarkable, that she was the sort of girl who is only sexy for the way she moves, whose entire appeal would be dismantled in a photograph? Even now, after two days together, you can't figure it out. She has flat brown eyes and wide thin lips and dark hair parted and jagged up the middle, chopped at the collarbone. She's skinny in a sort of gawky way, her knees

too bony and her belly round like a teenager's. Maybe she *is* a teenager. You couldn't tell; you still can't, and you haven't asked.

Was it deliberate or not: how long you smiled in that pause, both your eyes on those orange birds, how close you leaned in behind her?

I have a secret, she said suddenly. Do you want to know it? Yes.

My name is not Gayle. I lied to you before.

It wasn't just that she'd dropped the accent that she'd been slipping in and out of all day: her voice sounded different than it did earlier. Soft and vicious, somehow. A child with a spider in her fist.

I'm Irena. She smiled. It's nice to meet you, Richard, she said, and held out her hand to you.

· · ·

You don't know why Irena has been calling you Richard. You haven't asked, and you haven't corrected her. You took her hand and you shook it. You let her fingertips stay too long on the inside of your wrist.

And here is the truth: you *did* think about Kay, for once, in this moment. Here is the memory her touch sparked, though at first you weren't sure quite sure why:

Sharp rust on a doorknob. A crane-necked faucet that spat a brown coil the first time you asked it for water. The sound your suitcases made on the hardwood, the hardwood the landlord painted over with discount-sale maroon house paint that had been gradually peeling away for ten years. Kay's hair, white-blond on maroon as she lay on the floor. It's perfect, she said. I don't think we'll even need a bed.

You made it five and a half weeks before the first big fight. If

you could call it a fight: you, standing in the center of the room with your hands at your sides, Kay, on the bed you'd bought last week, staring at the wash of sleet in the window. She'd found a job at an architecture firm in Midtown five days after you'd arrived. You had picked her up there that night, for a date you couldn't pay for, and that was when it happened.

The architecture firm had broad sweeps of steel everywhere, exposed girders and angular drafting tables and long strips of metal rimming all those massive window panes. Someone was paid to polish everything; Kay didn't do it, and certainly not this coworker she introduced to you now, this Coe, his glasses rimmed in the same steel as everything and polished to the same glow. Coe's hands were covered in X-Acto knife cuts, and he held one out to you. He shook your hand and—that's it—his fingers glanced off the inside of your wrist in the same peculiar way Irena held your hand.

You looked him in the eye and faked a smile, a feeling like cold water spreading in your lungs. You took the elevator with Kay in silence, and told her that you didn't want to go out anymore, and took the train home nine silent stops and hiked up six silent flights of stairs before you started to yell.

Kay didn't yell back. Coe is my coworker, she said, her voice whispery and hurt. I don't understand why you're saying these things.

Why did he shake my hand like that, then?

Her face was like a crumpled paper bag. Shake your hand like what?

The floor of your apartment was full of ragged mouths, spreading snags in the maroon latex. You looked at them, and then you tightened your jaw and stared her straight in the eye.

Here is something you'll regret: that you didn't even think about being kind to her. You didn't realize, then, that this can

be the first thing to erode, after you've settled into loving some-one: you lose your obligation to be kind.

Here is what you didn't say: that you'd booked a tour upstate that morning, a tour that paid nothing. That it set off a rush of guilt in you that you couldn't process, so you reversed the situation: you told her that she had already done the thing you were about to do to her, that your leaving was her fault. The next day, while Kay was at work, a refurbished school bus that stank of biodiesel pulled up outside your building. The bus had long rows of Mardi Gras beads stapled across the ceiling in three places, each strand like a rib in a Technicolor rib cage. There were bricks of hash stashed under the seats, and a girl, of course a girl, named Zephyr. The company was into the theater of cruelty. You didn't even have any lines; you played a chair, a pillar, a couch that other actors sat on and delivered monologues from Artaud. But in your head, you were not the kind of person who would do this—who would leave the girl he loves to play a chair. That was not something that you could admit to yourself, and certainly not to Kay.

So instead, you said: He shook my hand like a man who was fucking my girlfriend, is how.

You said: I can't live like this. I can't live with someone who doesn't respect me.

You showed up in the apartment again six weeks later, your body wrecked from the show and reeking of fryer oil and drugs even after the gas station shower. You didn't tell Kay that you slept with Zephyr, because you didn't: Zephyr sat on your shoulders for thirty minutes a night and shouted about the apocalypse, her mime makeup sweating off the backs of her calves and onto your black sweater. You told Kay you were sorry, and that's all you had to say. She took you back. Easy as that.

Here is another thought that your brain rejects: that you are in Colombia, shaking hands with a girl with brown eyes that turn gold-black as the sun goes down. That you are in Colombia, and over the course of the next two days, you'll spend all day on set with her, palling around while the director doesn't call either of you up to shoot. That you are in Colombia, and you're doing it to Kay all over again.

. . .

In the lunch tent, you sit with Irena and watch the effects crew haul the prop body through the back doors of the bus.

Hey, how do you know it's my body? you ask Irena, flipping a card, tilting your head toward the lot.

She squints. Well, it's a little fat, she says, and you punch her in the arm.

Seriously.

Irena laughs. Well, I don't know. But if Ugo doesn't shoot with you again soon, he's probably about to kill your character off.

You sneer. He wouldn't kill me off.

Oh? And why not?

Because I'm the fucking lead. You say it like a brag, puffing up your chest.

She cackles.

What! you say. My agent told me!

Your agent hasn't met Ugo.

If I'm not the lead, why'd they fly me three thousand miles to be here?

He's done it before.

He's flown someone three thousand miles and then just replaced them with a pile of hamburger meat?

Irena stops laughing, tosses a peso in the small pot, and looks you straight in the eye. You really still don't know anything about this film, do you, Richard?

I really don't, Irena-Gayle. You toss your peso in the big pot. And I don't know why you keep calling me that.

She turns a card, a little grin playing across her face. Well, then. Let me tell you who you are.

· · ·

Richard Trent. He's the lead reporter on the film crew, the one whose idea it was to shoot the footage within the film. The film's working title is *Jungle Bloodbath*; the footage is labeled *Reels 1–4*, twenty-minute spools of Super 8 locked in gray canisters, ostensibly discovered on a recovery mission seventy-nine days after the crew disappeared. Irena says everything you shoot here will be presented like that: as found footage, white text on a black screen: What You Are About to See Is Real. This Footage Has Not Been Edited or Altered in Any Way. The Whereabouts of Richard Trent, Gayle West, and Joe Michaelson Remain Unknown.

You don't watch horror movies, but even as Irena describes it, you know this hasn't been done before. Cinéma vérité, she calls it, "found" footage, eventually a guerilla marketing campaign to match: it's a breakthrough. A new addition to the entire horror genre.

Next to that, the premise is cartoonishly simple, but you're too excited to notice. Richard has led his crew down to the jungle to recover Veronica Perez and the presumed remains of her parents, bumbling anthropologists that they'll probably cast in Italy and shoot quick takes of on a soundstage. They're presumed victims of the tribe they studied, the Yanomamö, a reclusive people known only for cannibalism, tribal war and nearly constant

nudity, save the occasional braided straw skirt. The crew has only three members: a cameraman named Joe, Gayle with her shotgun mic and her sound meter and Richard himself, straightening the hems of his safari shirt, his hair brushed to a gleam.

Here is what Irena doesn't spell out: that the crew spends an entire act in transit, on canoes and on foot, full of gory digressions. There are long shots of eagles shredding the innards of rodents, grand caimans sunning themselves after a river massacre, the water full of mud and pink. Ugo will get the footage in the morning, out on the river on his own with a long-range lens, and then he'll cut in your reaction shots later from the outtakes. Truthfully, it's aimless, all the dead animals, the gratuitous nudity, a full five-minute sequence that she and Ugo will shoot by themselves of Irena bathing lasciviously in the brown river. You've never seen an exploitation film, and Irena can tell. There's no sense trying to explain what it is, why so much of the movie will be devoted to ocelots gnawing on corpses, tits and safari khaki, blood spattering on bark, all of it set to a minor-key synthesizer drone.

So she sticks to the plot points.

Richard finds the village, stands awed under a tree full of human-sized nests. They scout out the tribe, spy on their fertility rituals and their intertribal war, watch them rape their women with stone obelisks. They formulate a plan to infiltrate, to make an attempt at rescue, and here there is a standoff. A twist. Ugo hasn't even told Irena what it will be.

It's part of his method, to keep all of you in the dark.

· · ·

All day on set, you can't sit still. All day, Irena and Ugo and a few extras go off into the jungle to rehearse, and it takes every

ounce of self-control you have not to stomp straight into the trees and find them. You just want to get started—to take the prosthetic leg up to the director and hack it to bits before his eyes, to show him that you're ready. He didn't make a mistake. He's got his man. Now that you know what kind of film this is, you are in this. Hyperrealism. Now that you know, you will do anything he asks you to—you just needed to be told what to do.

Irena stays late on set with Ugo, so you sit alone on the canoe and then the bus, your mind still racing over the possibilities: Richard with this tic, Richard with this kind of walk. Back at the hotel you can't sleep, so you pace the room, faucet to bedframe and back, your feet tripping on the thick, pebbly gristle of the carpet. You try to turn on the twelve-inch TV staring blankly from the corner of the room, get frustrated, give up. You decide to do Meisner exercises until you're tired, a favorite of your improv classes back in New York. You're supposed to have a partner, and you think of finding Irena, of her golden legs against the purple stripe of the bedspread, but you beat the thought back. You'll do it alone. You stare into the mirror and speak your character's intentions aloud, alternating assertions with questions until you've fully convinced your own reflection.

You are ready for this. I am ready for this? You are ready for this.

You are here on a mission. I am here on a mission? You are here on a mission. You are here on a mission? You are here on a mission.

You will find Veronica Perez. I will find Veronica Perez? You will find Veronica Perez.

You are Richard Trent. I am Richard Trent? You are Richard Trent. I am Richard Trent? You are Richard Trent. I am Richard Trent? You are Richard Trent. I am Richard Trent? You are Richard Trent. I am Richard Trent? You are Richard Trent. I

am Richard Trent? You are Richard Trent. I am Richard Trent?

You are Richard Trent. I am Richard Trent.

PROCURATORE CAPO: And what do you say to the testimony from certain female crew members that the atmosphere on set was unnecessarily sexually charged?

VELLUTO: I fail to see how that is relevant to the accusations I'm facing, Signor Procuratore. This isn't a harassment trial.

PROCURATORE CAPO: We've heard testimony from one of your special-effects artists, Agata Binasco, that the native women were often subjected to—

VELLUTO: Agata didn't speak the native language. She had no idea what the Indians were saying.

PROCURATORE CAPO: But you must admit that *you* don't speak the native languages of the region, either. That you were unable to communicate with the native members of your cast and crew throughout the entire production. Is that correct, that you didn't hire a translator of Ticuna or Yagua?

VELLUTO: Our expectations were explained to them before filming started.

PROCURATORE CAPO: By whom?

VELLUTO: By the man who coordinated the extras for us.

PROCURATORE: And who was that?

VELLUTO: The local proprietor, Hank Vance.

PROCURATORE CAPO: The proprietor of what, Signor Velluto?

VELLUTO: The hotel. The bar. The canoes, just about everything, I gather. He built the town from nothing

PROCURATORE CAPO: And is this the same Hank Vance who has since been indicted on charges of aiding and abetting major figures in the Brazilian and Colombian drug trafficking cartels, including the Comando Vermelho, the Medellín, the Primeiro Comando da Capital; this man was your translator?

VELLUTO: I don't see how his criminal history has anything to do—

PROCURATORE CAPO: All I'm saying is, Hank Vance was certainly a busy man.

VELLUTO: He was a periodic resource to us. We couldn't afford the expense of a full-time translator on set. That's all.

PROCURATORE CAPO: Then what about your lead actress, Irena Brizzolari? She wasn't a member of your usual ensemble, is that correct?

VELLUTO: No, she was not.

PROCURATORE CAPO: Your casting agent found her at an acting conservatory in—what was it, Switzerland? And she had no experience whatsoever on feature films? Why was that necessary?

VELLUTO: We wanted to cast fresh faces.

PROCURATORE CAPO: *Fresh.* You mean actors who no one would miss if they went missing.

AVVOCATO: Objection.

PROCURATORE CAPO: Withdrawn. Signor Velluto, did Irena Brizzolari understand what would be asked of her during the filming?

VELLUTO: I'm sure she did.

PROCURATORE CAPO: But we can't ask her. She's among the missing, correct?

[Whereupon Velluto pauses.]

PROCURATORE CAPO: Can you produce Signorina Brizzolari in this courtroom? We'd all love to hear her testimony.

VELLUTO: Watch the tape. She knew what she was getting into. She was game.

PROCURATORE CAPO: Or maybe she was just a fine actress. Maybe she was terrified and decided that sexually exploiting herself was the best way to protect—

[Whereupon Velluto laughs.]

VELLUTO: You've clearly never met Irena.

PROCURATORE CAPO: The question stands, Signor Velluto. Did Signorina Brizzolari understand the sexual things she would be asked to do in your film? Did you pressure her in any way?

VELLUTO: Let me reassure you, Procuratore: Signorina Brizzolari could take care of herself.

IRENA

Ovidio

When Irena screams, it starts from the core of her, scrapes up the walls of her throat and past her teeth and changes the air. When she does it again, it's the same, and the fourth time, and the tenth, and the twentieth and on. The trees shake with it. The river pulses. She articulates her tongue and makes the sound kick and rasp. She pivots and does it in a sprint.

Ugo never talks much on set, but she can tell he is impressed.

This is what Irena is best at, and it's what she did all day, alone with Ugo and the cameramen in the jungle. Ugo told her to writhe in the mud, afraid, and she did it. He told her to take off her clothes and step into the river and she turned a dial in her brain and she was a different girl. She closed her eyes and moaned, rolled her head around on her neck so her wet hair trailed over collarbone, neck, shoulder blades.

These were all throwaway shots and she knew it, just some gratuitous nudity and violence to pad out the first act. But she was so good that Ugo ended up spending hours on it, choreographing extras from the Indian village to spy from the reeds or the trees or a boat on the horizon line. He stopped once,

near dusk, and asked if she was tired. She broke character and laughed: Are you kidding? Let's keep going. Let's film all night.

·   ·   ·

She really would have done it: if the light hadn't gone and the DP said they should call it a day, if she had just been able to convince the director to stay out and keep rehearsing.

The crew is all exhausted and sweat-soaked by the time they're done, but Irena has so much energy. She springs after Ugo as he helps them pack up the canoes, chattering about how *good* she felt out there, and could she at least hear the audio playback, and when will he have scene work for her? When will she get to film with Richard?

Ugo sponges the back of his neck with a handkerchief, stiff-jawed. The new American isn't ready yet.

Why not?

He hoists a boom pole over the edge of the boat. You'll know the shot order when everyone else does.

She smiles. Well, can I warm him up for you, somehow?

But the sound guy had dropped his DAT recorder in the river, and Ugo had gone stomping out into the water after him, barking instructions.

When they get back to the hotel, Ugo goes straight to his room and the extras to wherever they live, down wood-chip trails winding past the edge of the lot and out into the trees. Irena is supposed to go to bed, too, but no part of her is tired. She smokes in her doorway, scanning. Richard must already be asleep, or at least locked in his hotel room, reading acting manuals or elocution texts, rehearsing for a part he might not have.

Irena is thinking of going to wake him up, when she hears Teo under the awning where they eat their meals.

Irena pauses, considering the back of his head, the shape of the four beer bottles lined up on the table in front of him. She could run up and surprise him, clap hands over his eyes and shriek. She could tease him about the little hotel maid she's seen him harassing the last few nights, the only reason she can think of why he hasn't been spending any time with her. She blows a smoke trail out of the side of her mouth, inhales again, and feels all the air in her lungs simmering off. An idea blooms in its place.

She strides straight over, slams open a beer on the side of the table before Teo has a chance to offer.

So I just talked to Ugo, she lies, and I think you need to start working on your American accent.

· · ·

Irena has always been the best at elocution.

Because that's all speech is: a tool you have to concentrate to use, a weapon that you aim. If talking to the new American was like making a glottal consonant in an accent that isn't yours—the tongue bucking against the skin of the soft palate, the secret, lush precision that can make anyone believe—then lying to Teo feels native, double-speed, Katharine Hepburn galloping through a monologue to a cowed Cary Grant.

Irena tells him that Ugo isn't sure that the new American will play Richard. She leans in across the picnic table and whispers it like a secret: don't let this get around, but he's thinking of casting you after all.

The only problem is, your accent is terrible.

Teo looks bored and skeptical, but Irena makes him improvise with her anyway. Teo says he just wants to drink, says he doesn't care what part he plays, but she goads him until he repeats all the Richard lines she can remember, critiques his

accent with every pass. Get a shot of this, quick, Gayle. Get a shot of this, quick, Gayle. Get a shot of this. But he has no control over his palate. She can hear how tight the back of his throat is, how it makes the vowels round up like Italian. When he says the word *shoot,* the *O*s gather at his lips and pinch off too fast, and Irena feels it like a flick straight to the nerve.

She leans over the table and puts a thumb into his mouth.

What the fuck are you doing? He chokes.

She swills. I don't have any candy, or I'd use that.

Candy?

She shrugs. That's how I learned to do it.

What are you talking about?

My dialect coach. She swirls the beer bottle in her hand and watches the foam twist like a vortex. That's how she taught me to do the American *O*s.

Teo sniffs and runs his tongue over his teeth behind his lip, tries not to look curious. How?

You suck on a peppermint until it's sticky, she says. And then you have to fix it to the roof of your mouth, as far back as you can stand.

And then, what, you talk around it?

Irena grins. No, you sing.

Teo rolls his eyes and spits, tugs the top button of his shirt open. Irena tilts her head.

Why don't you know know this stuff, anyway? You've never used a dialect coach?

No, I haven't. Teo picks at his beer label, annoyed.

Why didn't Ugo hire one for you? I thought you worked with Ugo on these jungle films all the time.

I don't know.

Irena sneers. What do you mean you don't know? Ugo doesn't want you to sound like actual Americans?

I mean I wasn't an actor before. I was a grip. I don't know.

Irena lets a pause hang in the air between them, her mouth hanging open, staring a straight line through the dark. Then she laughs as loud as she can. No shit!

I mean, I've worked on a lot of these, Teo says defensively, picking at his beer label. I was there.

You're *crew*?

The actors he hires aren't virtuosos, Teo says, his voice a shade too mean. He made those films for about fifty lire each. He shot them in front of green screens and put in a bunch of stock footage later, palm trees and apes and shit. They *were* shit.

Yeah, but you still take *pride*—

I'm saying it wasn't like this film. I'm saying no one was looking for realism.

Who's *no one*? Irena laughed. You mean Ugo?

Yes, Ugo. Of course Ugo.

Irena unbuckles one of her sandals under the table and rubs at the raw spot between two toes. I know you're just crew, Teo, she says, but you've got to realize: the director isn't the one who makes the film.

What are you talking about?

I'm saying, who cares what Ugo thinks anyway?

He's our director.

He's some crazy guy who got an idea for a movie. She grins. You're an actor now. You *are* the movie.

Teo hesitates. You'd never say that to his face.

Fuck no, but you know it's true. Irena points the tip of her cigarette at him. Actors are the powerful ones.

Teo scratches a new mosquito bite on the side of his throat and squints into the dark behind her, thinking. He's not crazy.

Half the crew thinks he is. You don't hear them gossip?

No.

They think he's gone full Colonel Kurtz. They think he's going to run away into the jungle to live with the natives and leave us all stranded.

No one's saying that.

I don't know. I heard him walking laps around the hotel last night. Four in the fucking morning.

He's working out the script.

He was murmuring to himself. *Richard, Richard, Richard.*

You're making that up.

Hey, I'm not insulting him. She laughs. I'm sure he's a brilliant, brilliant maniac.

He's not—

I'm just saying, I'd watch out. Irena leers, preparing for a lie. If you don't figure out how to pronounce your *O*s, he might not give you the part. Hell, he might even snap.

She claps her hands together fast, but Teo doesn't startle. He keeps clawing at the new mosquito bite on his throat, hard enough that Irena can see the welt start to rise. As she watches it, she thinks: even if the new American wasn't playing Richard, she could probably get him to kiss her. But Teo is harder. Teo she'll have to convince.

She kills her own beer, grabs Teo's out of his hand and swallows down the last of his, too.

Well, huh, it looks like we're out of beers now, she says, holding the bottle up to the light. Why don't we go into town?

He laughs. What town?

There's a little town, down the road. You really haven't been?

To get the beers, yeah, but not at night. And I'd hardly call it a *town*.

Well, let's go now.

You know we're not supposed to.

Everything is open at night.

You'd have to cut through the jungle.

There's a *road,* scemo.

Yes. A road. A road through the fucking jungle. He gnaws at something in his cheek and looks away. Those fences don't keep anything out.

We'll be fine.

Teo looks at her. You don't really know the producers yet, do you?

So?

Baldo is crazy about the insurance. He'd kill us.

She tilts the empty bottle in her fist, aiming the neck of it at him like a flashlight. Teases: You're scared.

Teo looks away. She can tell he's picked up on the provocation, floating over her words like a phantom note in a chord, and he's deciding if he should answer it, or if it's better just to disengage. Engage, she thinks. Come on. I'm ready.

But then his features flatten.

You know what, he says, I'm tired.

No you're not.

You're right. I'm not. Teo slides off the bench, picks up the bottles, and starts to walk away. But *you're* drunk, and *you* should go to bed, he calls over his shoulder.

Irena stubs out her cigarette and watches Teo go. Asshole, she calls after him after a while, but he says nothing, focuses on finding his footing in the dark. She could make Teo her boyfriend, but he'll never be able to make a glottal consonant: he couldn't make the uvula flare, the soft flesh shifting in the dark. He has something steely about him that she doesn't like, that she can't bend, no matter how much heat she applies. She tells herself: I don't want you anyway.

So Irena goes into the town alone.

. . .

The road to the town has fences, but they're low enough for something well muscled and wild to leap right over. It's paved with wood chips half decomposed by the winter rains, mossed over and made soft underfoot. Irena could tell someone had tried to hack back the tree limbs and the vines to clear the way, but the taller branches lean down, weighted by new nests made overnight, new clutches of just-grown seedpods that clatter as she brushes against in them in the dark.

Irena stumbles, but it doesn't bother her. She's paying more attention to listening than to looking. The jungle releases a constant sound that fascinates her: it buzzes over the sweat on her skin like sonar locating something in the dark. She thinks it could be insects or frogs or night birds, but it seems more elemental than that, somehow. Irena's taken this path into town almost every night since she came to Colombia, and she's come to think of the sound like an electrochemical force, an invisible process that works directly on the cells.

As she walks, she practices releasing her jaw and tenting the soft skin at the roof of her mouth to imitate the noise.

The town should be familiar to her by now. But there's something about the way it comes up out of the bush; the random arrangement of low-lying buildings and the single crooked street; the kerosene lamps that hang a low orange haze in the air between branches; the shadows of men; the sprinting shadows of children. There's something about the imperfect silence of the town that makes it feel mobile, somehow, like the buildings can shift and scuttle and become something else whenever she turns her back. Irena can't shake the feeling that if she ran up on it from behind, she would see a flicker of a different city for a moment: someplace bright and lean, halogen

and metal, full of music and vivid smells. As she comes up on
it, she watches for a gleam brimming out of the trees, as if by
watching she could somehow summon it.

She does summon it: the lit end of a cigarette. Then a silhouette in the doorway; voices. As Irena walks closer to the
town, she knows it will look the same as it has every night. But
she wills it to open just another millimeter to her, to flirt, just
a bit, with showing her its true arrangement. She knows soon
it will call out her name: Irena, once, in an American accent.

When she hears it, she will call back: Hank!

. . .

Hank is the one who built everything in Ovidio: the hotel,
the bar, the store, the airport, all the huts for the workers. He
had come to Colombia, broke, twenty years ago, from a city in
southern Georgia Irena had never heard of, and he'd built himself up here, sent for freighters loaded down with particle board
and buckets of plaster, whole buildings flat-packed inside boxes.
On the night they'd met, he'd tapped the edge of the pool table
in the middle of the bar and said, This thing had its own damn
boat. He was the one who brought in workers from Brazil and
gave the Indians jobs, made a civilization here out in the middle
of goddamn bedlam. The president of goddamned Colombia,
as he put it, had written him a letter a month ago; the president was sending a crew through the jungle with a telephone
wire, bringing the phone system all the way from Puerto Asís
to his town. *His* town; Ovidio was somewhere, because Hank
had made it somewhere. He never stopped saying it, but you
could tell even by the way he moved, the firm-knuckled sense
of ownership in the way he grasped at things, his hand pawing
the dip in Irena's waist as she leaned into a corner shot.

But tonight, something is different about Hank. He doesn't call out to her like she'd imagined he would, doesn't even go outside when he sees her waving through the window, loping through the darkness and through the door. She sees his face fall for just a moment as she steps inside, and then he fakes a wide smile, kisses her on the cheek once and says Bongiorno, bella, in his shitty Italian accent. Then he passes her a pool cue and a beer—practice for a second, we're just finishing up—and turns back to the man at the bar.

Irena practices kiss shots, tries to pretend that she's not listening. Hank is muttering something hushed and angry in Spanish to the man behind the bar and picking at the label of a beer bottle he isn't drinking from. There's sweat pooled in the hollow of his neck and between the lines of his forehead, the mermaid tattooed on one triceps blurry with it, his whole expression soaked and vague. Hank doesn't seem to realize that Irena can understand Spanish, or that anyone who speaks Italian can puzzle out the basic cognates, and he certainly has no idea just how good an actress Irena is.

He grabs a cue and cranks the chalk around the tip. He says to the man behind the bar, I'm telling you these little teenage assholes are gonna get themselves killed. You just watch.

Irena jumps the cue ball and giggles, Hank, look! Hank glances over at her once and tells her to keep going, baby, you'll get it.

The barman sighs and picks up another can, moving it around like a chess piece on the card table that serves as a rail. I think you're underestimating the M-19s, Hank, he murmurs. They can handle themselves.

They're fucking kids, Hank says.

Kids with Uzis.

Uzis they don't know how to use.

It's called a trigger. You don't exactly need to get a university education.

Irena's skin tingles at the word—*trigger*—but she plays dumb. She makes her voice sorority-high: Take a turn, Hank! Come on, play with me!

Hank circles the table and aims his shot, but he keeps his eyes on the man as he arranges his scratch. Have the rebels ever cut out a man's eyelids? he says too loudly. Tell me that and I'll tell you if they're tough.

Irena translates in her head: Eyelids. Párpados. Palpebre. If she listens hard enough for just a few nights more, she's sure she could learn this language like music.

The barman closes his eyes. Come on. You can't compare—

Just for seeing the boss' face when they weren't supposed to? Huh? Do they know tough like *that*?

They've been planting bombs all over the capital. Blowing off people's legs. What's worse?

I sure like my eyelids. I don't know about you.

The barman gives an exhausted laugh. And you don't like your legs?

Hank chews the edge of his tongue, decides to ignore the question. Do they even have a boss? I thought that was their whole deal.

But that's why they're dangerous, these socialists. The man squints and draws the neck of the beer to his eye, uses the socket of bone to pry the cap off. 'Cause there are so damn many of them. 'Cause they *all* fight like they're the boss.

Hank squints. *Are* they socialists?

Not exactly. Nationalists? He sighs. I don't know what the fuck they are. But I know they think they're some kind of saviors of the working class. I know they don't like being ordered around.

Well, they need to listen to me, now. Hank scoops the cue ball out of the pocket and underhands it to Irena. They need to let me be the boss, now. Where would they be if I hadn't set them up with the cartel?

The barman looks at the floor, stifling a sad laugh.

I'm just saying, if they're supposed trust me, well—they need to *really* trust me. He ambles to the other side of the table, taps at the spot he wants Irena to aim at on the felt. Tell them they need to assign a new delegate. Someone they haven't sent before. One of their women, if they're smart.

Why—

They need to negotiate something. They don't know these cartel guys—if they want more of the cut, they need to pay respect, not just fucking take a kilo. Then he switches to English, to her: Be careful on those pocket shots, baby.

Irena misses the shot on purpose. Hank, she mews. Show me how.

How does the cartel even know they took a kilo? the barman says, worrying a bottlecap between two fingers. The quantity they're shipping, how many places they're sourcing from and going to—couldn't it be an accident?

It doesn't matter if it's an accident. They're responsible. Hank says it to the man, but he's leaning over Irena's shoulder, now, guiding her cue.

But the cartel must have their own accidents, too. When they do their own shipments.

Still doesn't matter. It's about trust. Even if it *was* an accident—they counted down that shipment and it was short, period. They have to own up. They have to send a delegate. We'll go meet them together.

The cue fires, sends the ball into the pocket point. Close, Hank says. Practice.

The barman pinches the bridge of his nose, exhausted. At least tell me why they need to send a woman. If they're smart.

They might not kill a woman. Hank pauses, thinking. Well, not as quick as they'd kill a man.

The barman nods, digs for another beer in the cooler. Irena hasn't really looked at the barman yet, and she's surprised when she does by how old he seems compared to his voice. But old in a strange way, the skin not so much wrinkled as hardened.

I'll tell them, he says. But, Hank, you have to listen: the M-19s don't have to go through you like everyone else. Two bottles find each other in his fist and make a sound like music. You may have set them up with the cartel, but they don't need you to keep up communications between them. They can do it on their own.

Hank grunts.

I'm telling you, the barman says, it's not like those filmmakers and the Indians.

And why not?

Because they all speak the same language.

Hank laughs. They may speak Spanish, but only I speak the cartel's language. He points with his bottle. Make goddamned sure they know that.

He turns to Irena, and it's like a knob has turned somewhere behind his eyes, and his whole face has changed.

Now, honey—he smiles—you have to get closer to the table than that. Come on, you have to really get down there.

·   ·   ·

It's more powerful than simple elocution, what she can do with her body and her silence. Acting is about listening, and when Irena listens, she understands everything, no matter the

language they're speaking. This was a more powerful thing than talking—she was more powerful than all these men who were always *talking*.

. . .

On set the next day, they shoot one of the early scenes, more gratuitous nudity, more shock-value filler. Irena takes off her shirt and steps into the river to wash it. Teo yoo-hoos from where he's been hiding on the beach, tells her to wave for the camera. She starts and gasps, throws her arms across her chest. Then the costumers give her a dry shirt and she puts it on, wades out, does it again. Again. Every time, she can feel the new American staring from off-camera when she steps into the shot, and she feeds off it; her skin glows with that vibration. Teo is getting tired, but Irena never does. If Ugo is crazy for working this way, well, she is the same kind of crazy herself. She likes the way the lines become deliciously meaningless as she repeats them, until each word is not a word but a complex motion of the face, until she can perform the feeling with every muscle in her body, until her tongue itself is just another muscle.

What are you doing in here?

What are you doing in here?

Get out!

Get out!

Get out!

Get out!

At the end of the take, they eat patacones and beef stew in an oily red broth, a stale, thin bread that feels like coarse fabric in her mouth. The food is terrible, but Irena is starving. She swallows without chewing, her cheeks bulging, her teeth full of meat. Teo looks up at her, stirring a swirl of oil at the bottom of his bowl.

How can you eat this shit?

I'm starving.

I'm too exhausted to eat. Aren't you tired?

No. Why?

Sweat shines over the ridge of his eyebrows. Ugo just made us shoot the same take for three fucking hours.

She looks over at the director, furrowed and a little crazed, flipping through a notebook. She shrugs.

It's fine.

What time did you even get back to the hotel last night?

She squints her eyes, pretending to count on her fingers. Let's see. I guess I didn't.

You stayed out all night?

She smiles as she swigs from her Postobón, shrugs once.

Jesus. Teo prods at a knuckle of fat with his knife. You're not hungover?

Oh, God, of course I am. I'm dying.

You don't look it.

She grins. Thanks, handsome.

He hadn't meant to flirt. She can tell he resents her for taking it that way. Teo's expression snaps back like a rubber band, his face suddenly cold. He prods at his food with his fork.

What are you even doing out there? he says. There can't be anything to do in that shitty little town.

She thinks of Hank, cutting the lines with a razor on the side of the pool table, the dust-white and lush green under the kerosene lamp; the walk home, insect sounds vibrating up to the roots of her hair. She looks at the new American, scanning the lunch tent to find her, and waves him down.

Come out tonight, she murmurs to Teo out of the corner of her mouth. After everyone else goes to bed. I'll show you.

· · ·

She tells Teo to swallow the pickle juice and then throw back the shot in one mouthful. Then, when he's not expecting it, she cackles and puts her hand under his jaw to close his lips. Teo sputters and the men at the bar love it. Hank shouts, Careful there! I pay extra liability on this place for tourists!

We're not tourists, Irena shouts back. We're actors!

Hank hugs one arm around her. You little dummy! You sweet little thing!

Hank is drunk tonight, and in a better mood. He spills silver tequila over the pool table and Irena swipes at the gleam. He drags Irena and Teo out of the bar and through the jungle, a fog of insects swirling in the flashlight beam at their ankles. You've gotta see this, he shouts over his shoulder. Hurry up, you drunks.

Irena laughs and leaps on him piggyback. Teo walks ten paces behind, stumbling in the ruts.

Inside Hank's house, all the furniture is new. The porch has glass windows with butcher paper taped over them to keep the sun from bleaching the upholstery. There are wall sockets and long stretches of carpet, and when Hank slaps the sill, the sound is percussive and clean. He knocks on the windowpane. The Indians'll break this shit three times a year, he says, but it's worth it.

Irena spreads out her body and sinks into the plush, into the color of the fabric itself, dusk-orange, incredible.

It is, she agrees. It's so worth it.

Hank grins. He starts propping up a white screen.

We have to be at the canoes at five in the morning, Teo says into her ear.

So?

I usually show this to guests the first thing when they get here, Hank says, but your fucking director is all business. He

straightens the stand to make the screen level. Ted, he says over his shoulder, go ahead and flip that switch down by your left side.

Come on, *Ted.* Irena pronounces it in her American accent. Do what the man says.

Teo gives her a look. Who *are* you right now?

She thumbs the switch. As Hank jogs back to the couch, the projector flares on, turning him white and then a complex, twisting green.

On the screen, now, is another Hank, fifteen years younger, wrestling an enormous snake. There is no sound besides the clatter of the reel. The man and the snake are underwater, the water coffee-colored and spangled with beige sediment. The snake is as thick as the man, coiled around him so many times that she can't tell how long it would be stretched out.

Teo stiffens.

The snake constricts. The picture is too low quality to make out the scales, so the animal looks like a single rope of black muscle, loosed from a body but still moving.

Porca troia, Irena says, slouching into the couch. This is amazing.

On the screen, Hank's head keeps bobbing over the rim of the water, past the upper frame of the shot. The snake curls around his ankles, his thrashing knees, the lean muscles of his abdomen. But when his face returns to the frame, he flashes a grin full of bubbles, the sinews in his arms flexed taut. She was a big one, he says. Called her Magdalene.

Irena sits between Teo and Hank, the heat of the American bright on one side, the Italian rigid on the other. She smiles over at Teo. She puts her hand on the scruff of Hank's neck.

You have to hold the snake here? she says. This part of the neck? Is that how you do it? She strokes with the edges of her fingernails.

Exactly, Hank says through a half smile. That way she never gets a full grip with her teeth. How'd you know that?

I am—how do you say it? I am a natural.

You must be. He leans toward her. Maybe I'll teach you. If your friend doesn't mind.

He glances up at Teo. Teo keeps his eyes locked on the screen, a vein at the hinge of his jaw flickering in the green light.

Irena wonders, sometimes—why does she do things like this? It is not about sex, even if it looks like it. It is not about men, or even, really, about power—or at least, not the crass kind of power that men want. What she wants is to hear Teo's breath speed, to see his face change in the light. She wants to know how he feels before his brain has even had a chance to name the feeling *disgust,* to see it start in the farthest reaches of his body, in the fine motions of his mouth, his veins. This is why Teo isn't a very good actor: he can't summon these details up on his own. When he plays at the big emotions, anger and despair and fear, he does it with broad changes of expression but no real finesse. He is not like Irena; he doesn't have her control. The only way to get the shake in his fingertips and the twitch in his eyelid is to push him to it. It has to come up on him without warning, and grip him by the neck.

Irena does it before her brain tells her not to: she turns her back to the projector beam and climbs on top of Hank. She settles her legs on either side of him and grinds down, so he can feel the hot throb of the veins in her cunt as they press against the center button of his shirt. She puts her tongue in his ear, on the side facing Teo, to make sure he can see.

Teach me now, she says, loud enough for Teo to hear.

She watches the projection of the green flesh, twisting on Teo's face.

She reaches for Hank's belt. They all hear it unlatch, the leather sliding.

.   .   .

Four minutes later, she's following Teo through the trees.

They still don't have a flashlight, but Teo's walking in long strides, so far ahead of Irena that she can barely see him in the dark. The jungle is a wall of sound, the vibration of a million insect calls falling into a single, pulsing rhythm. Plants rush at her bare calves from nowhere. She jogs straight into them to catch up.

Slow down, coglione!

He doesn't say anything.

She laughs and grabs him by the elbow.

He turns on his heel and shoves her as hard as he can.

In moments like these, when she's reached the climax of her treachery, Irena thinks of airplanes: the feeling of the wheels leaving the ground, the little lift of her diaphragm as her breath catches and she feels her velocity change. Whenever Irena manages to push someone this far, she has this same sensation. They say you can't feel relative motion, that the body cannot experience 950 kilometers per hour, but that's wrong. As the heels of Teo's hands land on her collarbones and her body rockets back, she feels it all: her blood is full of that speed, that wind that can flay you alive. It is twice as good as sex.

This is why she smiles as her shoulder blades slam hard against the trunk of the tree. This is how she gets her footing so quickly, why she walks right back up to Teo and kisses him on the mouth.

He spits the kiss out. What is wrong with you?

She kisses him again, then jerks back away from him and

grins. She bites her lower lip and gazes straight at him through the darkness.

Stop it.

But I want to kiss you.

I don't. You're disgusting. That fucking American is disgusting.

She cocks her head in the dark. Well, I like you better.

He has a wife and kids, you know, Teo says. I heard the Colombians talking in the bar. Four kids. They were probably asleep upstairs all along.

I knew that.

He's twice your age. Three times.

Let's not go back to the hotel. Let's stay out.

He's probably diseased.

Cretino, I've never fucked him. I just teased.

You would have done more than that if I hadn't stormed out.

But you did. She softens the edges around her voice. And I followed you.

A charged pause hangs in the air between them, full of fury, mosquitoes, sex. Her skin is so sticky with the humidity and his must be, too. She backs up in the dark, finds a tree and leans. She lies again: Ugo still might recast you. As my boyfriend. We're probably going to have to do it on set tomorrow, anyway.

Teo hesitates. That's different.

It doesn't have to be, she purrs. It's your first time acting. Trust me, you'll see.

He thumbs his temple, exasperated. You've never worked with Ugo. You're not even supposed to be in this movie.

I am now. I'm your girlfriend.

You don't know that.

I am if you want me. Ugo's letting me choose.

You're lying.

Let me choose you.

You're a crazy bitch.

Say it again.

Jesus. No.

Do it. Call me names.

The third time she kisses him, he shoves her with both hands. The third time, he holds her against a tree with his palm at her neck and rifles in his pants, his breath ragged, his face a full foot from hers. Irena lets herself go limp, but she can see everything in the dark, and she does not close her eyes even for an instant.

Before the shove, the kiss, she had already decided: she would wait until he put himself inside of her.

She would wait until he thought he was in control.

Then she would hold him there. She would tighten. She would breathe the darkness like water. She would be like a constrictor, swallowing. She would use her arms and her legs and her whole mouth.

. . .

The next night, Irena goes to the town alone.

Hank is nowhere. The bar is closed, three padlocks hanging off the jamb, no light between the slats of the walls. She goes from building to building, cat-scratching at the doors, saying his name the way a small bell says *come*. No one answers. There's a shack full of stored fruit with one paneless window, an immense smell of sweet rot that fascinates Irena. There's only one shack with a sign on it, MÉDICO, and through a crack in the wall she can see one table, one chair, a shelf with nothing on it besides a bottle of white capsules and a roll of half-stripped Ace bandages, trailing its skin like a wounded animal crawling

away. There's a shack with three children in it, sleeping on the floor under a big orange sheet.

But what keeps drawing Irena's attention is the wall of dark behind the town, set like a blackout curtain at the back of a stage. There's a path to Hank's house somewhere, but she doesn't take the time to look for it. She kills her flashlight so the bugs won't find her. She steps high over the bush, past the edge of the clearing, and just walks the straightest line she can.

This is how she finds Hank, finally: fifty meters into the darkness, at a house she'd never seen before. It's a bigger shack than anything in town, hulking in a clearing near the water. Irena had wanted to show up at Hank's bedside, to loom over him and his sleeping wife until he woke and froze, but studying the shape of the building in the distance, she realizes it's even better to find this. It has a new straw-thatch roof that she can smell in the dark and a perimeter of razor grass that looks tended, somehow, coaxed to form a wall between the clearing and the river. At least, that's her best explanation for why there is so little light here, why the house is so hard to see.

That's why she doesn't see the six men standing guard in front of the shack's door, black rifles lolling in the shadows near their hips. That's why she doesn't see Hank, standing outside and smoking a cigarette that he flicks straight to the ground the instant he sees her.

What are you doing here? he mutters.

I came to see you. She pushes a strand of hair behind her ear and smiles. The motion displaces a bug that had settled somewhere in her ponytail; it leaps directly into the hollow of her ear and whirs.

You need to go back to the hotel.

But I don't think I could find the way back.

He looks both ways, toward the jungle and the river, toward

the men with the guns, who chew toothpicks and say nothing. Shit. He lowers his gaze to the ground then back up at her, speaks in a firmer voice than before. Follow your tracks.

But right then a fat man appears in the doorway, a man with rolls of skin on his forehead and under his chin and around the points of his elbows, and he is saying, Hank, Hank, this a lady you're talking this way to?

He says it in English.

Even just from the way he moves into the doorway, Irena can see that this man had an incredible physicality. His hips shift fluidly under the fat. His hands are small and careful in a way that is frightening; when he puts his arm around Hank's shoulders, Hank tightens every muscle in his body so the man won't feel him wince. Hank doesn't answer, so the man keeps talking, straight to Irena, his eyes roving all over her. What is your name, darling? Darling, would you like to come to our party?

Hank pronounces every syllable: She is leaving right now.

The fat man barks a laugh. Come on! Let her decide!

Irena meets the fat man's eye. He is still smiling, back-patting, but there is something in his look. Hard, masculine, commanding. It's amazing. Irena studies him, jealous. How can you make your eyes disagree with the rest of your face like that?

Irena smiles. The bug in her ear screes louder, like it's warning her of something, but she decides to practice the fat man's trick: she makes her expression innocent and wide, but she gives Hank a look that says, move aside now, and walks past him through the door.

·   ·   ·

The fat man's voice is different inside the shack, sweeter and lower: Gentlemen, I think we'll need the good cachaça.

He says it in Portuguese; Irena finds that she can vaguely understand that, too. The room is lit by one bulb and it is full of people. Shirtless men with wide scrapes on their chests and their inner arms. Indian women missing critical teeth. Children in big T-shirts who look tired. They are all speaking different languages, and they are hard to distinguish, all colliding in a blur of voices. She sits on an unlabeled cardboard box with something solid inside it. Hank stands next to her, his body like a wire pulled taut.

Don't be mean, she whispers to him. I just wanted to see you.

Where's your actor friend? Is he coming, too?

She looks at the side of his face, the bones in his temple buckling, like he's chewing something tough.

Relax, she says. You mean Teo? I'm done with him.

Anahi! The fat man sings, Guilherme, Dónde diablos está su hija?

Hija, figlia, daughter? Irena tries with half her brain to translate. And where has she heard the name Anahi? But she can't focus, can't stop looking at the line of Hank's profile, his skin colored whiskey-orange in the light. Hank; daughter. She can't keep the two thoughts in her head at once.

In the corner of her eye, a teenager in jean shorts walks anxiously into the room, carrying a bottle as big around as her own waist. Irena thinks she recognizes her—yes, she was a maid from the hotel, shit, maybe *the* maid that she's seen Teo following around—but she can't get a good look at her face to be sure. Anahi keeps her eyes on the floor, avoiding the room so intently Irena wonders if it is an effort of superstition. And does the room smell like blood? Irena considers. Meat, at least. Slaughter. There's a slaughterhouse smell about this place, something soaked into the dirt floor so deep it can't be scrubbed out.

Tazas! the fat man yells, jubilant, and Irena thinks, Cups.

No tenemos suficientes, the girl murmurs. We don't have enough.

The fat man turns around to face the girl. Something in his face twitches, once, like a machine activating.

What happens next happens fast, the mood of the room changing like a gearshift thrown back. The fat man grabs the girl by the hair, the part at the back of the head where the roots are thickest. Everyone stops talking at once. He pulls the girl's head back so far that her neck bends, so far that her tracheal vertebrae crane and her eyes roll toward the ceiling, searching for someone to help her. Irena can see the undersides of Anahi's eyeballs, wet and white and roving. The girl whimpers once—Pa—but she knows not to finish the word.

No one moves at all. The girl's hands stay clenched around the girth of the bottle, to keep it from dropping and breaking.

The fat man's face keeps changing: vicious and then smiling, like he's dipping his bride at their wedding. Irena feels something like hunger start to swell in her chest as she looks at him. She thinks: *How could I move like that?*

Encontrarás algunas. His voice is soft and reassuring. Eres una niña lista.

Irena can't translate it.

He lets the girl go. She falls back for an instant and then rights herself, hands the fat man the bottle, wipes her face with her hands as she hurries out of the room.

Friends! The man says in Portuguese, then, and Irena realizes that she can't tell what his native language is: his command of every accent is perfect. He has an aristocratic tilt to his nose that signals no nationality. His lips curl up at the edges in a permanent smile.

Friends, he says again, we have a guest tonight that I should introduce, someone who has just arrived in our town.

Something starts clicking underneath Irena's sternum and begins to speed.

Juan Carlos, the fat man says, Preséntete.

She deflates. A man sitting on the other side of Hank leans forward, clearing his throat. He's around her age, maybe twenty or twenty-one, with an overgrown beard and a green bandanna tied around his temples, filth soaked into his clothes. Juan Carlos tightens his jaw to look serious and nods around the room. But when his gaze lands on Hank, he stills.

The fat man continues, his voice teasing. I'm told that Juan Carlos is part of a new regime in this organization, and that he may be able to help us understand our little miscommunication about the last shipment. He coughs. Excuse me. About our last shipment *weight*.

Hank does not lean forward, but his voice does: We don't do this now.

The fat man wheels around. And why not?

It's not the time, he says, his voice leaning toward Irena, now, though again his body makes no signal.

I think we should get to know our friends in the M-19. Don't we all want to know our friends in the M-19?

Some of the men and the children clap uncertainly. Hank's eyes are full of words Irena can tell he's not allowed to say. She can tell he wants to tell the fat man to shut up.

Juan Carlos, you must know, just because we're requesting reparations doesn't mean we blame *you* for what your last co-mandante did. Maybe it was an error in measurement. We all make—

Hank stands.

You're worried about your girlfriend? The fat man laughs. Look at her, she's tough! She knows what men do!

The fat man walks slowly over to Irena and extends his

hand. The fingernails are clipped small and strangely cute, like little eyes opening.

Hermosa, he says, Cómo te llamas?

Irena can feel the skin over her own face, tight, tight, so tight it will show all her thoughts moving underneath it if she's not careful. She relaxes the way her acting teacher showed her: jaw muscles, scalp muscles, tongue. She shakes her head and smiles.

No Spanish? Okay. Beautiful girl, tell me your name.

English this time. In the corner of the room, Anahi returns with an armload of cups. She pauses in the doorway and stares at Irena.

He says it in Italian: Bella, qual è il tuo nome?

Her heart pauses. Her face is blank and smiling.

We're going, Hank says. He pulls her up by the arm.

But it's a party! The fat man says.

The men with the guns have their backs to the door. Hank pushes past them with both hands.

You'll leave your M-19 friend here alone? the fat man says.

Hank keeps moving, shouts something in Spanish so fast that she can't understand.

The fat man pounds his own chest once. Come on! That isn't the Jungle Hank I know!

One of the guards moves to bar them, but Hank keeps shoving.

Stay! The fat man starts pouring drinks, a fistful of shot glasses and teacups in one hand, sloshing silver liquid over all of them at once. Hey, hey, everyone, let's toast to Hank. Come on. Let's toast to Hank staying at the party.

The door rushes shut. The sound behind the door doesn't. As they stride into the jungle, Irena can hear the room shouting the toast, the liquid glugging in the neck of the bottle, the sticky sound of the men adjusting their grips on the rifles. She

looks back over her shoulder and sees them, the guards with their guns hovering just a bit higher in the dark. Hank drags her forward so hard that her gaze jolts. He grabs the flashlight from her and switches it on. She can see the guards' faces, but she can't make out their eyes.

The air in the trees has thickened: the heat is heavy like the dark is heavy, pushing against her legs and her chest as she moves.

Slow down, she says. Hank, come on.

You never come back here. Hank's hand is still heavy on her upper arm. His feet make a scraping sound against the ground plants.

Who was that guy back there? What did he call him, the guy from the M-19?

Hank exhales.

He was cute, she fakes. What if I wanted to party with him for a while?

He says nothing.

Hey, hey, she purrs. I'm not scared, if that's what you think.

Hank stops. He holds both of Irena's shoulders in his hands and keeps her there, his breath heavy in the space between them. The hotel is that way, he says, aiming the flashlight into a tangle of bush with a skinny path cleaved into the center of it. His face looks wild, like he'd been running furiously into a headwind. Follow the trail, he says. Forget everyone you saw.

Irena angles her face into the light, tries to make him look at her. Let's stay out. One more hour, come on. It's almost morning.

He gives her a look that says, *Stupid fucking girl.*

Then he clears his throat.

You forget everyone you saw, Hank says. You never come back. Stay in the hotel from now on.

He shoves the flashlight back into her hands, jogs off into the trees.

.   .   .

When Irena gets back to the hotel, there's someone waiting in the meal tent.

It could be Teo or Ugo or a hotel janitor taking a smoke break or someone she has never met. It could be anyone, but Irena knows, before her eyes confirm it, that it has to be the new American.

She knows because she wills it. She knows because her body signals her, before she even registers his height or the slouch in his shoulders or the boyish way he gnaws a cuticle, that this is who she wants to play her boyfriend.

Before he even sees her, she's practicing what she'll say to him, practicing the words behind her teeth. She will make her tongue flip like a tree frog's, a thousand times a second. Her mouth will be full of poison.

Just before he turns toward her, as he opens up his mouth and calls her toward him with a voice full of relief, Irena realizes: she can control him.

She can alter her elocution. It's as simple as that. This American, he will believe every word she says.

RICHARD

Ovidio

Here is something that fills you with shame when you think of it, three days later:

The morning after you saw the prop body and Irena finally told you what the film was about, after you'd stayed up all night doing Meisner exercises in the mirror to convince yourself that you were Richard Trent, you came up with what you thought was a brilliant plan.

You combed your hair eighteen times on each side. You did forty push-ups and walked a straight, fast line across the parking lot, your blood still jumpy under your skin.

You found Ugo at the meal tent.

I'm ready, you said. What are we shooting today?

The director pinched a piece of unbuttered toast between his fingers and looked at it, disturbed, like *it* had just spoken to him. We don't need you yet, he said, incredulous.

Something in you deflated, but you tried to smile over it. Is there a production schedule I could look at? You know, just to get an idea of what I need to prepare?

The director just chewed, gazing blankly past your shoulder.

You wondered if it was a translation issue. You tried again: Do you know when you'll need me next? For what scenes?

How would I know that? Ugo said, and then shoved the toast into his cheek, turned and whispered something urgent to his DP.

It happened three days in a row, some version of this conversation. The first day, you'd gotten on the bus like everyone else, waited on the sidelines in case he'd changed his mind. You watched Irena and Teo film a scene where Irena stepped half-naked into a river again and again, threw her arms over her chest when she realized he was watching. Ugo made her do a dozen takes, and every time, her body was a surprise—T-shirt tan lines and unexpected freckles. You were never desensitized to it. Every time, you waited for the director to say it was your turn, to call you into the scene with her.

He didn't.

The second day, you didn't get on the bus to set, just to see if anyone would notice.

They didn't.

You told yourself that maybe it's cultural; maybe American filmmakers are the only ones who are so neurotically organized, with their thick binders full of storyboards and shot orders, twiddling the sound levels for two hours before they let you say a word. They just have a different process, these Europeans, more associative, more free-form. They must.

The crew all speaks in Italian, so you didn't understand the things you heard them whispering as they loaded up: that Ugo had been filming nothing but the Indians hunting for days, close shots of spears bending into the surface of the river, close shots of impaled eels dragged out after. Close shots of Teo and Irena, gaping in reaction. You ignored the sound guy who

whispered, in English like he wanted you to hear, that maybe Richard's character has been cut altogether.

With everyone gone, you took long showers in the single outdoor stall that the cast and crew usually all have to share, studying the pattern of soap whirling down the chestnut-size hole someone's gouged for a drain. You felt the anxiety release from your muscles, and then you felt them seize right back up as the maid pounded once on the stall door, shouting in broken English: Water shortage, please, not a long time?

You tried exploring the town. Twenty-five mosquito bites just on the walk over; a collection of plywood shacks painted blue and pink and Creamsicle-orange, none of which ever seemed open in the daylight hours.

You sat in the hotel room and read *Respect for Acting*: *If I compare myself to a large, meaty, round apple, I discover that my inner and outer cliché image of myself is only a wedge of it—possibly the wedge with the rosy cheek on the skin. But I have to become aware of myself as a total apple—*

You closed *Respect for Acting*. You got the TV to work, finally. You watched a washed-out episode of *Petticoat Junction*, overdubbed in Spanish, the volume on maximum.

The third day, you didn't leave your room at all.

The third night, you tried to sleep. But hunger and anxiety worked on you, made all the air in the room feel like it was boiling. The table fan moved the hair on your scalp and it made you feel like tiny animals were running over your skull.

Around midnight, you went looking for Irena. You didn't know her room number, so you waited in the meal tent until she found you. You had planned just to ask her if she had heard any new rumors about your character or when in hell they might need you to film. But when you saw her, striding across

the lot with a worried expression on her face, it was like a seam ripped open in you.

Here is something else you are still ashamed of, the morning after:

That you cried on the shoulder of her little white T-shirt. That when you pulled away, when Irena looked you in the eye and spoke—listen, it's okay, we'll talk to him tomorrow—you saw that you'd left a wet pattern there like an archipelago.

After Irena put you to bed, you dreamed about Kay. She was sitting naked on your shoulders in mime makeup, shouting the same two words directly into the heat of the stagelight: Total apple! Total apple! Total apple! When you told her you were tired, when you tried to set her down, she said no; the audience is full of foxes, and they all paid full admission. How can we stop the play before we've given them what they came for?

·   ·   ·

The next morning, Ugo skips breakfast.

His seat at the picnic table has a ragged heart carved into it in the exact spot that's usually covered by his tray, the words *FAT PUSSY* carved into the center of it with a blue pen.

You look around for Irena, but she isn't there either.

You tense your jaw and drop your own lunch tray on top of the heart, pivot-turn and march over to Fabi's table.

You demand a script from him—any script, so long as you're in it. He only has the scene for the day, handwritten on four sheets of legal paper, the letters angular and dark. You snatch it from his hands and stride off toward the far end of the tent, willing your ears to shut out all noise so you can think.

Under the centered heading, you see your character's

name—RICHARD—and a monologue, thank God, a *monologue*, and it is a full page long.

Your heart pounds with gratitude. On the page, Richard is impassioned, shouting straight to camera about the ferocity of jungle life, the daily violence of the strong consuming the weak. If Veronica has been consumed by these savages, Richard says, and the authorities are no help, then we must become the more savage force. We will make them tell us where she is. We will find her. And if we don't—on the page, the word *BEAT* is written in huge letters—then this will be our revenge.

Then you're supposed to give a cue—*Gayle, Joe! Now!*—signaling the crew to torch the tree of hives.

You flip the page and there is a doodle of a cartoon girl shot through with arrows. You flip the page and it's the same girl again, a toothless crescent for a smile, *X*s for eyes, poorly drawn flames curling off her body. Someone's scrawled a few notes in the corner in Italian, a line of numbers and times, but there's no explanation. You flip the page over. The lines are blank yellow, stained with dirty fingerprints. There isn't any more.

Fabi is routing for something in a scrambled egg when you stride back up to his picnic table, slap the script back down.

I don't understand.

Fabi grins and chews.

You need to explain this to me.

You like it? Fabi says. Big—big words, for you?

Why does Richard do this? Where—how far into the movie is this scene?

Fabi nods, peppering his eggs.

I don't—God, you don't speak any English, do you?

He doesn't.

Then the voice comes from behind you. You don't recognize

it immediately: Baldo, the long-legged producer who drove you from the airport, still in the same powder-blue shirt. He's nattering in Italian to Fabi, crosses to Fabi's side of the table. He sits and starts eating somberly. His plate has nothing but meat on it.

Hey, you speak English. Do you know about this scene?

Baldo glances quickly at the page and exhales. I can't believe he still wants to do that.

So you've read it.

Baldo saws a sausage into thirds, exhausted. Yes. I'm going to have to beg the insurance company for forgiveness, but yes. We're doing it.

It's just that I—I thought the premise was that Richard was a journalist? You stutter. I thought this was, like, sort of a possible *rescue* mission—

So?

So this is crazy. This *tree of hives*, or whatever it's called—it's some sort of Indian dwelling, right?

Baldo sniffs, annoyed. Sure.

Then why would he attack these dwellings where Veronica might—

Why does it matter to you?

Because I need to understand his motivation.

Why?

You puzzle, stare into the mess of sliced ham on Baldo's plate. It's important for an actor. Motivation is always the most important thing.

Who told you that?

You blink. Baldo is looking you full in the face for the first time. There's a sag that tugs his left eyelid down, a brownish stain like a watermark on his cheek. You shouldn't stare. You shouldn't.

Then he sighs: Fine. I think he was talking about putting this scene at about . . . what do you call, the halfway point.

You nod vigorously. Okay. Okay, is this a *change* in his character, or—

Yes.

Okay, so, ah, he's compromising his ethics a bit, he's getting carried away by emotion, but his *intention* is still to find Veronica and—

Jesus, I can't listen to this.

I just need more information.

Fabi whisper-chatters something in Italian, points his fork at you and swirls it around.

Please, I just need to know why Richard would set a forest fire when he's trying to save someone inside it.

Then I'll make it easy for you, Baldo pronounces. You're not the director. You don't need to worry about what Richard would and wouldn't do.

The way Baldo says it, it's like a heavy stone has been set down on the table between you.

He eats. I *am* Richard, you try to say, watching him scrape up the meat with the side of his fork. I'm playing him, at least. But your voice sounds tentative, even to you.

Baldo rolls his neck once to each side and reaches for the salt. Richard is a bad man, he says. Okay? Is that enough motivation for you? Richard is a bad man. Why he does what he does is not your problem. He laughs. It's mine, if it's anyone's. I'm the one who'd have to pay off the lawsuit if this fucking stunt gets out of hand.

But how—

Baldo sets the saltshaker down and stands. Fucking ask your director. They'll film it this afternoon.

· · ·

Here is something you don't know:

Richard and his crew don't arrive in the Yanomamö village until the second act of the film.

You don't know it, because you'll film almost none of the lead-up to the scene you'll shoot today. Ugo will find an Indian who can serve as a body double, and he'll be the one whose silhouette stomps over the last hill and looks out over the town. Ugo will have a store of reaction shots he can draw from; you saying Wow, look at this. You saying Are you rolling? You saying Quick, over there! The body double will be the one who spies on the Indians for the first time. The body double will be the one who hides behind a rock with Joe and films their ceremonial meal; he'll end up as your voice double, too, since he'll be the one making the disgusted sounds into the mic as the Indians hack the shell off a giant tortoise for a stew.

You'll be the one who films the scene with Gayle where Richard decides that diplomacy isn't the solution here. She'll be the one who says, We need to find a translator to question them, please, they might know what happened, and you'll stop building the campfire, look up at her and say: No, Gayle. That's not what we're going to do.

It will be the body double, though, who handles all the close shots. It will be the body double's hand that pulls all the triggers in the movie, swings all the machetes, holds every Indian facedown in the mud.

You won't be there to film those scenes.

PROCURATORE CAPO: Signor Velluto, you must admit that at least one member of your production was harmed during your six weeks in the Amazon.

[Whereupon Signor Velluto does not respond.]

PROCURATORE CAPO: We have documentation from the local medic in Ovidio. Would you like us to reopen the exhibit, or could you summarize this document for us instead?

[Whereupon Signor Velluto does not respond.]

PROCURATORE CAPO: Signor Avvocato, please instruct your witness to answer the question.

VELLUTO: I will not.

PROCURATORE CAPO: Is it because you do not wish to implicate yourself?

VELLUTO: I was not responsible. It was a random event. It couldn't be helped.

PROCURATORE CAPO: That's not the legal definition of responsibility, signore. You wrote the scene where this occurred. You hired the production designer—

VELLUTO: He was a professional! He knew—

PROCURATORE CAPO: You did not advise your cast or crew of the risks! At the very least, we can call that a form of negligence, no?

VELLUTO: What am I on trial for? For not anticipating all contingencies? For planting the fucking Amazon rain forest? Did I found the nation of Colombia? What?

PROCURATORE CAPO: Criminal negligence is not about—

VELLUTO: Remind me, please! I've forgotten! Because I thought I was just there to film a movie.

PROCURATORE CAPO: That's exactly the problem, Signor Velluto. You filmed the entire incident.

VELLUTO: No. No, I didn't see it happen. I would have stopped it.

PROCURATORE CAPO: I apologize, you're right. You filmed the *aftermath*, and did nothing to intervene.

[Whereupon Signor Velluto says nothing.]

PROCURATORE CAPO: We can play the tape. It's in the final version of the movie.

VELLUTO: Don't.

[Whereupon the procuratore capo starts the video.]

PROCURATORE CAPO: You confirm, yes, that this shot is not the work of special effects? That this is authentic footage?

VELLUTO: The scene won't be in the rerelease.

PROCURATORE CAPO: Because you regret this.

[Whereupon Signor Velluto pauses.]

VELLUTO: Because the framing was off.

PROCURATORE CAPO: Signor Velluto, if you have any compassion for the man in this video, if you have any semblance of regret, you will identify him for the court now.

[Whereupon Signor Velluto leaves the witness stand and begins to move to exit the courtroom.]

GIUDICE: Signor Avvocato, please instruct your client—

VELLUTO: Turn off the tape.

PROCURATORE CAPO: If you don't feel some measure of responsibility, Signor Velluto, why—

VELLUTO: Turn it off. This isn't how I want my film to be seen. Turn it off.

GIUDICE: Signore, you will be held in contempt of court if you do not return to the stand this instant.

VELLUTO: I need water. I need a moment.

PROCURATORE CAPO: Who is this man on the tape, Velluto?

AVVOCATO: We request a formal recess, and we apologize for this outburst. Please.

VELLUTO: Open the doors. Open the doors.

PROCURATORE CAPO: Just say his name, Signor Velluto.

AVVOCATO: Signor Procuratore—

PROCURATORE CAPO: Why can't you say it, Signor Velluto?

MARINA, LA ARAÑA

Ovidio

They'd had the fight again last night, just before the comandante came to take Juan Carlos to the cartel: Marina sitting
up ramrod-straight on her cot on in the medical tent, Juan
Carlos lying on his side, facing away. They've been fighting
since they got here about this place, an evolution of the same
fight they've had a hundred times on the drive from the safe
house in Bogotá to Putumayo and the speedboat ride into the
bush and the awful hike from the riverbank to wherever they
were now. It was like they were following a script, by then, all
the gestures written in: Marina raked eight fingernails from
her sweaty hairline to the crown of her head and seethed. She
told him that this place wasn't what he'd promised. She told
him she needed to go home.

Juan Carlos said what he always said: they couldn't go anywhere, not until the war had begun.

Marina braced all her muscles against a fever chill and tried
not to yell. There is no war, Juan Carlos.

Not yet, he'd said, calm as always. But there will be. They're
planning a big siege down here, you know that.

They're planning it. Not us. Not the people.

We're not comandantes yet, Marina, you know that. We just got here.

If we're not, then this isn't true socialism.

You don't—

I want you to sleep outside tonight, she'd said.

But Juan Carlos hadn't moved. Even when Marina scooped up a mosquito net and wrapped it tight around her own shoulders, dragged her aching bones out of the cot and threatened to go outside herself, he hadn't said a word. This is my bed, she'd rasped, her voice raw and weak. This is my movement. I have a right to this.

Marina, we're both too sick—

If you're comfortable being on the outside of all this, she said, then go be on the outside.

The fucking bugs will eat me alive by morning, Juan Carlos mumbled. I'm not leaving this tent.

Yes, you will. If you love me—

And then he'd looked at her, and said something he couldn't take back: Marina, we wouldn't even be here if you hadn't done that to Andres.

The timing was too perfect, but it was how it happened: this was the moment she heard the flap swish open, the comandante grunting as he ducked inside. Marina was still standing, the mosquito net slung over her shoulders, and Juan Carlos' words hung like smoke in the air between them, when the comandante announced that Juan Carlos needed to get up now.

There was a new complication with the cartel, something they needed a new face to help smooth out.

We're sending you now, he'd said to him. Your associate can stay here and rest, he'd mumbled, tilting his head toward Marina.

·　·　·

But Marina doesn't need to rest.

Or rather, what her body needs doesn't matter to her now. What her body needs is the opposite of what her instincts have been screaming for her to do, the opposite of the thought that thrashed in her skull like a trapped bird as she lay in her cot all last night, awake and alone. Since she got to Ovidio three days ago, Marina and Juan Carlos have done nothing *but* rest, lying together in the medical tent with army-issue rehydration drips jammed into their arms, still malarial and sweating through nightmares, waiting for the comandantes to say they're well enough to serve. If what Marina needed was just sleep, she wouldn't still have this same frantic urge to run, this same brain-spun feeling she's had since the moment she stood over Andres' body back in Bogotá.

She wouldn't have waited up, shaking and furious, until she was sure she could not sleep and Juan Carlos wasn't coming back that night.

She wouldn't have waited until she heard the patrol guards douse the fire just before dawn, and then listened to their footsteps, taking them back behind the camp to piss or nap or screw before the comandantes woke.

She wouldn't have thought to herself: Go. Wouldn't have braced herself and stood, looped the strap of the Kalashnikov across her chest, and stepped as quietly as she could into the bush.

Marina doesn't know where she's going, or why, or what she'll do when she gets there. But if all she needed was rest, she wouldn't have walked as far as she has already, the mid-morning sunlight searing against her hairline and the skin of her heels screaming inside her boots. Marina knows no one is supposed to walk so far from base alone. Their camp is too close to the town. She is sick and lost and moving slow, and

196 · Kea Wilson

she knows that if she goes too far, any tourist on a nature walk could wander up on her.

But Marina hikes. It's been hours by now; she doesn't have a watch, but she can tell by the height of the sun over the tree canopy, the bright slap of light ahead that tells her the river can't be that far off. She can tell by the way her lungs suck against the wall of her lungs—she didn't bring water—and by the new ache in her muscles, deeper than the fever, twanging muscle fibers that she's sure she's never used. Marina starts to feel something running down her ankle, under the pant leg and down into the shaft of her boot. She imagines a fat bead of sweat, or an ant, as big as her thumb knuckle, with a bite that a compañero told her early on to watch out for because it will make your leg swell and purple and burn for days.

Marina stops. She slaps her ankle and seethes and then takes a deep breath and forces herself to be still. She knows she needs to think. She didn't bring a compass or water or a map. She has no food and she hasn't eaten more than a mouthful of anything in days and what she's managed to get down she's thrown up. The strap of the rifle has cut into her collarbone and with every step the gun pounds an oval of ache deeper into her lower spine. She turns a half-circle, scanning for a path or an edible plant or a reason to go in any particular direction.

She turns another centimeter, and that is when she sees the women.

·   ·   ·

One of them is naked and pregnant and staring at the sky. The other is tall with short black hair and a bucket full of what looks like blood at her feet, and she is using both her hands to smear the other woman's body red.

Marina lowers to her stomach as quietly as she can, hunkers so her chin digs a shallow cup into the mud. She widens her eyes to see through the black tangle of the bush and tries not to breathe.

The women aren't alone; Marina can see past them to what must be a village, the sunlight vivid through the gaps in the trees. There are dozens of people there, and smells like food and woodsmoke that make her throat feel hollow. When she squints, she realizes there's a huge structure strung up in one enormous tree: a grid of what looks like huge nests tipped on their sides and suspended from the branches, like rooms with their fourth walls knocked out. She sees a man in blue jeans ease a huge ladder off the side of the tree, and then she sees the people that must have just climbed it: brown people with long black hair and grass skirts, curled up one to each nest and staring like they're waiting for something to begin. Something slithers over the back of Marina's knee but she doesn't react: she is maybe three meters from the women, twenty from all the rest.

The tall woman says something that Irena thinks she almost understands—Girare, like girar, could she be speaking Spanish? The pregnant woman looks puzzled, until the other takes her gently by the shoulders and rotates her a quarter turn.

The pregnant woman laughs. Oh.

Marina is thinking, *Is she one of the Indians?* when suddenly, something happens in the distance.

A whoop, a gunshot, then the low rumble of startled people. The tall woman stands up from her bucket of blood and turns to face the sound. Marina cannot believe she is close enough to see all this but there it is: at the base of the tree, a skinny white man talking into a camera in what sounds like English. A skinny white girl with brown hair, posing with a sound recorder. Another man with a lit torch, striding fast behind him, setting fire to the lowest empty nest.

A film, Marina realizes. They're filming.

But the fire is real. It is small at first, and then it rushes, turns the nest into a sphere of light.

The voices louden, and then there are the sounds of shrieking women, stabbing at the air. She can see the people in the lower nests leaping out and sprinting. She can see the people in the higher branches brace themselves and peer down at the long fall.

She can see the fire climb, searching for the nearest tangle of dry vines.

Marina's heart races, but the women close to her are calm. The tall one's hands are at her sides, palms out, so the blood won't stain her clothes. She is not pretty but there is an honesty to her posture that is unusual and magnetic to Marina; she is exhausted, and she shows it. She watches the fire leap from nest to nest like she's seen this exact scene so many times. Marina does not know why, but hot tears clot in the corners of her eyes now, a feeling like jealousy filling her mouth. She blinks the tears out, stunned, like a sudden wound has opened on her brow and leaked down.

The Indian says something, and the other woman looks at her and smiles, says something that must mean, It's okay. It isn't real.

The tears slick over Marina's cheeks and into the corners of her mouth, but why? Marina flattens one palm and swipes the wet out with the thinnest edge of her hand, quick as a knife draw, but the tears keep coming. Snot balloons inside her sinuses and she exhales hard as she can without making a sound but it refills. If she keeps on this way, she thinks, the women will hear her, the fucking people in the tree will see her crying in the mud when she should be invisible, and this—this is when the madness returns. This is when the wild thought starts pulsing desperately in the center of Marina's brain, forces out a tendril, and unfurls:

She could preempt it.

She grits her teeth around the sour taste of her own crying.

She could kill them all right now.

The semiautomatic is slung over her back like an afterthought. She has her fists if she runs out of ammunition. She has her teeth. They are all distracted, and whether she wants to admit it to herself or not, Marina has done terrible things before—done them so recently that when she closes her eyes at night she still feels the muscle on the inside of her trigger finger flare with blood and pulse until she has to make a fist. As Marina watches the women, silhouetted against a distant backdrop of fire, she cannot help it: she pictures herself rising out of the reeds, the wet whites of many eyes reflecting fire, looking at her. She could do it to protect the mission, or to slaughter the bourgeoisie. Or she could do it to ruin everything: the revolution, the cartel, so many plans. She could do it for no reason. She could do it alone.

How good would it feel: for the whole world to be, for once, as violent as the memories in her head? To force that symmetry with her body, her gun, her voice?

Marina pictures herself after it is done and they are all dead, waiting for voices to come through the trees behind her. She can almost hear them: compañeros shouting Bitch and then Coño, a gun firing off, What have you done? Then they will gun her down into the mud, and for the first time since she killed Andres, she will know relief.

She closes her eyes, thinking of these things.

She opens her eyes, and that is when she sees it: a man on fire, running toward the trees.

The people by the tree don't notice for a moment, but the women do. The Indian angles her chin like a strange animal has just loped past her, studying. The tall woman stiffens. Then she sprints.

She calls out a name, but Marina can't make it out.

The burning man is sprinting, too, and now everyone else sees him. The burning man is running toward the river that Marina didn't realize is just there through the trees, and then their voices and the fire and the river are so loud that Marina knows this is not part of the film, this is not a stunt, this is her best chance, right now, to run.

But then Marina realizes: the Indian woman hasn't moved at all.

She's still standing less than three meters away from Marina, her head cocked at the same angle, bloody from neck to knee, studying the beach. Before, it had seemed like the Indian didn't understand what the cameras were or what the movie was, but now, Marina realizes, she's grasped the concept, an instant too late. The Indian chews the tips of two fingers and smiles, amazed. It's like she's watching something remarkable on a screen.

When the rain comes, Marina seizes the moment and scuttles back, but the Indian still stands there. Marina runs, but when she stops behind a tree a dozen meters out and peeks, the woman hasn't moved. She is peeling her pregnant belly off her body, a prosthetic glued on with some adhesive that the rain must have melted. The people on the beach are screaming and the fire in the tree is battling the rain but the Indian woman is just there, holding the belly in front of her like an enormous bowl, blood running down her shoulders like it's coming from the sky itself.

· · ·

By the time Marina gets back to camp, the rain has stopped.

It's almost dusk; it took her longer to get back than it had taken her to walk away, even walking what she thought was a straight line. She'd expected panic and fury, but no one seems

to have noticed she's been gone. The comandantes are nowhere, which means they're probably all huddled together in one of their shacks, discussing whatever they sent Juan Carlos to do last night. A few of their women are out in the cook yard stirring cans of beans in metal bowls, their children sprinting around the yard hollering. A compañera in a braided belt glances up at Marina as she passes, and from the woman's expression, Marina can imagine how her own face must look right then. She hasn't seen a mirror in over a week but she can picture the hollows of her cheeks, the animal shine of her eyes, the mud smeared down her front.

Juan Carlos is back in the med tent. He has one arm thrown over his face, the elbow pointed up at the ceiling like a shark fin rising through dim water. She can smell liquor coming off him in fumes, and something sweet, like wet rope and vomit. She lies on her back on top of the cot next to his and tries to breathe through her mouth.

Where were you? In the chuntos? Juan Carlos asks, so she knows he's been passed out, probably for hours. Marina exhales; at least she doesn't have to explain herself.

You mean the toilet, Marina says, flattening her voice to play along. Don't use their fucking lingo.

I'm just wondering.

Don't pretend you were worried. She turns onto her side. I'm going to sleep.

She can hear him exhale, deciding whether or not to push it. She can almost feel Juan Carlos' thoughts working, plotting his approach, trying to sidestep the fight. He decides on this, and says it in a careful voice: I know you're mad that they kept me out all night. I wouldn't have left if I had a choice.

Marina holds her breath, doesn't dispute him.

A shipment came up short, Juan Carlos says. A shipment

we delivered from Brazil. Maybe three kilos. The cartel thought we were skimming.

Were we? Marina thinks, but she's too tired to say it out loud.

We weren't, of course, Juan Carlos says. We would never. We do this to fund the revolution. Drugs aren't our business. It must have been an accident.

She can tell by his voice that Juan Carlos believes this completely. Marina breathes, something hardening inside her.

But anyway, it was the American's idea, Juan Carlos says. For us to send someone new to smooth things over, for them to send *me* instead of one of the comandantes. In case the cartel feels like they can't trust the people they know anymore. It's better to send a new face. It's basic diplomacy.

If this conversation had happened yesterday, now is when Marina would have sat up straight, spitting venom, shouting out how dumb he's been, how dumb it is that he's let himself be used. Here is where she should be saying: This is not our fight anymore, and we have to get out now. But Marina feels something strange creeping through her now, a sick heat, like vomit welling up. She is thinking of a wall of fire in the jungle, and beyond it a river, wider than they can swim across. She is thinking, despite herself, of Andres: a ghost who would cling to her back even if she ran straight through the flames, if she managed to kick hard enough to make it all the way across the water.

She is realizing: even if she convinced him to escape with her, they couldn't.

Juan Carlos softens his voice down even more. I know, it wasn't fair to you. I wouldn't have left you if the American hadn't said they really needed me.

She makes her dry lips move. What American?

There's an American who runs interference between everyone here and the cartel.

I thought we hated the Americans.

Juan Carlos sits up, wincing and groping for his tobacco. Well, we'll have to work with a lot of people we don't like if we want to win this war.

Marina flips onto her stomach, listens to Juan Carlos pinch the tobacco flakes out of the pouch and thumb the paper open. She thinks of war—she used to love to think of war—but when she closes her eyes she can see nothing but the place they're in, nothing but rot and rain and dead things left to soak, razor grasses and legions of invisible insects vibrating the air.

They thought about sending you instead, but they thought you were still too weak, Juan Carlos says.

Marina thinks: their war, now, is not an invading thing but an invading place. Their enemy, now, has no brain and a billion arms and can send spores rooting in wetlands of their bodies. They are all too weak.

But she doesn't say a word.

When the pause goes on too long, Juan Carlos softens his voice.

I'm glad they didn't send you, he says, setting his cigarette down, standing. I'm glad they let me keep you safe. He sits down on her cot and reaches out for her.

Marina can hear his voice, but it's like he's at the bottom of an ocean. She can feel the weight of him lying down behind her on her cot, and then his hands on her, pulling her close. He moves slowly, like the attack has already happened and he's dragging in his kill. She keeps her face aimed away from him.

Baby, he says, underwater. Are you awake?

Yes, she answers, staring down into a flat black sea.

They got me drunk, he laughs. The cartel. They acted like it

was all a party. The American was there, and I think he invited some fucking Italian girl. She must have been some tourist he's fucking, I don't know. My point is, they weren't being secretive at all.

Marina flinches, thinking of the tall woman in the jungle and the language that she spoke. Girare, Girar. Could it—

And in some ways that was scarier, I guess, Juan Carlos wonders. That they were so confident about it all, you know? They barely even asked me about the short shipment. I'm not sure how well I did.

He holds her fist in his hand and thumbs one of her knuckles like a worry stone. She can feel the dried filth flaking off her.

I'm sure you did fine, she forces herself to say.

And here is where the hitch of doubt creeps into Juan Carlos' voice, for the first time since they came here: he says, The thing is, he says, I got the feeling that it doesn't matter what we do to pay them back. Like they're going to pretend like everything's fine, until one day, they just—I don't know.

She can tell Juan Carlos wants to tell her more, but all Marina wants is for him to be quiet, so she can focus. She shifts her body closer into his and pretends she wants it there. She sweetens her voice and makes herself talk.

Will you keep me safe? she says.

He kisses the back of her neck. Of course, he says, reaching across her hip. Anything, he says, his hand creeping toward the button of her jeans.

When Juan Carlos is inside Marina, she can think. She uses her body like a flare thrown into a field, creating a diversion. While he's tending to it, her mind can go elsewhere, out of the tent and away. That's the only way she can be alone.

When he's done, she has decided.

She won't tell him what she saw out there in the jungle.

．　．　．

Juan Carlos sleeps.

This is always the worst part of the day, for Marina: worse than the sex or the flies stuck to her sweat or the hours they spend fighting. When Juan Carlos sleeps, he tumbles into sleep completely, like he's been pushed underwater. He barely even breathes. The only things that move are his eyelashes.

And this is when the thought comes, each night, despite her, in the silence of the tent: the thought Marina's been avoiding every moment since they left Bogotá, the reason *she* can't sleep at all. She thinks about the day Andres let the Patient escape.

She'd studied his face just like this: his eyelashes longer than Juan Carlos', the neat grooves of his combed hair. He was in the kitchen and she was crouched behind the false wall in the pantry, staring through the knot they'd gouged out in the pine. She could see only small parts of him this way: his boyish doughy ears and sweating temples, the skin over them tensed. This is how she'd realized: he was lying.

At the same instant, she heard the Patient upstairs, just over her head, in the secret compartment where they'd kept him for thirteen weeks and six days.

In the tent, Marina's breath goes shallow and quick, anxiety rushing up from nowhere and tightening around her lungs. She tries to focus on Juan Carlos: his breath leaving just slightly through his open lips, his eyeballs spinning under the weight of his eyelids. Why can't she look away, from this man she doesn't love? Why didn't she look away from Andres, as she listened to a man's bare feet scrambling on the floor a centimeter above her head?

Why did she study the sweet curl of hair behind Andres' ear

as she heard Matón die, right above her, as she heard a voice above her whispering, I'm sorry, I'm sorry?

Marina still remembers how it felt: all her skin hot with fury, her teeth tight around her tongue. She remembers watching Andres drop ice cubes into a cup and smile. She remembers what she thought: Jesus, you are so beautiful; what the fuck did you just do?

How can these two things coexist: the specific heat of compassion, the specific heat of rage? Marina thinks she can remember when that used to be what it was all about for her, this revolution. Now, in this jungle, it makes no sense to her at all.

She crouched in the pantry, and the chord came sounding through the ceiling.

A bolt of fury struck her chest and vibrated straight through her.

And then the record player was explained away as a malfunction, and the landlady was gone, and the Patient stuffed down into the chamber again. Then Marina kicked out the panel in the pantry.

She took her rifle and stepped into the kitchen light.

She looked around once, slowly, her head swiveling like a carnivorous flower sensing the approach of meat.

And that's when she makes herself stop the memory: at that instant when Andres rounded the doorway back into the kitchen and stopped, stared back at her. She remembers the muscles in her hand and arm contracting, the weight of the gun growing lighter in her grip, and then she forces herself to think of anything else.

In the jungle, Marina watches the sleeping man who told her once that he'd save her sleep, and knows that he will never save her, that there is no escape, and she will never sleep again. Her eyes are open and her brain is in Bogotá, stunned, in a white kitchen with her rifle at her elbow and her tongue numb in her mouth.

She watches night fall through the walls of the tent: the

shadows leaning into the fabric, the color draining down to gray. Then the compañeros light the cook fires in the yard, and Marina watches the light brim up from the ground.

. . .

Hours later, when the fire is doused and the quiet hour comes, Marina makes a choice.

She tries not to rustle as she stands, stays quiet as she tucks her pants into her shoes and buckles up her belt.

Juan Carlos doesn't wake. There's a crate of supplies in the corner of the tent, a shoulder bag full of bandages and iodine that she empties out and steals. There's no food, but she will find food later. The gun is right where she left it. A machete, too, is lying by the tree line, halfway up the steep incline that separates camp from the bush. She picks it up and thumbs the point to test it. She'll probably need this more.

Marina doesn't think anyone sees her move into the woods. But if someone does, she has the gun and the machete.

She still doesn't have a compass, but she knows where the river is now.

. . .

The patrols find her less than an hour later.

She'd stepped into a nest five kilometers from camp, climbing over a fallen moriche palm with an infested hollow. She'd heard the humming, but the jungle was all humming, and so she'd walked straight into it. When they bring Marina back to Juan Carlos, he doesn't recognize her. Her clothes and boots and all her skin are covered in mud, and the mud has dried as pale as chalk, and under it her face is not her face.

Her eyes are swollen shut. She is stung and stung and stung. She is almost walking on her own—she is alive—but her skin does not look like something you can call skin.

Outside the med tent, in the pitch dark, Juan Carlos drinks and paces, waiting for the med tech to apply the poultices and get the poison out. He can hear the man mention hornets, or maybe beetles; they have an awful kind down here that spray poison straight into their bites. He can hear her suffering, little yips and whimpers, and then a low, horrible sound, once, like they're ripping her skin slowly off. He can hear a comandante standing over them both, demanding to know why she was out there alone.

When the comandante finally comes out of the tent, he runs a handkerchief over his soaked face and looks at Juan Carlos.

This girl, she's your associate?

Juan Carlos hesitates. My girlfriend.

Associate. That's what we call them here. The comandante is bald and has a heavy, fleshy forehead that makes it hard to look him in the eye. I need you to tell me what you know about her, he says. I need to know right now if you think she was running tonight. If you think she might even be the *type* who might run.

Juan Carlos swallows. No. No, she believes in this mission more than anyone I know.

The comandante bites the tip of his tongue with his back molars, nods and sucks. We're concerned this was a kidnapping attempt gone bad, he mutters. Retaliation for the short shipment.

Juan Carlos does not allow himself to think: but no one heard anyone out there with her.

But to be honest with you, it's probably better for her if she were running, the comandante says. I need you to know this. Sometimes compañeros don't take to the life down here. We

know how to deal with that. But if this wasn't a defection—
here he pauses, aiming two fingers at Juan Carlos—if the cartel
did this, you need to know that we won't strike back. She may
be your associate, but what we have with the cartel, that is
bigger than her.

Juan Carlos wants to believe it, so he says it like he does:
She wasn't running. No. Marina isn't the type of person who
would run.

· · ·

When the med tech finally leaves, Juan Carlos goes back into
the tent.

Marina is lying on her side on her cot. She is facing the wall,
and all the lights are out, and he is grateful.

Are you awake? Can you talk?

She answers so fast it startles him: What do you remember
about the night that Andres and El Matón died?

Her voice is not her voice; is her tongue stung, too? Juan
Carlos closes his mouth and tries to make his voice kind. We
shouldn't talk about this tonight, Marina. Why are you talking
about this?

Do you remember what I did?

You did what you had to, he pronounces. We do what we
have to. It doesn't matter, especially not now.

Not that. Not killing Andres. I mean after.

You need to rest.

She goes silent, stays still.

Marina? he hears himself say.

After Andres, I went upstairs to the Patient. You remember?

It is done now.

She is in the same filthy clothes as before, and he can hear

them shifting as she breathes harder, starts to cry. I beat him, she says.

You taught him a lesson. I've done the same—

I beat half his teeth out. I beat him unconscious.

Juan Carlos takes a step forward.

I almost killed him, too, she says. Did you know that? I almost killed two men in one night. Do you know why?

Someone passes in the yard with a lantern, and the light surges through the tent wall and over Marina's body. Juan Carlos winces, glimpsing how much the shape of her has changed, and he's ashamed of his reaction. He makes himself lie down on the cot next to hers.

It was revenge, he says too firmly, compensating. The Patient killed one of ours. It was for El Matón. Why else?

She turns onto her back and tilts her head toward his voice.

Juan Carlos doesn't let himself blink, looking at the woman he loves, at the face that isn't her face. The red knobs of skin, everywhere. The seams where her eyes should be. The grotesque swell of her lips. The heat radiating.

It was because he said he was sorry, she pronounces.

He makes himself look at her, mutilated. He makes himself look at her, the monster who shot his best friend in the gut and left him to die on a kitchen floor. La Araña, the girl he loves.

It was brave of you, Juan Carlos says, reaching for her hand. I love you for it. You did it for all of us.

·   ·   ·

If Marina could open her eyes, she would look at Juan Carlos the way she looked at the Patient that night. He had the garrote slack between his hands, two wooden handles and a piano wire like a thread of light in the bottom of the hole. Her

head is full of the same violence now as it was then: silent and pummeling and sick, her muscles surging with acid but her breath even and true.

She hit the Patient hard enough to make her knuckle skin split.

She was nineteen years and seven months old, and death was not a light she could stop from coming through the window.

As she hit him, she thought of bodies in government cars, Andres' long eyelashes skimming the kitchen floor in the forty-two minutes it took him to die. She thought of what a dying body was: all those colors. Not just red but yellow, diluted fluids, acids and froth. She beat the Patient to make sense of it. She beat the Patient because she knew, that night, that death was not an injustice. Her alias was La Araña but it was not her name. She did not kill Andres, because death was not something you accomplish. Death is a place full of bush and trees with no road out, and that is where she lives now.

She thinks of telling Juan Carlos what her stupid plan had been—to kidnap one of the Europeans whom she saw out there in the jungle, to ransom them to get upriver, that she would have killed again if she had to—but she is too sore and tired to open her mouth.

When Juan Carlos speaks again, his voice is dim, a murmur beneath acres of water.

Listen to me. You didn't kill the Patient.

Marina turns back onto her side.

You beat him pretty bad, I'll give you that, but he was ransomed three days later. He's still alive. You know that. You remember.

She tries to swallow.

You still feel guilty. It's natural. But you can't let it get in the way of our work here.

And here is when Juan Carlos' voice changes, brightens and hardens at once. He says all the things he has said before, by rote, because there is nothing else to say to stop the noise.

That what they are doing is about the future of the nation.

That every killing is a sacrifice so there will be no killing someday, soon.

That the cartel will kill them if they do not do their part, and Turbay's police will kill them if they run.

That they will stay here as long as they are needed, until they die, even, because that is what compañeros do.

He talks and talks until he thinks she is asleep. He talks until he falls asleep himself, half drunk from the rum he swallowed to calm down, deep enough that she knows he won't wake up. He does not wake when she sits up, when her skin screams and her mouth opens and she slaps her hand across her own burning mouth to stop the noise.

He does not wake when Marina stands and gropes the edges of the room for her gun.

When she leaves the room and goes outside.

When she staggers out into the yard and up the hill toward the bush and to the place where, in ten minutes, they will find her ruined body.

When the rifle falls from her hand and tumbles off into the dark undergrowth, so no one can tell she fired the shot into her brain herself, that it didn't come from someone hiding in the trees.

When she does these things, Juan Carlos, still, will sleep.

He is exhausted from all this talking.

He cannot explain it to her again.

RICHARD

Ovidio

Here is something you don't know:
How many things are out there in the jungle.

It's 4 a.m. You've been walking for an hour in the trees alone, something you thought that you would never do here, something you regret as you soon as you feel the screech of the fox bats rake over your eardrums. The path is too dim for you to see well, so you keep your eyes glued to the ground, strain to sense changes in texture through the soles of your boots. Mosquitoes cling to the sweat in the hollow of your neck and you can't stop swiping at them there, even though you know they're everywhere else on you, too. You know that the jungle is full of things that can swarm and leap and glide out from nowhere; that you are not safe here; that you should not have refused the bus from the river mouth to the hotel with the rest of the crew, shouting after them that you needed a walk to clear your head and you'd be back by dawn; that you should not have ignored the producer's scowl and demand that you get on right fucking now, don't be stupid, Richard; that you should be in your bed.

But after what you saw on set today, you're not sure you're safe there, either.

Here is something you don't know:

That at this exact instant, across the river, a guerilla soldier named Marina has pressed the mouth of a rifle into the space between her eye socket and ear and fired.

Here is something you don't know:

Six feet from where you stand right now, a red flower that smells like carrion begins to open, and the flies alert.

Here is something you don't know:

The hotel is only a hundred yards away as the crow flies, but the path will wind so much before you reach it that you will be sure until the moment you hear the muted growl of a generator that you are lost.

You don't know what the fuck you're doing.

You stop. You breathe. A clutch of squirrel monkeys you can't see leaps into the canopy and a thousand leaves scatter like an explosion. You close your eyes to shut it all out. You make yourself remember what happened on set today.

·   ·   ·

You arrived this afternoon ready to shoot your first big monologue, and Ugo handed you a double-barrel shotgun.

Revision, he said, spitting into the dirt.

You'd been taken to a new set fifty yards into the forest, the river barely a glint through the trees when you looked back. Irena had told you about the tree of hives, but you hadn't seen it for yourself. It was about ten feet taller than you'd pictured, the nests rougher and sharper looking, hanging heavier off the branches than could possibly be safe. The set dressers had strewn a few clay pots around, dug out a campfire pit and tried to make it look like a village. A clutch of Indian extras milled around, tugging uncomfortably at their loincloths.

You looked down at the gun. A set of initials you didn't recognize were carved into the grip.

Why do I need this? you mumbled. I thought the script said we were burning a village down.

But Ugo was already walking away.

Sweat sprang up on your forehead and the backs of your hands. Excuse me. What do you mean, there's been a revision?

Ugo turned back toward you. There was something in his face: maybe exhaustion, hardened over into something else. The sun found a gap between the branches and flared into your eyes, but thinking of it now, you're sure that wasn't it: that wasn't why he aimed that look at the shirt button at the center of your chest, why he wouldn't look you in the eye.

When he talked, it was too careful, like he was thinking about every micro movement of his tongue. You still say the monologue, yes. We still burn the village. But first—he tilted his head toward the beach—you shoot the dog.

You looked out toward the fire pit. The dog was tiny and black, snarfling happily for insects in the ash. A bored assistant stood over it with a long stick, in case it decided to run off.

Why?

Just do it.

But why?

Because Richard wants a shot of something dying, Ugo said, like it was evident. Because you are Richard. Cristo. Do I really need to give you reasons?

You heard your mouth saying it: No. Sir.

He didn't smile. Good. Shoot the dog, then say the lines. Then you burn the village.

The dog turned in your direction. You could see its shining round eyes, the white of its chin as it snouted at an anthill. For

some reason, you found yourself looking around for Irena, but she was nowhere.

You mumbled, But I don't think—

You can.

No, no, it's just—I don't know how to use the gun.

The Indians were beginning to look at you, curious. The makeup artists, Paolo and Agata, were smearing mud onto two women's knees, and they glanced up, too.

You have to.

It's a movie. Can't you just get the effects crew to—

Just pull the trigger. Ugo pantomimed it. Do it quick. Not too gentle. And don't mess it up. We only have one dog.

He'd already turned away from you before you got the nerve up to say, finally, I won't.

Ugo looked back toward you, then down at the shotgun. You were holding it in front of you with both hands like it was a lunch tray. He sucked his teeth and grabbed it from you with one fist, a gesture twice too fast for how tired he looked, the words snapped off too quickly.

Fine then. Teo.

The skin across your face stung with a sudden heat.

The veins in the side of Ugo's neck stood out like axial cables. He barked an Italian word you didn't understand, and Teo—the actor who held Fabi in the headlock your first day on set, who must be playing Richard's cameraman—ambled over and took the gun from him. Ugo looked back to you for a quick instant, dead-eyed and chewing at something in the pocket of his cheek.

Positions, he said.

Here is something that you can't believe happened only sixteen hours ago, the sun stuck overhead at high noon like an indecipherable stain on a ceiling:

You stared into the lens of a Super 8 camera and tried to remember what was supposed to happen next. You knew the scene started with a monologue. You had to make your voice work, and aim it straight to camera: in the jungle, every day is about survival of the fittest.

But then you heard the gunshot in your periphery. It punctured your memory like a balloon, and just like that, the words drained out. The camera panned in your direction, an alien beast turning to you with an open mouth. You looked, despite yourself, at Teo, the rifle still balanced on his shoulder and his eyes leveled to the sights. The dog leaned onto its side, its neck arching back so you could see both its eyes were open. Then it arched down the other way, stared at something deep beneath the mud.

The sky over you was white with the grit of dirt in it.

You heard your own voice enunciating the monologue, mangling it—The daily violence. Um. The strong overcoming the weak. Yes. Violence! For Veronica! Gayle!

The wound in the dog's side didn't bleed like you would have expected. The blood only pooled, a shallow thumbprint of dark liquid sunk into the curve of its belly.

And then Irena was suddenly next to you, prodding her prop sound recorder into your face, egging you on. Then revulsion and relief collided in you, so powerful it should have disabled you, but you heard yourself yell the final cue anyway—Joe!—your voice scattering like a bat across the air. Teo switched the gun for a torch and jogged up fast. He dragged the torch up the seam of the lowest nest, painting a narrow thread of flame all the way to the top.

Here is something, hours later, that you still can't believe: There were people in the nests.

You blinked. It couldn't be.

But you could see them through the gathering smoke: a dozen of them, yipping in a frantic language as the flames reached. They were naked with cropped black hair; the Indians, yes, the extras, you had seen these people before. You hadn't noticed the producers herding them up ladders and into the nests before the shot began, and at that moment, you could see them only in thatches: naked bodies and dark, swinging hair, swelling rib cages and white teeth.

No.

The ones in the lowest nests dove, landing with hard, wet sounds on the mud. The ones in the highest nests clung and stared.

No. No. Your mouth was shouting it.

The ladders had been taken away.

A muscle in your temple throbbed.

There were cameras everywhere, and they were all filming.

The branches shook and bobbed. A man in the sky was clambering out of his nest, trying to get higher, away.

The director shouted, Va', va', va'! He laughed. Yes!

No, you have a mark to hit, you need to move—

Then, somehow, the soft clatter of the camera reel was louder than everything else: the fire, the screams, the gun firing again and again and again into the trees.

Then you all saw the man on fire, sprinting toward the river.

Then, like an act of God, all the rain rushed in at once.

Here is something you didn't really register until now:

When Ugo ran after the burning man, he grabbed a camera. He kept rolling as he ran.

Between the smoke and the roar of the rain and everyone running, the realization didn't strike your brain for hours. The cameramen ducked under tarps with their equipment. The PAs doused whatever the rain didn't, leaned ladders back against

the trees, and waved the terrified extras down. Irena sponged rain and sweat off her forehead, laughing—that was amazing! You were dumbfounded, shaking, asking yourself: What did I just see? Was I the only one?

. . .

You said it out loud: Irena, I think someone's hurt.

The man on fire was named Paolo: he was one half of the makeup and effects crew, the man you saw carrying the pile of meat that was supposed to be your corpse out of the bush. A spitfire had caught the front of his shirt. Ugo had told him to fan the flames toward camera, and they'd fanned back toward him.

The rain put the man out, but there wasn't a medic, afterward, to treat the burns. Baldo fumbled in the first aid kit. Paolo's wife, Agata, sprinted from the bush where she'd been prepping an extra for the next scene, stood over him and tried everything she could. The rain stopped, and the river water was too dirty to cool him down. The bandages in the kit were too narrow, so she found some plastering strips she used for mold-making and laid them across his chest, his neck, his chin. The crew gathered on the beach and watched.

Here is something else that you didn't notice:

Ugo recorded the sound Paolo made, as the cloth met his flesh. He recorded the boat, pulling away with the burned man and his wife and the producer on it, and planned to dim the shot in postproduction, to say that it was Richard and Gayle and Joe.

Everyone thought that you'd all go back to town, but Ugo was too keyed up. He'd sweated through his shirt. His face was stern but ecstatic, his hat stuffed into his back pocket so you could see the gleam on his hairline. He jogged through the ashes of the nests, yelling for his cameramen to follow, to

film a specific heap of embers, to get a close shot of a burned straw doll. He directed them in mixed Italian and English to move quicker, yelled that they were losing the light, this was the only fucking scene they've shot so far that's been worth anything.

Then he switched to English and called you over. He told you to sift through the mud with your bare hands, the gun slung across your back by a strap for effect.

What am I looking for, you asked, too quiet, still shaken.

For anything, Ugo said. Crouch lower. Look meaner.

You raked through the wet ash. You did it, until your fingertips hurt, the soft tissues inside your nose stinging with heat and the sharp smell of carbon.

You stalked over the burned ruins and squinted, looking.

When Ugo told you to accost an Indian, you did that, too: you faked spying him in the distance, a short man languishing under a rubber tree with fake burns pasted across his feet and shins and knees. You stood over him like you were told and you leered like you were told, though you had no idea what you were supposed to be telling the man to do or why.

I want something from you, you said in the sternest voice you could manage.

I don't know what I want from you, you said, and pointed at the hollow of bone at the center of his chest like you were making a demand.

No one could hear you, of course. Your voice will be a distant gurgle on the final cut; the camera's filming from twenty yards off. You had no idea where you were supposed to be going when the Indian pointed you deeper into the trees and told you, in a language you didn't understand, to walk.

You did dozens of takes, again and again, until the light was changing too fast between shots and everyone but Ugo was

exhausted. You did it until it was too dark for the light meters, and then Ugo made the set dressers build a fire, shot another three hours of you and Irena and Teo stomping around in the dark, until one of the cameramen finally murmured, It's a waste of film stock.

At midnight, a PA doused the last embers with a bucket of river water. The set dressers tried their best to tear down, put aluminum flashlights in their mouths so they could use both hands to haul. You tried to help, but as you hoisted a light stand over a tree trunk, you heard it: someone in the crowd was laughing and laughing. You squinted, and it stunned you to realize that it was Ugo.

He was on the beach with Fabi, nattering in Italian. He slapped the producer across the chest with the back of his hand and wrested his flask away from him, swallowed hard. He held the drink up to a moon hung a mile too low in the sky. One eye was squinting, all teeth grinning. Then he pointed his viewfinder at something down the beach and jogged after it.

What the fuck is he laughing about? Why the *fuck* is he laughing?

You didn't realize you've said it out loud until Teo answered you. You didn't even realize Teo was *there* until you heard his voice and turned to see him kneeling in the grass, tying up the broken strap on a camera bag.

He's happy.

You'd never talked to Teo before, except in passing. You didn't know what the flatness of his voice signaled, and so you didn't know that he was annoyed with you, that you should probably stop talking.

You said: What is he so happy about? He almost killed that man. He almost killed *all* those people. He set a fucking forest fire. If that rain hadn't come—

Teo pulled hard on the stuck strap and grunted. Then it wouldn't have come.

You stared at him. There had to have been a plan, though. It was a stunt.

He can kill anyone he wants, Teo said. It's his movie.

He hoisted the bag across his back and left you blinking in the dark.

This is why you refused the bus from the river mouth to the hotel, why you've spent the last four hours wandering alone like an idiot, losing the trail every ten minutes:

Because you can't stop thinking of the man on fire.

You can't stop thinking of him when he hit the river, the sound of steam and howling. You think of how filthy the water must have been, rushing up against his wounds, and of the sharks Fabi mentioned—the ones that swim up from the Atlantic Ocean, that feed on piranhas and other sharp-toothed fish. You think of parasites that can swim through a pore and lodge in the lung, that can flit into the mouth and live under the tongue for years.

If you could talk to anyone about it, it would be Irena. You'd looked for her on the beach, but it'd been too dark to find her. On the boats, you'd looked again, and then you'd realized: she was sitting right next to Ugo.

You follow the darkening road for hours, and count the things you don't know.

Why won't they show you the rest of the script?

How many miles would you have to walk through the jungle until you reach the airport?

Why did they take your passport?

What happens at the end of the movie?

And because you don't have answers, because the jungle is full of chaotic sounds of a million animals and you can tell

none of them apart, because you are scared and you wish that you had anyone with you, here is the sudden memory that your brain spits out:

A year after you arrived in New York, eleven months before you boarded the plane to Colombia. It was winter; the lighthouse shuttered; she didn't understand why you'd taken her all the way out here.

Why do you think of it: in this, this moment of real panic? In this jungle, in this dark that reeks of soil and decay, why do you think of Kay?

You told her you were sorry, and you started to cry—or at least, the muscles in your face that participate in crying seized up, the way you'd trained them to do in acting school. You weren't trying to pretend, but the frozen wind pushed into your eye sockets and rifled your hair, and the drama of the moment must have gotten to you. You had another tour, yes, down to Delaware and back up the coast for three weeks, but that wasn't why you were doing this. You took Kay's hand, spoke in slow syllables. You took her here because you had something beautiful together, and beautiful things should end near the water.

That was actually the line you used on her.

Kay said nothing. Her face revealed nothing, her skin blue-white in the cold, her eyes blue-white like always. The sand was full of black shells and plastic bottles. You were both wearing goosedown vests in sun-bleached colors, wool sleeves, thick socks. Everything looked exactly how you'd pictured it. You closed your eyes for dramatic effect.

I love you, you said. I always will. But I *need* to act.

When you opened your eyes, she was halfway across the beach.

You had only closed them for an instant. An *instant*—how

had she moved so fast? But in your memory, it was not *even* an instant, just a slim black split between frames, a tiny gap that undoes your understanding of time, renders the moment discontinuous. Kay was there, and then Kay was gone. You barely shut your eyes, but in that lost time, the reel spun, and she was at the shoreline.

You sprinted after her. This you remember. You behave differently around water than you do around fire; you were brave. The sun was dull and your footsteps thudded on the frozen gray sand. The water was silver and full of knife edges, and she was walking as fast as she could alongside it, away from you.

This is how your memory has always repainted it, anyway: you didn't hesitate. She only got a few feet away before you caught up to her and reached out for her shoulder.

Then why was Kay so out of breath, her skin flushed with cold and wind and crying? Why were her eyes so wild when she turned to you, fifty times bluer than usual, the whites bright pink? You had never, never seen Kay angry before, and you'd certainly never seen her cry. It stunned you. Every time you'd broken her heart, she had just taken it in, had waited patiently until you came to her senses, had held you when you came back through the door.

But you'd never said it to her face before. You'd always just left a note.

Kay, you remember yourself saying, Kay, calm—

Why the fuck are you doing this again? Her voice was high with disbelief.

Your brain raced, your mouth moving. I don't—I'm sorry, okay? I'm not like you. I'm not so *sure* about everything. You're superhuman. It's just not that easy for me to—look, maybe someday I'll be ready.

You reached out to touch her face.

When she shoved you away, you remember, you were astonished at her strength. More than the impossible winter cold of the water, more than the punch of the sand as you lost your footing and landed on your ass and the heels of your hands, more than the way the air in your chest instantly clung to your organs and seized.

You were astonished by what Kay said, standing over you ankle deep in the water, in a quiet voice that should have been a yell: That she wasn't *sure*. That she wasn't *ready*. That she wasn't *superhuman*. Jesus.

I am *decent* to you. You remember it now: that's exactly what she said, spitting out your name like a seed. Decent. That is all I've ever been.

Kay didn't help you up out of the water. She turned and stormed back to the parking lot, toward the road that led to the station, and you walked back with her, ten paces behind and watching the white flag of her hair whip in the wind. You sat in the next seat over on the train, the two of you melting all over the orange plastic seats. Then you switched trains, and you took the seat next to hers, and after a while she was exhausted and let you hold her hand.

You didn't go on the tour. You never talked about it again. The radiator was busted so you took hot showers and ate soup for breakfast in the morning. You watched her pull a white towel over her hair and told her she was pretty. You kept a fragile thing suspended in the air between the two of you, and you tried not to break it. You didn't break it. You weren't the one. You didn't.

· · ·

In the jungle, you stop and breathe again, overwhelmed. You look at your hands and the fine details of them are gone: cuti-

cles, tiny hairs, wrinkled skin over knuckles. This is all you can see: the texture of loose gravel scattered over mud. The narrow clearing of the road stretching before you and behind you. Nothing is on either end. No one is coming for you. The road is straight in both directions.

.   .   .

In the final cut of the film, Richard will look at his hands in just the same way, in dark outside of the village. They'll light you through a blue CTB gel to simulate the moon, wave a palm frond in front of the bulb to make it spookier. They'll increase the f-stop for a brighter close shot on your hands: dirty fingernails clutched around two scorched white stones.

Like everything else, it's filmed on handheld, this time by Gayle. She'll approach from a distance, before Richard notices her. When he does, he'll stand up quick off the rock he's been sitting on and shout for her to put the camera away.

I was just getting some establishing shots, she'll say. I tried to get Joe to do it, but he wanted to sleep. The moon over the river is insane.

Well, turn it off.

She'll drop the camera to her side, but the reel won't stop. There's a shot of the ground, black and leaf-littered.

The audio is clear, though. The insects hum. Richard whispers.

I have to tell you something.

What happened? Gayle whispers back.

When we made contact tonight, after we smoked out the villagers at the tree of nests—

You shouldn't have done that. Her voice is thin and alarmed. Richard, I *told* you you shouldn't have done that—

One of them surrendered.

Gayle pauses. What do you mean?

I mean they took me to their graves.

Another pause. A snake as wide as a wristwatch winds its way through the bottom inch of the frame.

I don't understand, Gayle pronounces slowly.

Esteban and Amanda Perez. The researchers.

What about them?

They weren't—shit. Richard laughs, exasperated. They died of some fucking disease. The villagers were saying something that sounded like *malaria* over and over: Mal-a-*ri*-a, Mal-a-*ri*-a, they were, like, *chanting* it—

Slow down, slow down.

They didn't know what to do. They tried to shaman them back to health but it didn't work. Fucking animals didn't even try to row them to a hospital.

Shamanism isn't—

They're savages, Gayle. They killed those people. Their negligence.

Gayle sighs, crosses her arms over her chest. The camera swings wide and scans a new patch of ground behind her, settles and stares down the rotted-out core of a tree stump.

How do you know for sure? she asks.

Know what?

That they're dead.

Of course they're dead.

Richard, how do you know they were even buried where the Indians said?

Richard pauses. Gayle breathes hard, and then she realizes.

Oh my God, Richard.

I *had* to.

You didn't.

I needed to know for sure.

You dug them up?

I'm a journalist, Gayle. I had to check my facts.

Jesus!

You should understand that.

What are those stones you're holding?

Richard says nothing.

What did you do, Richard?

What the fuck are those stones?

Why would you even need a grave marker out here? Richard is speaking quietly, a laugh in his voice. It doesn't make any sense.

Those are their grave markers?

Fucking everything that dies in this jungle gets eaten up within an hour.

You can't just *take* a grave marker.

Richard laughs openly now. Even if the bodies don't get eaten—one rainstorm, the river could just wash them away. Why would you even bother with a grave?

Gayle pauses, then speaks slowly. We need to be able to find the bodies again. To give them back to the families.

Richard laughs.

This isn't funny, Richard. How are the families going to reclaim the bodies if we don't—

They're not.

Gayle is speechless. The camera shakes.

We're not going to tell anyone about this.

Richard—

This isn't the right narrative.

What do you mean?

I mean I didn't come down here to report on a couple of fucking malaria cases.

But that's what happened.

Richard pauses. His voice is strange, echoing hers: *Happened.* Yes, I guess you're right. That's what *happened.*

In the silence that follows, you can hear a sound like stones clinking together, like Richard is turning them in his hands.

Then Gayle speaks: Richard, why are there only two grave markers?

Richard says nothing.

Richard, who was buried there?

Esteban and Amanda are gone, Gayle. That's all you need to know.

What about Veronica?

Veronica. Veronica.

Richard says it like an incantation, a spell to summon something.

Richard, is she alive?

Don't worry about it, Gayle.

Then they are both walking; the camera roams the ground.

Richard, what are you planning to do?

This is when the reel runs out.

PROCURATORE CAPO: Signor Velluto, I have to ask: What was your real intention, when you made this film?

VELLUTO: I don't understand that question.

AVVOCATO: Objection. My client is not required to testify against his best interests.

PROCURATORE CAPO: I'm not asking your client to implicate himself, Signor Avvocato. I'm inquiring simply from an artistic perspective. What was your vision? And more specifically, how did the . . . conditions of filming contribute to that vision? Why were they necessary?

VELLUTO: You're asking why I didn't shoot it on a soundstage in Italy. Plastic trees and stock footage of monkeys, stuff like that? You're asking why I'm not like other directors?

PROCURATORE CAPO: But you *yourself* shot that way. Fourteen films before this one, all at Safa Palatino here in Rome. I can present the contracts.

VELLUTO: Don't.

AVVOCATO: Objection, relevance.

PROCURATORE CAPO: I'm trying to establish why Signor Velluto changed his vision so drastically for this production. It goes to his state of mind at the time of the alleged crimes.

[Whereupon the giudici popolari nod.]

PROCURATORE CAPO: So, signore, why did you leave the soundstages? Why knowingly put your actors and crew in danger?

AVVOCATO: Objection!

PROCURATORE CAPO: Withdrawn.

VELLUTO: You would rather I build animal puppets and pay some marionettist to flounce them around? Put Italian

actors in brown face and Tarzan costumes, tell them to pretend?

PROCURATORE CAPO: You would have avoided allegations of animal abuse that way. Abuse of *humans*. Not to mention the charges you face today.

VELLUTO: It was the *state* that leveled these charges, friend, not—

GIUDICE A LATERE: Signor Velluto, sit down.

PROCURATORE CAPO: And to your point about brown face—the Indians you used were acting, too, weren't they? We've heard expert testimony from an anthropologist that they were likely from the Ticuna and Yagua tribes, that Ovido is many thousands of kilometers from documented Yanomamö territory where you claimed the film was set—

VELLUTO: Have you seen the goddamned horror movies that are being made today in Italy, Procuratore?

PROCURATORE CAPO: Not many, I'll admit. But I've read Napoleon Chagnon's account of the Yanomamö tribal life, and your film is not exactly a documentary in that regard.

VELLUTO: It's my understanding that Signor Chagnon's treatise isn't considered exactly unimpeachable either.

PROCURATORE CAPO: I haven't heard of this controversy.

VELLUTO: Well, then I'll tell you. American anthropologist goes down to Venezuela in his battle khakis and a bucket hat. American anthropologist takes a goddamned crate of weapons into the bush and passes them out to whatever Indian he can find. Then American anthropologist writes a goddamned book about how the awful, warlike Yanomamö savages won't stop killing each other. Now you're all caught up.

PROCURATORE CAPO: But there have also been claims that

Christian missionaries were the ones who supplied the Indians with hunting weapons that were so tragically misused.

VELLUTO: Well, if the *Christians* did it!

PROCURATORE CAPO: And more to the point, what about you, Signor Velluto? You manipulated the Ticuna and Yagua into performing unspeakable—

VELLUTO: Did the film scare you?

PROCURATORE CAPO:—acts, and then you call *them* Yanomamö, call your film a documentary for marketing purposes, sullying the name of that largely peaceful tribe—

AVVOCATO: Objection—

PROCURATORE CAPO: If Chagnon's work is problematic, you must admit, signore, that you're at least a part of that problem.

VELLUTO: Did it scare you?

[Whereupon the procuratore pauses for a long while.]

PROCURATORE CAPO: Yes, very much. When I thought of what sort of man must have made it.

AVVOCATO: Objection!

VELLUTO: Never mind why. You were frightened.

PROCURATORE CAPO: I can never mind why. This is a court of law. I've already stated—

VELLUTO: Then I'll restate it for you. You were scared. That is why I made the film. Why I did what I did so that the film could be made.

PROCURATORE CAPO: Is that a confession, Signor Velluto?

AVVOCATO: Signor Giudice, this is a flagrant—

VELLUTO: Let me off the stand. I've answered your question.

PROCURATORE CAPO: I have more questions.

VELLUTO: Let me off—

GIUDICE A LATERE: Signor Avvocato, give the witness some room.

PROCURATORE CAPO: Signore, it's becoming increasingly clear that we need to pursue a line of questioning about Signor Velluto's mental state at the time of filming.

VELLUTO: I can't breathe.

PROCURATORE CAPO: This is a tactic.

VELLUTO: I can't breathe when this bastard is in my face, breathing my *air*—

GIUDICE A LATERE: Do we need a medic? He's turning purple here—

VELLUTO: You were scared by my film. Watch my film. You people. Let my work speak for itself.

UGO

Ovidio

He could do it on his hands and knees in the mud.

Ugo rips out a hunk of elephant grass so he has a better sight line. He aims his viewfinder and imagines in the scene postediting: backlit, close shot, the camera laid down sideways with half the lens steamed opaque by the heat of the earth.

Or he could move the camera along the ground slowly, snake's-eye view. Blades of grass edged in blood, then more, then everything drenched flat to the earth red and red and red until finally, the body: staring milky-eyed into the lens.

Ugo stands, crosses his arms, chews the inside of his cheek.

Behind him, it is dusk, and a dozen people are packing up the canoes or vainly trying to tear down the remains of the burned nests. They glance over their shoulders, anxious. They are waiting for him to tell them they can go. They don't know what he's doing, with his viewfinder on his knees.

But Ugo can't leave until he decides how he wants the American to die.

. . .

But to make a decision like that, Ugo would need to watch every horror film since 1896 in sequence and map the shot order to the instant. Then he needs an impulsive concussion, a jerk to his system that slaps his brain flat against the wall of his skull and makes the history of cinema drain out. He needs a crane and a thousand-dollar rig and then he needs his camera to liquefy in his hands, to stand in the humid void of the set with nothing between him and the actor. The paradox has been keeping him awake for days: he needs to systematically eliminate all alternatives, to know no one has ever died like this on camera before, and then he needs to feel the idea come howling out from within him with no referent.

Sweat has gathered in the creases behind Ugo's knees, and he feels it suck as he stands. Today was the best day they'd shot so far, but it's not enough. The whole film is worth nothing if this one death is all wrong. He exhales, runs the back of his wrist over his brow ridge and tells production they can all go back to the hotel.

He stays on the set until darkness comes, listening to the insects purr and yammer. A native boy hangs around to row the boat back for him later, crouching in the weeds near the bow to make sure it doesn't float away. When Ugo can't stand still anymore, he climbs the low branch of a tree and tries to imagine the American's spine draped over it, or no: an aerial shot of the American's torso hacked into three ragged steaks on the muddy jungle floor.

In the weeds, the boy pulls his T-shirt over his knees and rocks, making small sounds to himself.

Ugo aims his viewfinder away from the boy, brushes a dead fly off the lens. What if the American dies bloodlessly—a hot poison boiling, pushing against the inner shell of his body until the veins pop and drown him from within? Or what if he is drained, every cell of his blood in an empty canoe, and they film just that: a boat drifting south?

. . .

Even after he lets the boy row him home, Ugo still can't sleep. He's going to order the blood from props in the morning and shoot it by sunset, and he plots the thing all night: a follow shot from the shore, smooth as a dolly, an Indian carrying the camera at waist level and walking slowly. By dawn, he's decided: at the last minute, the Indian will turn the camera around and aim the lens up at his own face and leer.

But when Ugo gets to the breakfast tent, the American is not there.

He sets his tray down next to Fabi and Baldo, aims his gaze at the empty seat the American usually takes. He can see straight across the lot to the hotel, a spasm of sunlight reflecting unevenly off a plastic window. He can smell whatever's on Fabi's plate, something ricey and sweetened.

He tries to sound detached: Where's our Richard this morning?

I think he's cracking, Fabi says around a mouthful. Prima donna shit. There's always one, eh?

Baldo glares. We should all be cracking, after what happened to Paolo yesterday. Ugo, we need to talk.

Ugo ignores him. What do you mean he's cracking?

Because we asked him to film for once? Fabi laughs. Because he's an amateur who can't improv? Who knows.

Baldo leans forward, his fork hovering over his meat. We should all be as disturbed as the American. We need to talk seriously about halting production until we can assess the safety of the next—

Fabi interrupts him, big-voiced and big-gestured. He's tired! The guy's tired! He just can't hang, that's all. Give him an extra hour of sleep, he'll be fine.

Ugo brushes a strand of hair off the rim of his plate and feels a muscle along the roof of his mouth tighten.

Well, Paolo is not fine, Baldo says. The medic in town says it's mostly second-degree burns, but he's not going to be back. Agata either. They're trying to get him healed enough to transport to Bogotá tomorrow, where they have a real burn unit.

Who cares? Fabi says. The set dressers can cover the effects! We're pros!

We care because a lawsuit could shut this whole production down in a minute.

Fabi snorts. They signed a nonindemnification clause. We all did.

Indemnification without coverage is worthless. The insurance won't—

Ugo stares into the wet, pink core of a guava, thinking.

Fuck the insurance! Fabi cheers, swinging a speared sausage around. We're making art here!

We aren't making anything until we take a step back and think about this, Baldo says. And, Ugo, I should remind you the insurance wouldn't cover us for starting a wildfire in a fucking national park. You told me you would simulate it.

Fabi waves a hand dismissively over his plate. Come on, it was a controlled burn. The nests were the only thing dry enough to catch fire.

Jesus, what pyrotechnic specialist told you that?

Ugo sets down his fork, doesn't look at either of the men. We leave early today, he says. We leave now.

Fabi stops chewing. What, *now* now?

Baldo huffs over his plate and waits for Ugo to change his mind.

Now, Ugo says, swinging his legs over the bench. Get them ready.

Baldo rubs his eyes. I guess I'll go wake up our American.

Don't.

What do you mean, don't?

Ugo walks, shoves his plate into one of the maid's hands without looking at her. I mean that if he doesn't show up, he doesn't show up.

How?

We shoot with who we have, Ugo says, sparking a cigarette. If we don't have who we need, we block.

What do you mean, we—

I mean I'm going to the bus.

It's that feeling: everyone scrambling behind him, the hotel doors all flung open, the shouts of *where is the*—and *hurry, get*—. It's the vibration down the bones of Ugo's forearm as he pounds the door to the bus open with the side of his fist, and how it feels to walk down the long empty aisle between the seats. He needs this: to find his place at the very back and settle in to watch them all come running. The floor is coated with sawdust and smells like livestock, which is probably what the bus is used for in the off-season when they don't need river shuttles. The crew runs like livestock, and that's what Ugo's been looking for: the feeling of being in front of a stampede, the hoofbeats of the herd coming up through the ground.

He needs to decide how to kill the American.

And he will, when they get here. It will be like raising a shepherd's crook and pointing in one direction, the answer coming to him when it has to, when they are close enough to trample him, when he sees the shine of their eyes.

· · ·

Ugo thinks: strangler vine, piranha swarm, a single falling stone.

He tries them all out.

An Indian holds another Indian by the nape of her neck and shoves her facedown into the river, but an underwater camera would violate the whole premise and from land it doesn't look like anything. An Indian fakes a tumble backward onto the blunt end of a spear and his body opens like a book. An Indian strikes another Indian with an ax at each wrist, each knee, each elbow.

He hates all of them. He calls for a new set up, new props.

They've been doing test shots for the American's death for the better part of six hours when the light starts to wane. He's thinking of calling it a day, but Irena announces that she wants to help, so Ugo lets her climb the tall tree by the river and model a stunt. She mimes trying to force her ankle out of the place where it's wedged in the cleavage between two branches, but then she twists too far. She falls. She does the stunt just like they've choreographed: the acrobatic tumble that breaks the ankle and leaves her hanging and screaming upside down from the branch, the painful twist in her neck as she looks over her shoulder and sees the Indians circling the roots of the tree.

The whole crew gasps. Irena is three meters off the ground and thrashing, her hair waving like a flag. The prosthetic leg in the tree gushes, and the rig that's holding Irena's real leg in place is invisible no matter what angle they shoot from. Ugo doesn't know exactly how the effects crew managed it, but he knows about the squib they strapped just inside the neck of Irena's shirt, just beneath the hollow of her throat. He is the only one who doesn't shout Oh! when the Indian shimmies up the tree and reaches out with the machete and bleeds her like a sheep.

The crew applauds. The cameras stop. Irena does a little

upside-down bow and then someone climbs the tree and helps her back onto the branch and back down to the ground.

That's our fucking poster image right there! Baldo shouts, slapping his hands together once. Start putting together the press kit! That right there is our moneymaker!

What did he think? Irena says, pushing her bloody hair back from her face. Will it work for Richard's death scene?

What do you think, boss! Fabi yells, but Ugo isn't there.

The set dresser is the one who sees him, from the tree branch, when he looks up from dismantling the climbing rig: Ugo in the distance, stumbling over mud ruts with the oar in his hands. Ugo in the boat alone, pushing off into the darkening water.

. . .

He will make the bus come back for them. They have enough canoes without the one he took.

He will shoot it tomorrow. He will kill the American tomorrow. He will think of a new way.

He just couldn't stand to watch it again: all the death cues played out in the same order, the hitch in the breath, the eyelid shiver, the corn syrup blood dripping off the ends of her hair. Ugo has seen actors die this way so many times, it's become abstracted, like someone shouting the same word into your ear again and again for hours. It makes him feel furious and insane and restless. It makes him walk.

But when did night come, and has he ever been this far down the road? The village is small but Ugo has barely seen any of it yet. When he can't sleep, he wanders, but he stays close to the hotel. He walks circuits around the parking lot, or once, he sat all night on the floor of the shower stall and

listened to a single drop of water thunk again and again against the clay floor. Sometimes he goes to the abandoned breakfast tent and stands on the picnic table like it's the deck of a ship, closes his eyes, and waits for an epiphany to reach him. He hears the same sound now, walking through the bush. Biology tells him that nearly every insect in the air right now will die by morning, and Ugo knows that for the rest of his life this will be the sound of death for him: the backdrop of a hundred thousand minuscule wingbeats under the bark of tropical bats, and somewhere in the center of that sound, the crackle of a hundred thousand new eggs hatching.

When he thinks about it, has he slept more than an hour a night in the last six days?

When he comes up on the house, it takes Ugo a moment to realize he's arrived. The trail stops. His flashlight beam roves, encircling a glass window, a thatch of roof shingles, the beveled lip of a porch stair. He steps back. He can't put these things together. He can't believe these things are in the jungle, and he swings the flashlight wide to check.

The American proprietor hadn't told them he had managed to build two stories and an attic all the way out here, or that the house was propped on stilts to keep it out of the floodplain, or that it was painted this shade of power-washed pale purple. He had told the whole crew only to follow the road past the main square about three kilometers, to stay left at all the forks and look for a clearing. He'd told them he had a movie to show them, that it was tradition for every guest who came through town to see it, to come anytime, day or night.

Hank doesn't turn on the light when he opens the door. He yells for Ugo to stop shining that fucking thing everywhere, and what is he doing here in the middle of his kids' goddamned bedtime, and he might as well come on inside.

• • •

Ugo and Hank sit together in silence in the dark in front of a screen, watching a woman lean toward the peephole in a hotel room door. The ax blade comes through the wood with an atonal jolt of synthesizer, nicking her forehead, her body tumbling back onto the Persian rug. She presses both hands to her face. A gush of orange blood surges between her fingers, and her tongue is the same orange when she screams; the color calibration is all wrong.

The murderer pounds the door open, and this is when the projector hitches. The woman flips onto her belly and crawls, but the picture flickers: Ugo keeps missing the fine details, the pattern of the rug, the color of her fingernails.

Ugo's mouth twitches. The American proprietor stands up and slaps the machine.

This goddamned thing. It would cost me about a million dollars to ship it back and get it serviced, but one of these days—

Wind it back, Ugo says.

I can make it work if you just give me a—

Ugo leans forward and finds the switch on the side of the machine himself.

The woman flips onto her back, stands. The blood siphons back into her skin.

Ugo can feel Hank looking at him, but he keeps his eyes on the screen. The woman walks slowly backward, away from the door, to the white hotel bed and the book laid open across it. She lies down and reads. Then the scene cuts: ballerinas sprint backward in ragged toe shoes toward a retreating shadow.

Ugo thumbs the switch back to play again.

The American huffs, sits back down on the couch and kicks

up his feet on the coffee table, swipes a beer from the space between his boots. So you had a rough day on set? Hank says. Need to unwind? To what do I owe the pleasure of this visit?

Ugo doesn't answer.

I mean, I'd love to hear more about this movie, Hank says. God, it takes me months to get new reels shipped down here. Is yours—

Ugo hushes him.

Ugo decreases the frame speed as low as it goes, and suddenly he can see everything. The pores on the bridge of the woman's nose as she leans toward the peephole. The minute curvature of the peephole itself, the glass as blue as her eye. He studies the velocity of the splinters that race past the frame as the ax comes through the wood, and this is when Ugo presses pause. Focuses. *There.*

Come on! Hank yells.

Ugo tents his hands in front of his face. In the center of the woman's eye, there is an odd dark shape.

He winds it back again.

Hank laughs a little, coughs. You know, Hugh, when I invite guests up here, it's usually to *watch* a movie.

Splinters, eye shine, the same synthesizer lick. He can't make out the shape, even on the second pass.

I mean, really, what I wanted was to show you the movie from my snake-wrestling days, but when you told me you were making a *horror* film, I thought, hey, let's show off the collection.

Fast-forward: the woman scurries. The door opens and the murderer's knees appear. They bend to lunge.

But if you're just going to skip around all night—

Freeze frame on the cross-fade: the edge of an ax blade blurring into a wide shot of a stone fountain, the water sparkling like fairy lights.

Ugo unthreads the film fast, yanks the reel off the projector and puts it back into the canister. The room is flooded with white light. He rifles through the box on the table, holds a few films up to read the labels: *Who Can Kill a Child, The House with Laughing Windows*. He opens the case.

Well—Hank laughs—I'm learning a lot about you tonight, Hugh. You're certainly not an Argento fan.

Ugo threads the film through the sprocket, says, We saw the only part worth seeing.

What's wrong with the rest?

The rest is all predictable.

Hank's voice is surly and full of laughter, only halfway through with swallowing his beer. I tell you what, buddy, I hate to say it, but your movies must be goddamned terrible. You don't get horror at all.

He turns to look behind him, finds Hank's face in the dark. He is glassy-eyed and slouching, paunchy and overtanned. Ugo's never really looked hard at the man, certainly never had a conversation with him, but he's heard him plenty, speech-ifying in the lunch tent, in the bus he insists on driving to the trailhead most days so he can go on bragging about how the bus itself was sent down on the ferry in pieces. How the president of Colombia himself had ordered a telephone line installed there, Julio César Turbay Alaya himself, look it up, a thousand kilometers of wire strung on foot just so the capital can bend the ear of Hank Vance. How they were witnessing the birth of civilization, here and now.

Hank runs a toothpick through the space between his two front teeth and smiles.

Tell me what I don't get, Ugo says.

What?

About horror movies. What do you know that I don't?

Hank collapses back onto the couch, sighing. I'm drunk, guy. Come on. Don't make me explain it. He studies the darkness inside his bottleneck, reconsidering. Tell you what—play this next one from the beginning, and we'll talk.

Ugo thumbs the switch.

A car roves between green hillsides. The camera takes in the height of the mountain, the flowers brimming over the edges of the road, the gray castle towering over the peak. They're *supposed* to be all the same, Hank says, these movies. That's the point. You're supposed to be able to predict them. Watch this.

On-screen, the man drums his fingers on the wheel, the camera registering the fine wrinkles in his knuckles. The music is sunny, full of synthesizers. The sun discolors everything, three shades too brilliant and full of lens flares.

It's a classic setup, Hank says. A guy drives up to a cabin in the woods, right? Ghost stories and marshmallows, everything's great, until—boo!

On the screen, nothing happens. The car slows onto a dirt road and the man opens the door, inhales the mountain air.

Well, not now, I guess, Hank says, But that's the fun of it, you know? You're waiting for the jump scare. You know it's coming, and it comes. You want to get what you paid for, and you get it.

Ugo says nothing. The man walks to the house.

It's about catharsis. Hank pauses. Didn't you say you'd directed a dozen of these things? You've gotta know this.

What is catharsis? Ugo says. I don't know this word.

Hank takes another drink and ignores the question. This guy, he says, pointing to the screen, he's going to die. All these damn movies are exactly the same, so we know it, no doubt: by the end of this thing, we will see him bleed. Then let me ask you something: Why do we watch? Huh?

Ugo grits his teeth in annoyance.

Why do we watch a movie if we know exactly what's going to happen?

I asked you.

Hank smiles. Because we don't know *how* it's going to happen. It makes us feel powerful, to be able to find out.

The man on the screen walks into the castle. The camera slow-pans to a stained glass window, a human shape inside.

Hank grins, his teeth silvery in the dark. See?

Ugo looks him in the eye. He jams the switch and the reel fast-forwards, double-speed.

Pause: A nun strings a woman up by her wrists, laughs as she cranks at the mechanism. Toes rise and hover over a dirty floor.

Hank says, See! What did I tell you!

Ugo mutters to himself. No, not this scene.

Smash cut to a close shot of an old book. Pages flip in a startling wind. Bible or grimoire. Ugo prods the switch, getting angry.

This scene is great, Hank says, Hold on—

A long fast-forward, and then the man from the beginning of the movie is dying: a serrated knife, a priest in bloody vestments.

Hank erupts. That's not fucking fair, he yells. Is this the end of the reel? Man! That's not fucking *fair*!

Ugo studies the angle of the camera: high right, fish-eye, a dolly shot. You can see the back of the priest's skull partially eclipsing the victim's face, a sliver of the victim's forehead and his eyebrows raised in terror. An arch of a stained glass window yawns over them, turns both men shades of orange and blue. You can see their bodies struggling against one another, the blood racing across the floor, but that's not where your eye

goes: the camera is more interested in the sunset, the violence that the window does to the light.

This isn't funny anymore, guy, Hank mumbles. All this film studies bullshit isn't cute.

Don't watch, then, Ugo says.

What are you doing, are you just looking for shit to plagiarize? Scanning through for the greatest hits?

Ugo controls his voice. My movie will be nothing like this.

Don't bullshit me, Hugh. *Every* horror movie is like this.

Not mine.

See, but it *is*. Hank is up now—pacing, Ugo thinks, but then Hank crosses to a closet on the other side of the room. You know, I've been watching your production. Hank laughs. You know I've got eyes in the field.

Ugo thinks of the boy who rowed his canoe yesterday, seventy pounds in an oversize *Columbo* T-shirt the American must have given him, his tiny shoulder blades straining to move the oar.

Hank rifles around on a high shelf, shouts his words into the dark of the closet. I mean, I appreciate the thought, doing a horror movie cinéma verité style, but you don't really think that'll *work*, do you?

The movie is still running. The priest stabs and stabs and grimaces.

Killing is killing, Hank says. Even if you shoot it handheld, smear a little pig's blood on things to make the props look more real.

I'm not just going to smear pig's blood, Ugo murmurs.

I know, I know, but even if you have the best effects crew in the world? Whatever brilliant strategy you come up with? You get this movie in front of an audience, they're not going to be any more scared by it than they are—ah, heeeere we go.

Hank hoists something down. He crosses the room.

All I'm saying is, do you think whatever you shoot out here is going to be any different than these?

He plunks a heavy box down on the coffee table. Ugo tries to keep his eyes on the screen, but then Hank thumbs the projector switch to pause.

He glances.

A dozen more film canisters, labeled in masking tape:

Savage Rites, Dir. Ugo Velluto.

The Swarming Hour, Dir. Ugo Velluto.

Cannibal Purge, Dir. Ugo Velluto.

Half of them never saw theatrical release. Half of them *he* doesn't even have proofs for anymore.

Hank grins. The projector whirs. I've enjoyed your work, sir, he says.

This is when they hear the knock at the door. Or at least Ugo hears it, flinches at it, tries to look away. But Hank keeps staring into the side of Ugo's face, straight through his skull, smiling. The knock comes again, soft and slow and six times, like a code, but this time, Ugo is sure, it's not coming from the door knocker outside. It's coming from the hallway, just beyond the room they're in.

Ugo turns the projector back on, winds it back a scene, tries to focus on the screen. Ugo tries to think about his film, about the American actor covered in boils or poison darts or bound up in ropes tight enough to make the skin bleed.

He tries not to listen to what Hank is saying in the hallway, in Spanish that is too easy for him to parse.

You can't be here.

I know.

Fuck, you smell drunk.

I needed to talk to you.

How did you get here?

I took a boat. I hiked.

Jesus. All that way?

The man he is talking to is filthy; Ugo can tell without looking. It is not just in his smell but in his voice and the sounds of his soaked shoes on the floor, jackboot-heavy, squealing when he pivots. A chilled sort of fury extends like a membrane between Hank and this man, and Ugo can sense that without looking, too. He feels the membrane vibrate, like it's been flicked. He pauses the reel and studies the face in the corner of the frame: it is blank, genderless, and totally impassive, but there are small muscles at work beneath the skin, an expression starting to form.

He starts the film back up. But still, Ugo can hear the men behind the doorframe, whispering in quick Spanish.

I had to talk to you.

The fuck you did, not this late at night.

Listen.

You know better than this, man.

Listen—they killed Marina.

Ugo fast-forwards the film, jams the play switch again.

The man on the screen tries to run, leather shoes squealing against a polished floor.

A deep sniff; a jostling, as Hank pushes the man farther down the hallway. Don't use names. You know the rules.

She's dead.

Well, what did she do?

I don't know. They never even met her. *I* must have done something that night when I was at—

But Hank hushes him.

Ugo pauses, lets the reel slip forward for a microsecond, freezes it. The face does not change. It does not even blink.

Hank sighs. When?

Last night.

Listen: How do you know it was them?

Because they're fucking animals.

This town is full of animals. Think. How do you know?

She left the tent in the middle of the night to go to the chuntos. Our bathrooms. She was . . . very sick. She couldn't see. It was a bullet. It came—

Lots of people here have guns. Think harder.

It must have been them.

Or—

You were the one who connected us with them. The man sobs. You know it!

The skin along the side of Ugo's face tingles. He locks his jaw. The man speaks again, more whimper than word, but Hank interrupts him.

Juan Carlos, breathe in. There. Good. Explain it to me: How do you know they did it?

I can't—

Give me the evidence. Spell it all out. Did you see one of them, with your own eyes?

The man on-screen raises his hand to shield his eyes. The priest slashes at it and the blood fans.

The man in the hall sobs once. It was them. It was them. I know it.

Hank's words are careful and somehow strangely pleased, every consonant landing like a pebble dropped carefully in a lake. You didn't see. You couldn't have. He laughs. We both know they're not that stupid.

Ugo doesn't know why he turns from the screen, now, toward the darkened hallway past the doorframe.

You're responsible for this. The man's voice is desperate and

exhausted. There is the sound of his shoes again, turning away, but he does not take a step.

Hey, buddy, come on, don't do that. I was up here in my house. I was just watching a goddamned movie.

I love her.

Call it a war casualty. You're a foot soldier. Casualties aren't your concern.

This isn't supposed to be a war, the boy says. That's the point. The war is later. We're preparing for the war.

Friendly fire. It happens sometimes.

They're supposed to be our allies. You said they were our allies.

Well, then it's more complicated, isn't it? What can you do?

She wasn't a war casualty.

Then what was she?

She was murdered. Goddamn you. She was murdered.

Asesinada; assassinata.

Ugo doesn't need to translate. The membrane between himself and these men is that thin. In the pause that comes, Ugo turns back to the screen. He switches the projector on again. Hank starts laughing—slow at first. Then he loudens. He riots and wheezes. He laughs in a way that is so huge it must be exaggerated, so Ugo can hear the spit in it, the bucking muscles that line his throat. Ugo hears Hank's shoes stomp back quick toward the living room, leaving the man in the hallway alone.

The fadeout starts on the screen, and the priest is still over the man, stabbing. The face in the window is dim and unchanged.

You're a psychopath. The man's voice is low from the hall.

Hank coughs once to steady himself, sighs. Kid, he says, however you may have felt about your little dead girlfriend, don't let it make you stupid. He flops down on the couch,

shoves a fistful of popcorn into his face and yells over his shoulder. There's no such *thing* as murder in the jungle.

Hank turns to Ugo. Switches back to English. Now, Hugh, where were we?

He leans forward and swipes at the lens with his thumb; the face on the screen, a piece of remarkable dust, is gone.

· · ·

When he gets back to the hotel tonight, Baldo will be waiting for Ugo in the parking lot, smoking a cigarette at the picnic tables. He will not whisper when he talks, when he says that he is furious. He won't lower his voice when Ugo tells him to, when he says that no, it can't wait, they need to finish the conversation that they started this morning.

No, it's not just about the fire.

It's about what they're all doing here. It's about making sure they're safe here. Especially in the town at night.

I just went for a walk, Ugo will say.

But Baldo thinks too many people are going for walks. Baldo's even followed some of the actors, once or twice, after midnight when they run out of beers to drink in the parking lot or their rooms. He'd seen the actress go into the American's house. He'd seen her go out into the jungle and not come back for hours. Of course the actors could do what they wanted— that actress, she seems like a wild one, they probably couldn't stop her if they tried—but suppose something happened to one of them? To Ugo, even?

Suppose that what paid for everything in this town wasn't just canoe rides and nature walks?

Suppose they had more to worry about than just snakebites, out there in the bush?

And this is when Baldo will finally lower his voice, will lean conspiratorially close to Ugo, and stare urgently, trying to catch his eye. I know it doesn't feel like it, but we were lucky with what happened to Paolo, he will say. He lived. We're out an effects crew and I won't let you pull anything like that stunt ever fucking again, but ultimately, on-set accidents are what we have insurance for. What I worry about is off set. What I worry about is the town.

Ugo doesn't respond. He studies the line where the light from the hotel rooms meets the darkness of the bush, an abrupt blackening two-thirds of the way across the lot.

If something happens to one of us, and the insurance doesn't pay out, Baldo says, I need you to know, it won't be me. I won't lose my shirt on this. Especially the actors. Especially the American.

Ugo murmurs: What about him?

Baldo brings the cigarette to his lips, chews the filter for a second in thought and spits it out. We don't know anything about where he's from. If he has family. What if he's, I don't know, the son of an international lawyer, a million-dollar trust fund? What if he's *someone*?

He isn't.

You don't know that.

They found him at some acting school. He isn't anybody.

What if he is? Eh? Baldo points the lit end of the cigarette like a laser. What if something happens to him and it's our fault?

Ugo sniffs.

You know he's been hanging around with the actress, Baldo will say. If she gets him into the same kind of trouble she's been fucking around with, that's international press, right there. It's not the same as one of these Colombians, shit. Even one of

the Italians. Our courts don't let us sue like theirs. American lives are worth something. Real money. Don't tell me you don't agree. If the American is in any danger, Baldo will say in a harsh whisper, then I'm out. I need to know right now that you will do everything you can to keep him insulated from this place.

Baldo will wait for a response.

·   ·   ·

But Ugo will have the same feeling at this moment as he does now, a rage that does not belong to his brain. A thought crawling out of him despite his better judgment, hand over hand from his gut to his mouth, slick with bile, intent on coming. He will look at Baldo the way he looks at Hank, across the darkness. He will be queasy with the thought, but when he speaks, his voice will be slow and sure.

In the lot, he will say it to Baldo with the softness of a genuine question. Then maybe we should care a little bit less about American lives?

In Hank's living room, for now, he holds the feeling in his throat. He can hear the man's footsteps striding down the hallway, out the slamming door. He feels the weight of the reel in his hand like the body of a small, dead thing.

He says: About what you said earlier, Hank.

The reel settles on the spool. He pulls out the film to thread it. He pauses to swallow, to study this new, flashing thing that spans the air.

What you described before, how the movies are all the same—we have a word for it in Italian. I think in English it is *camp*.

Yeah, Hank said. That's the word, you've got it.

It is for the stupid. Ugo feeds the sprocket. His hands are

shaking but his voice is not. It is the thing you use to make them watch. For most filmmakers, that's enough. For most audiences, that's enough. Most audiences are that simple.

On Hank's side of the room, there is a change of temperature, an inaudible frequency set wailing. Ugo can't stop talking.

And see, I need stupid people. He winds the reel. I want them. Even if I didn't, I would have them, because the world is full of them: stupid, violent people who want to watch girls being shot in their heads and men cutting out the eyelids of boys and children tortured—oh, but stylized, giallo, always giallo, so they can stomach it and heckle at it and eat while they watch it in a dark room with their hand on their lover's thigh and never *really* feel it—

He switches the projector on.

These are the ones who will come see my film.

And you're gonna make them *really feel it?* Hank chuckles. Guy, I've seen your movies. You can't do any better. You don't have a better idea in your head.

This film I'm making now is different.

How's it going to be different? Huh? What's the big revelation? What's the *real* way to make a horror movie?

Ugo can feel his heartbeat in the bones of his face. He looks toward Hank, slouching into the shadows on the couch, and he speaks slowly.

What do you think? It will show them what you do to people in this town.

It is too dark to see Hank's expression. The room is quiet, and he does not apologize. He does not stand and scream in Ugo's face. He does not force Ugo to admit that he understood every word he said to the guerilla in the hall. He does not call out a name, and a man with a pistol does not charge through the door to beat Ugo senseless with the grip. All these things

are possible, Ugo knows they are, but none of them happens. Ugo looks at Hank's vague expression in the dark, and thinks about the American actor, and how he will make him die. The answer comes to him in a rush and he holds it there, tight and hot in the fist of his brain.

He has his thumb on the switch, and next to the switch is a dim red light that flares like a pulse.

Ugo, Hank says, pronouncing the name perfectly. Where are you from?

Dust motes swarm in the blue of the projector beam.

Genoa.

It's supposed to be real violent over there right now. Hank smiles. At least the last time someone brought me a newspaper three goddamn months ago, it was. What was it called, the Red Armies? Red Brigades? Some other terrorist groups, communists and nationalists and everything fucking in between, blowing up half of Rome. He chuckles. Those are your people, right? Almost as bad as this shit down here in Colombia, huh?

The screen is full of darkness and names.

So I'm wondering, Ugo—what space have you got to judge? What makes you think you're one to talk about violent people?

Ugo focuses on the movie. When he speaks to the American, he pronounces every word.

Remind me, he says. Where are *you* from?

RICHARD

Ovidio

For the three nights after you film the village-burning scene, you skip the bus home from the river mouth.

Ugo is keeping you on the sidelines all day. There's no explanation of why, no mention of a rewrite or announcement that you've been fired, just a quick gesture with his arm: stand over there, we don't need you. The first few times he does it, the crew tries to keep you occupied: the costumers fuss with your hemlines, someone who's filling in for the makeup and effects team pads a glare-proof foundation over the perpetual sunburn on your forehead. But soon they don't bother. The script supervisor whispers to you: You can probably go for a walk, but don't go far.

So you stay. You watch everything.

You start to overhear the rumors. That Baldo is mad at Ugo because of what happened to Paolo, the effects guy. That Baldo is back at the hotel pouting because Ugo won't cut stunts that the insurance won't cover. That without Baldo there to keep him on track, Ugo has thrown out the whole script.

Whatever happened, no one talks about it, and Paolo doesn't come back from wherever they've sent him.

Ugo arranges extras in a circle with drums and palm fans, makes them do a tribal dance with choreography Ugo made up. Ugo makes an Indian row out to the center of the river and stand upright in his canoe for an hour, pretending he has just spotted something coming downriver. Ugo has Irena sprint down the beach, screaming, pursued by no one. Every shot takes hours for him to get right, and then three days later he shoots it again, this time with the Indians naked instead of in grass skirts, this time in mid-morning light, this time at the beauty hour. It's surreal, watching the movie in parts like this, everything repeated and out of order and strewn out over so many days, the drama flattened by randomness, by how god-damned long it all takes. It's like watching the worst kind of art film, the kind designed to test your endurance. The sun beats down on the part in your hair. Your heels ache from standing, so you crouch. By the end of each day, you feel nauseous and insane and convinced that this is a form of intentional torture. You tell yourself, on your walk back from the river mouth, that tomorrow you just won't come to set. No—that the instant you get back to the hotel, you'll demand your passport back. You'll demand a flight. You won't forget what happened to Paolo, even if everyone else is acting like it never happened. What happened to Paolo will not happen to you.

But every morning, you get back on the boat.

Irena tries to visit with you sometimes, when Ugo's getting establishing shots or has finally allowed you all to get lunch.

It's strange between two of you now, since the night in the lunch tent when you cried into her shoulder, since she broke her promise to help you talk to Ugo. You've felt strange *around* Irena, ever since you saw her climb into Ugo's boat after the village burning scene, since you heard her laughing with him in the dark.

You want to ask her to explain, but Irena chatters, sunny and bright and oblivious. Oh, it's always like this, she tells you, ladling hogao sauce over rice. He's an auteur. This is just how he works. It's how a lot of directors are.

You chew. Has he told *you* what we're doing next?

No—she laughs—he had me go out in the jungle and practice running while he critiqued. He says I'm bad at it. He says I flap my hands like a weirdo.

Why does he make you practice it in the jungle? I thought he was shooting that scene on the beach.

She shrugs. He doesn't want me distracted, I guess.

You exhale as you laugh. That's fucking nuts.

Why?

He doesn't even tell you what the scene is? Do you even know what you're rehearsing for?

Not really, no.

How do you decide how you're going to play it, then? How do you pick your motivation?

She looks at you, puzzled and smiling. I just run. God, you're weird lately.

After a few nights, Irena tries to get you to ride the bus back with the rest of the crew, to sit in one of the back rows with her. You refuse, say you need the walk. You bend down to tie your shoelaces so you won't have to look her in the eye.

But tonight she pauses as she climbs the stairs to the door, gives you a look that you can't avoid or parse: innocent but with something off about it. The little turn at the corner of her mouth, her eyes a little too open and shining black in the dark. Her eyes find you again once she's in her seat, staring through the window as the bus pulls away.

You stand a moment alone at the river mouth after they're gone, trying to decide what the look meant. Then you walk,

listening to your own footsteps, the chewing sound of gravel and the suck of mud.

You remind yourself of the things you know: I have a return ticket in four weeks and it is zipped in the inside pocket of my suitcase, safe. I have a life I can go back to. I can find a way to get my passport back from whoever has it now. I will go home.

But your mind wanders to things it shouldn't: fires and women with eyes like animals, gangrene spreading over a kneecap, a plane surging toward the ground. They're the same things you've been thinking of all day, sidelined on set, your paranoia rising every time Ugo calls for a new take and doesn't ask for you to be in it. There's a question at the back of your mind that you can't shake: Why is Ugo keeping you around? What is Ugo going to do to you?

When you get back to the hotel, you go to the main office first and ask if you can use the telephone. I need to call my girlfriend, you say, and when the woman behind the desk just smiles, you say it again, gripping an invisible receiver to your ear. She stares at you for a long time, and then she shakes her head. No teléfono.

In acting school, your teacher used to freeze you in the middle of scene work, straight onto the stage, and crouch down to whisper questions in your face: How do you feel right now, in this instant? She did it just as your thumbs found the pulse points in Desdemona's throat, as your Willy Loman careened off the stage and the guy in the booth cued the car crash sound. Stop. Now. How do you feel?

Joyful, but in a bizarre way, you'd tell her. Anxious. Hungry. Like something terrible's about to happen, but if I try to guess what it is, it'll make it real.

Usually, though, your emotions were still roiling. You couldn't think of anything to say at all.

Back at your room, you slide the key into the door a tooth at a time. You take in a last mouthful of humid air. You ask yourself a question, and then you step into the room.

· · ·

How do you feel right now?

The lights are all on, three half-dead bulbs simmering. The television is running, too, the rabbit ears aimed so they register a dim Latin soap opera. The picture is bright and corroded by static. The characters have no nostrils and their eyes are faint black under the snowdrift.

And then the door swings open another inch, and you see her: Irena, her feet golden on the bedspread, her tan a gradient fade as it moves up her legs and over the bend in her knees and under the little white shorts she always wears. The mosquito netting is tucked up, and her back leans against the wall, her head just underneath the framed macaw. She is laughing, and that sound is what sends your nerves crawling toward the surface of your skin.

How did you get in here? you say.

She keeps cackling, doubling over, her face buried in her bent knees. You have to watch this, Richard, she says.

You take a step into the room and ease the door closed.

Enrique just told Ymelda that he's her long-lost twin, but if they're brother and sister, that means the matador they *both* slept with is—oh, God, it's too *funny*—

You don't know where to sit. She's in the exact center of the bed.

Irena sighs, collecting herself. Hey, she says. I'm sorry you've had a rough few days. Her eyes are glittering and dark and she's grinning, her lower lip bitten a brighter pink by her upper teeth. I've been thinking about you.

Above her head, the cross-stitched macaw's eye is a stitched black X; not a circle, but an X, like an eye sewn shut.

You sit down on the bed next to her.

· · ·

Here is why Irena came:

To tell you that she's sorry she didn't help you talk to Ugo, a week ago, after you found her in the lot and cried that you were scared. To tell you that she couldn't talk about it before, but she's been conferring with Ugo on her own, and Richard—Richard, I think I've convinced him to do something amazing.

She's convinced him to make Gayle and Richard lovers.

You look at her: the hungry expression like a kid with a birthday cake, her bare feet dirty on your bed.

Irena explains. Since the first draft, Ugo has made Gayle lovers with nearly everyone in the cast—Joe and even a few of the villagers, a mud-orgy scene with most of them, which, in the end, they hadn't been able to properly choreograph. But when you arrived, when Ugo saw the two of you walking on the beach, playing cards in the hotel these last few days, he started to think that maybe he'd found the right partner.

She imitates Ugo's matte-eyed thousand-yard stare, his voice murmuring in Italian around a pantomimed cigarette. Then she translates what he told her: Get to know him tonight, Irena. Keep getting familiar. Tomorrow we shoot a love scene.

· · ·

No matter how it starts, this is how it ends:

Her tongue, slick against the inside of your cheek. Her arms around your neck, skinny ankles crossed on the bed, at the base of your spine. She paws at your shirt buttons. She laughs into your open mouth.

You tell her no, at first. You tell her this is crazy.

She tells you, of course it is. That's why it's fun.

But what you meant is that it shouldn't be this easy: to let her convince you. To forget the mix of nausea and fear that you've been swimming in these past few days and kiss Irena back. To forget Kay so completely as you lean closer to Irena, to say Okay, okay, we can. You do not think of Kay as you hustle out of your underwear. You do not think of her as you dig into Irena and stir, a wide circle and then again, like you could scrape her body out. Kay, every piece of her hair alive in the wind. Kay soaked and blue, opening her eyes to find you in a flare of light.

When you kiss Irena, you do not close your eyes.

Here is something that does not happen:

Guilt finds you, finally, in your sleep. It shakes you, makes you look at what you've done, insists that what you've done is real, that you were the one who did it.

Here is what you dream of:

Irena. Still Irena. The topographic perfection of her body. The pockets of shadow that pool in the crooks of her elbows and the hollow between her breasts. A gentle eddy of hair below the navel. A thin scar arching over the hip. The dream has a distinct temperature: the molten core of a planet, suspended in the airless dark. The hotel room smells like wet carpet and suntan lotion and something else—something melted, melting—and as your eyelids twitch awake, the scent enters your brain without your permission.

Tomorrow:

You wake, an awful current of heat still spreading in you, shimmering. Irena is not there.

You felt guilty, didn't you? You felt guilty, and that's why you pushed her off you, why you said what you said next.

Irena, go back home. I have a girlfriend.

You said it. Didn't you?

I can't do this. It's not fair. Everything that's happened—I just feel so fucked up, and I—

But she smiled. Richard. Richard, listen.

She traced the outer shell of your ear and wet-whispered into it.

I am your girlfriend here.

How did you feel?

However you felt, this is what you did: you swallowed once, an enormous effort. You tried to say it as gently as you could: Please put on your clothes, Irena. It's late.

·   ·   ·

You do shoot the love scene. Three days later.

The movie is shot out of order, but of course you don't know what the real order is. In the final cut, Richard makes love to Gayle a full forty-five minutes before he burns down the village, an entire hour before the climax of the film. No one tells you just how long this scene comes before Richard finds Veronica, before the final showdown at the rival village. You don't know about the showdown. You don't know about anything. No one gives you the context for the love scene.

You are not prepared.

When you ask for a script, Ugo says fuck a script, that the script is what he tells you.

And really, what difference would it make: if you knew Richard's motivations, if you knew why *anyone* does the things they do?

By the time you shoot the love scene, Irena has not spoken to you for three days—not a word since she left your hotel room at 3 a.m., straightening the hems on her white shirt. When you tried to talk to her, she pretended she couldn't hear, shouted a loud joke to Fabi in Italian, or threw her arm around a cameraman and nuzzled close.

On set it was the worst, because Baldo, you were sure, was definitely gone, and Ugo had suddenly ditched all the scene work, decided it was better to feed you individual lines that you couldn't tessellate into a story. Here we are at the edge of the world—cut. Put it on the fire!—cut. Film it! Keep filming!—cut. You felt each line flare in you and then pass, like your emotions were sample licks you could call up from the tape deck, play for four seconds and then switch off, toss another on the reel. You felt Irena on the edges of the shot, shouting scattershot lines to her own cameraman: Richard, they're coming!—cut. Richard, I love you! Don't do this!

At first, you had tried to plan what you'd say to her—I didn't mean it, or About the other night, or I'm sorry, I should have let you stay. You were going to apologize the very next morning, but the silence that Irena threw up between you was total and bizarre. She would not speak to you, but she *smiled*, any chance she got. Her mouth kept moving, throwing out the punch line to a joke in Italian that made everyone roar, but her gaze stayed fixed on yours, straight across the four feet of dusky water between canoes, a look on her face like she'd just found a kitten on the side of the road.

Fabi was in the back of her boat rowing, rioting with laughter. You saw him out of the corner of your eye, dropping the

oar, mumbling Merda, thrusting one arm over the prow to fish it out. It made your heart rate spike, made your mouth open to shout No. You were thinking of the river sharks he told you about, sharp-toothed things in the water.

But then, with one awful throb in your frontal lobe, you began to understand.

Irena kept looking at you with that mix of bemusement and pity. A dragonfly hovered in the air between you, drew a zipping X in the air in front of her face, and you knew the truth and made yourself say it in your head:

Irena is not angry with you; she has no more use for you.

There were never any sharks.

You are not the lead in this movie.

You don't know when you'll leave. You don't know anything. Everyone here has lied to you.

·   ·   ·

The day you shoot the love scene, you ride in the front of the canoe alone.

One of the extras is in the rear, rowing and steering both, and he doesn't manage to dock the boat so much as drive it into position, the keel slamming into the rough mud of the bank. The boat tilts and leans and everyone yells, Whoa, whoa. Your knees are still shaking as you clamber onto the shore, your shoe catching a loose mudslick and sliding you into the splits. You straighten yourself up, look around to see if anyone has noticed.

No one has noticed. Everyone is staring at something moving down the beach.

It is Ugo. He is ten yards away and getting farther, and it takes you a moment to realize that Irena is with him, her elbow

clamped tight in one of his hands. They are twenty yards away, then thirty. She is rigid. She does not look at him, but he stares straight into the side of her face, never breaking stride.

This isn't right. Ugo usually takes his time at the beginning of the day, setting up cameras and testing sight lines through the trees. The two of them stop twenty yards off and right away they're speaking fast, loud, him in Italian, her in meek nods and single syllables. They're too far to hear, but based on what happens in a moment, you'll be able to guess at what they're saying.

Something like: I don't know what the fuck happened between you and the American over these past few days, but today, Irena, you are in love.

Or:

Today, Irena, you fucking talk to him. Today, you *get* him to talk.

When she turns back to face you, her expression is stern and terrified. But then, just like that, it's like a gear turns. She smiles. She waves, just a flicker of her two little fingers, and then the hand drops. It sends a chill over your whole body.

Ugo gestures: Va' laggiù. Irena jogs over to a thick-trunked tree, half the branches hacked off by set dressers to let in more of the light. She looks back to him, and he nods once. She leans against the trunk, settles into what's left of its shade.

You are alone for a moment, watching her: her spine a loose S-curve under the same white shirt. Exhaustion and fear pull over you like a sleeve.

Then Ugo's voice is shouted over a distance, from behind a camera five yards away. What are you waiting for, Richard? Porca puttana. Go fucking get her.

· · ·

What that means, though, you're not sure. Irena described this scene to you in your room, and the best you can remember, Richard is supposed to creep up behind Gayle, to lunge at her from out of frame, and shout *boo* before overcoming her with kisses. You're supposed to keep kissing her through her screams, and her screams are supposed to evaporate into laughter, and then into something else.

Ugo could have changed his mind by now. But Ugo signals you to enter, and you don't pounce, you don't surprise and Irena opens her arms to you like she's expected you all along. She tastes the way she did before, smoked salt and coffee, and she touches you the way she did before, both thumbs pressed to the bulges of bone behind your ears. You can't shake the strangeness of it. Your mouth moves but it's like all the nerve endings in your lips have gone dead. You have one hand on her waist and one forearm leaned against the tree over her head, and the bark is sharp against the thin skin there.

You keep going. Spit wells in the back of your throat and heat stings at the whites of your eyes but you don't stop. This is the important thing: to remember your training, to keep acting through accidents, through pain, to use the pain to add dimension and heft to your performance.

But it shouldn't hurt to kiss someone.

Irena yelps, too: a splinter of bark has slipped into her elbow. She doesn't break character, either—no, it's more like she *relishes* the pain, her hips tilting deeper into you, her tongue finding its way between her lips. You startle. You shy. You keep kissing her, but your mouth moves without intention; your hands still rove over the small of her back, but robotically, like they don't belong to you. A cameraman takes a step forward, and you can hear him breathing. You look up and into the lens,

and realize that it's not a cameraman: it's Teo. He's holding a camera, but he's a part of the scene, too.

Cut. Richard!

I'm sorry.

You do the scene again, but it's worse. You lunge this time, but it feels like she lunges back, your teeth clicking against each other, your sternums colliding, and everyone can see you wince.

Cut!

You receive her kiss like a fist to your mouth.

Cut!

You're shaking; why are you shaking? She can probably feel it in your fingertips, gripping her hipbones, her jaw, the base of her neck.

By the end of the twentieth take, Ugo's face is stone. He keeps his fist at his mouth, the muscles of his jaw knotted tightly behind it. He's standing right where he's been standing all day, behind that distant camera, watching you. You've never had a director who stood during shooting before, the sinews over his knees raised like he's ready to walk straight into the shot and kneel down to scream more directly in your face. You've never shot a movie before, period, besides some short films by pretentious NYU MFAs on their thesis years. Even the MFAs shot mostly in the university theaters where they could control the light grid, could sit in plush chairs in the dim shadow below the lip of the stage.

Irena's whisper is harsh in your ear, the first words she's said to you in days: Don't you get it?

Get what?

What he wants you to do. She grips you around the side of your head and pulls your ear closer to her mouth. He wants you to force me.

You stare at Ugo, the short silhouette pacing and smoking. Irena's fingers are still entwined in your hair.

Stop looking at him. Her voice is urgent. He hates that.

It is too late. Ugo is at your elbow already.

. . .

A revision:

Now, Ugo wants you to act as if you *know* that Teo's character is filming you.

He gestures, aims the lit end of his cigarette at your throat. You understand? Richard's a pervert. He knows his friend is right there, and he wants them to see everything.

Would Richard do that? You ask yourself. But you don't dare ask Ugo, and Ugo, of course, doesn't bother to explain.

He says, When you take her shirt off—he puts his hands on your torso to demonstrate—move her body like this, so you're showing her tits to the camera. He maneuvers you roughly, to show how he wants it done.

You look over at Irena, still leaning against the tree. She is facing away from you like before, her body angled toward the river. She is still, and slivers of light fall between branches and land on the side of her face like a tangle of scars. You wonder if it's method acting. If it is, it's good.

I don't know. You say it aloud despite yourself.

Ugo looks at you. His tongue moves in his mouth, like he's just on the edge of a word. His hands hang at his sides, twitching a bit at the knuckles. You brace yourself for a slap.

Then, he exhales. You feel no relief from it, but you smile like you do. Ugo walks away, rubs the ridge of his eyebrow with the heel of his hand and laughs like he is tired.

He doesn't know? Ugo asks, gesturing toward the crew.

Listen to this, Richard Trent, the *director* of this *film*, doesn't fucking *know* if this is what he wants to do. Scemo.

Ugo seethes.

No, wait, he continues, I'm sorry. Excuse me. This actor. This fucking *actor*, thinks he *has* to know everything.

I didn't say that.

He thinks this is his movie!

I didn't mean—

But you do. Ugo says, turning toward you again. That *is* what you think, isn't it, Richard? Like everyone else on this fucking set. Everyone in this fucking town, with your insurance, your precautions—

The crew starts looking around at each other, feet shifting in the mud.

This is when Ugo takes a step back and smiles. This is when a thought sparks behind his expression, and he pivots to face the crew.

You know what? he says. Go home. All of you. Take the canoes.

Fabi looks up from his Corona to object.

Send a boat back for us at sunset, Ugo says.

Fabi mutters something in good-natured Italian. Ugo screams back in English.

I don't give a shit about the insurance. He spits. Baldo flew back to Italy four fucking days ago. I thought I'd heard the last about the fucking insurance.

Your skin lights up with anxiety.

And don't talk to me about the production schedule, either. You're all professionals. Figure it out.

Fabi tries his limited English: But the cameramen—

Do I look like I can't operate a camera? A shock of sweaty hair has come unglued from Ugo's forehead; dry spit pearls in

the corners of his mouth. He grabs a camera bag from a startled crew member, throws the strap over his shoulder. Fuck, we might not even film this. He laughs. We're going to rehearse. Okay? We're going to rehearse this thing all day if we have to, until he gets it right.

He points at you.

The props and make up crews are halfway down the beach already. Fabi just stands there, staring and looking helpless.

I need to work with Richard, Ugo says, willing himself to be calm. For the rest of the day. I need to work with Richard.

Irena starts to leave, but Ugo stops her. You stay, too.

· · ·

Two birds thrash in the trees. The crew ambles.

Let's go into the jungle, Ugo says. You're too distracted here.

The birds scream and collide and tumble out into the sky over the beach, still mauling each other. Irena's expression is impassive; she walks forward like a string has pulled her. You have to will your feet to move, to follow Ugo in the direction that he's going. You have to. Why won't your body do it?

You're standing still when Ugo leans down and picks up the machete.

You try the ligaments in your jaw. Where—

We need to go where it's quiet. Ugo hacks once through the bush and finds a place between trees where you can walk. He takes another step and has to hack again, mutters, Shit. Shit.

You follow. You keep your eyes on your feet as they push through the mud. You keep walking until the mud recedes, and then you navigate over roots. As you walk, you listen to the crew

gathering up, bending your hearing behind you until you've walked so far that you can't hear anyone anymore. There are no zippers or snapping cases or canoe prows moving through water, no voices whispering questions. Now, there's the shimmering sound of birds and insects and leaves, all of them loudening the farther you walk. It's getting darker as the canopy thickens, a weird brown-yellow darkness like a room with old paper taped over the windows.

Ugo's voice is calm, a little breathless as he hustles. Tell me, Richard—do you read the European news?

You high-step over a tree root, somehow gnarled two feet out of the ground. No.

Have you ever heard of the Red Brigades?

No, I don't think I have.

That's part of my inspiration for my film. He hacks. That's part of why—Irena, tell him, I don't feel like translating.

Irena tiptoes onto a tree stump and springs straight off, eyes glued to the ground. The Red Brigades killed the prime minister, Aldo Moro, a few other hostages. When we rehearsed in Italy, Ugo set up a projector and showed us all these photographs they took of the bodies.

They put the bodies in the trunks of cars, Ugo says. They wrapped them up in the white sheets with the bullet wounds here—he points to his own torso—and here and here and here. Front page of the national newspaper. All that blood.

Ugo sends the machete through the bush again, hits a sapling that disintegrates instantly, releases a smell of rot. The camera over his shoulder jostles.

You swallow. Why did the Red Brigades do that?

To send a message, Ugo says. There's an edge to his voice, a hoarseness like an impending laugh. The government had killed rebels first. It was an act of *justified retaliation*. He hacks

again. Of course the newspapers didn't show those pictures. It's hard to photograph so many dead.

I don't understand.

Easier just an *important* one. A prime minister. That's an image that they'll print. You can't take a picture of a whole system of control.

It sounds like—

Do you know about Italy, Richard? Do you know about the blood in our streets?

I don't.

What about Colombia, do you know what happens here? What's happening here right now?

It's not my—

America. Fine, then, America, tell me you know about American violence, at least.

You pause, trying to come up with something to say. Irena is five yards in front of you, looking out into the trees. Her white shirt looks like a handkerchief blown down a subway tunnel.

Finally, you manage: There are some terrible people, sure.

Do you know what this film is really about?

Ugo stops, turns to face you. His face is furious, in total disagreement with his voice. You stand there, staring, trying to put the two together.

No.

Do you know why I—why *I* wrote it?

No.

He buries two fingers in the cap of muscle above his heart.

This is my film, Ugo says. You play the lead journalist who filmed the footage *within* my film. But you know what?

His glare is unblinking and lands cross-eyed between your eyes like a dart.

That film, that is mine, too.

There is a wildness in Ugo's face. The muscles under his eyes struggle to contain it. The machete is still in his fist.

He sniffs once, gestures toward a bare spot on the rain forest floor. Now, you two, lie down there.

What?

Lie down there and kiss her.

. . .

This is why you do not see the man who comes through the trees:

Because Ugo tells you to kiss each other with your eyes open, and to stare right into each other's eyes as your mouths move.

Because Ugo keeps the machete close, squats down and plants the blade in the ground and braces himself against it. Because Ugo is two feet away from you and giving so many commands.

Arch. Better. Put her on top.

Because you are an American from a state with wide fields and quiet water, and you don't know how to listen for footsteps in the trees.

Because the man who is watching is a trained guerilla operative, fleet on his knees, and has been tracking you for days.

Because Irena tastes like rum and vomit and it's all you can do to kiss her back.

Because you are supposed to be Richard, who does not mind the way she tastes.

Because this is not your body you are in right now. Because Irena is not in her body, either. Gayle is the one who grinds her hips into yours. Richard is the one who feels the pressure

of it, the heat. Their bodies were never yours to do with as you like, not her, not you, not while Ugo is watching.

Because Ugo is watching.

Because Ugo is watching, and he is unzipping his camera bag and about to start filming. But even he cannot see the man coming up behind him, or the Kalashnikov in one of the man's fists, the knife low in the other. Because you are an American and you have not trained yourself to see things moving in the mud, a face streaked in mud, hands coated in mud so that every part of him blends into the trees.

Irena is on top of you, and then suddenly the Kalashnikov is digging into the center of her spine.

You see the fear in her eyes before you see the shape of the man behind her. You don't even notice the knife until it is shining like a necklace at her throat.

PROCURATORE CAPO: Signor Velluto, we have questioned you for fourteen days.

VELLUTO: I'm aware, Signor Procuratore. I'm tired, too.

PROCURATORE CAPO: Then why continue? What's the sense?

VELLUTO: I agree. But you won't let me go that easy.

PROCURATORE CAPO: I mean that *you* could end this. If you would simply produce your actors for the court, you could prove incontrovertibly that they are alive.

VELLUTO: My attorney has submitted the film into evidence. Draw your own conclusions. You will anyway.

PROCURATORE CAPO: The film shows them being murdered, sir. Eaten. You would confess to the court that these are all special effects?

VELLUTO: I would not. No. That would ruin the film, I would not.

PROCURATORE CAPO: Then you would confess to our giudice that you were a documentarian?

VELLUTO: I would ask them to watch the film and draw their own conclusions.

PROCURATORE CAPO: Are you conceding that human lives were lost during the making of your movie, Signor Velluto?

VELLUTO: I would. Of course I would. Aren't they always, in some sense?

PROCURATORE CAPO: We're in a courtroom, Signor Velluto, we don't have time for you to speak in this sort of artistic—

VELLUTO: I've said what you wanted. I've said what you wanted me to say.

PROCURATORE CAPO: You seem tired, signore. Perhaps—

[Wherein Velluto turns to the avvocato and whispers.]

AVVOCATO: Signor Giudice, may we request a recess? My client would like to discuss a deal.

THE ACTOR

Ovidio

In a way, this isn't happening to you.

You're still lying under Irena, and the rebel is behind her, his knife flashing in your eyes. You know this, but your body doesn't; you cannot make it move.

You could say that it's happening to Richard, but that's not true, either. He doesn't react when the rebel repositions his gun and presses it to the white nape of her neck. He doesn't bargain or yelp or swing. He cannot move, either.

This is the kind of terror that blanks a mind and leaves a body empty. This is not happening to you: you are somewhere else watching from the black-green shiver of the trees, not on the ground with your heart in your mouth, certainly not in control.

So let's not tell it that way.

The American actor is the one this is happening to. He is the one whose hands fall off the actress' waist as the rebel forces her onto her knees. The knife at her throat is the brightest thing, flecked in black dirt. It reflects the V of bone under her chin, the tiny press of her tongue inside her jaw as she tries to swallow.

The director throws his machete in the dirt behind him

and raises his palms. The rebel barks a word in Spanish—
Levántate—and the actress staggers to her feet.

The American can't stop looking at the reflection of her jaw
in the knife blade. I was just kissing her, he thinks. I was just
kissing her.

And then the rebel jerks the rifle out from behind the actress and points it straight at the American, and then suddenly
everything is real and so terribly green and he is scuttling back
and up and there is mud smeared up the length of him.

Ponte de rodillas!

The American stands; the rebel screams again.

He dicho ponte de rodillas!

He falls to his knees.

· · ·

Here is something the American actor doesn't know:

The rebel is named Juan Carlos. The rebel has been in the
jungle for less than two weeks and he is still not used to the
maddening way his sweat never dries, or the way the lines
in his palms are always veined black with filth, or anything
else about this place, though the American actor would never
guess. Two weeks ago, this rebel was pretending to be a busi-
nessman in a safe house in Bogotá. Six months before that,
he was a university student who listened to Gang of Four
and read Rosa Luxembourg in his dorm room, who came
home to his mother's house for dinner every Sunday and
told her lies.

Here is something the director doesn't realize yet:

That this is the same man who was at the American proprietor's house, sobbing in the hallway about a girl who had been
killed. That when he left, he slammed the American's front

door, surged down the porch stairs and then paused. Pivoted; listened to his own breath, which was ragged and desperate, like he'd been running. Juan Carlos waited for an instinct to tell him what to do, and then his arm decided. He overhanded his lantern into the American's front door, and watched the glass explode.

The director tries to speak but the rebel is shouting again. The director can pick out some of the rebel's words from his Spanish—*kidnap* and *don't move*—but he can't parse the rest.

The rebel stayed outside the American's house for too long, waiting to see if the fire from his lantern would catch. He was drunk and furious and he wanted to see the house burn, to see smoke rise to the doorknob, the brass clouding with smoke shapes as the fire climbed. He knew exactly how much work it must have taken to get that doorknob there, how much the American must have paid to ship it down from Tarapacá, and he knew exactly where that money came from. It came from their backs, their blood, their women, their hands hauling coca paste into the hulls of planes instead of fighting their war. He'd been shipped down here, too, on cars and shuddering motorboats and on a hike that made his girlfriend cry from the sores on her ankles and feet and the bites that studded her whole body, that made him shout at her to focus, to remember what all this was for, to remember what Andres died for, to pick her gun back up and walk. He'd been shipped down here with his girlfriend with an ideal, and now she and Andres and the ideal were all dead.

The rebel thinks of this as he pulls the actress closer to his body, points the rifle out at the men and starts to back away.

The fire didn't catch. The house didn't burn. He had to find his way back to his camp without a light, six kilometers in the dark, and as he swung the machete through vines he couldn't see, he had time to think, and to get angrier.

He thought about the American proprietor. He thought about the girl he'd been with at the cartel house, his Italian girlfriend, purring in his ear. After the stunt he'd just pulled, he knew the comandantes wouldn't give him the chance to leave camp again, not for days at least. But even then, as he swung his machete so hard he heard his shoulder joint snap, he was already making plans.

The actress tries not to breathe. The way the rebel has the knife pressed against her throat makes it hard to, makes her chin tilt up at an angle that hurts. At first she tries to keep her gaze down, so she can see what the others are doing to help her, but it makes the muscles in her eyes strain and ache. So she lets herself look at the sky, or what little sky there is out here: a scrap of white hatched over by tree branches.

Her brain spins. Her lungs burn, and she doesn't know what to do with her hands. She makes herself take little sips of air through her nose, and when the actress smells the man she realizes: I know him. He was at the cartel house that night, with Hank.

The American actor's mouth hangs open; his breath won't get in any other way. His heart feels like a stone hurled against a salt flat, over and over. The director is to the left and the machete is ten meters behind them both and the rebel is the fourth point of the diamond, the actress pulled tight to his chest. He tries to plot the arrangement of the trees but there are too many of them. There is no opening. There is nowhere he could run.

He is thinking of running anyway, when the director realizes who the rebel is. He is thinking of running when the director begins to speak.

The rebel can't understand a word the director is saying. The

rebel is crying and that was not the plan: he wants to swipe the tears off but he can't let the girl go. The plan was to take her, to ransom her for seven million pesetas, and bribe a pilot to take him to Cuba. Or the plan was to kill her like they'd killed Marina; no, to kill her like they'd killed an M-19 soldier, a sister-in-arms; to kill her because, when he saw her at the cartel house, he knew the American proprietor was fucking her; and that asshole should see how it felt. The plan kept changing, he'd had too much time to think.

For the last week, the comandantes had been keeping Juan Carlos under watch, made him shovel new chuntos, as punishment for leaving camp without permission. They must not have known he went to the American proprietor's house; if they had, it would have been worse for him. If they had, the comandante wouldn't have given him a stiff-jawed lecture about grief and self-control and the importance of the mission. He certainly wouldn't have left him alone to work.

Juan Carlos dug too deep, a grave's depth, farther, until brown water seeped up around his ankles and then his shins. He dug past sundown, through meals, manic, until the children from the camp crept up to the edge of his hole and stared. He'd planned and planned and waited until a moment he could break away, and he was sure, when he found the Italian girl, he would know what to do.

He still doesn't know what to do, not really, and so he presses the knife blade closer to the girl's throat, until he hears the sure sound of her choking on it.

The director speaks in his slowest Italian, in the shortest words he can summon, hoping that the rebel can puzzle it out:

Listen, listen. I know you. I *know* you.

The rebel turns and stares down at a man on his knees.

The director holds his palms out as he speaks, to halt him. You are the one—they killed your girlfriend? You are the one that came to Hank's house? He pauses, searching his memory. The girl, Marina?

Here is something you don't see in a horror movie:

The fear at the center of a violent act. The hurt.

The rebel bites his lip like a child. He lets the lip go and leers, pivots to make sure no one else is watching.

The director's palms are still in the air, two white shapes, like targets. If you think we are with him—he pauses. If you think that because *I* was in Hank's house that night—

The American actor's breath is shaking in his chest. The mud on his face was smeared there by a makeup artist.

We're not his friends, the director says, his voice hitching. We're not a part of what he does. I swear it.

The actress sobs.

So you're going to do the right thing here, the director says, more slowly now. You're going to let us all go.

The rebel drops the knife to his side.

He stares straight at the director. There is something complicated in his face. The gun is still there, pressed to the back of the actress' hip.

There, the director says. Good.

But then the actress jerks forward like she's about to run, and the rebel throws the rifle diagonally across her body like a seat belt and pulls her back in. He presses the rifle hard to her sternum with one hand, uses the other to reach across her body and slash her once, deep, into the flesh just below her elbow crease.

The skin parts, pink. Then the blood streams.

The rebel puts the hand with the knife over her mouth, keeps the knife in his grip to stifle the sound she's making: a keening that is not quite as human as a scream.

The American actor's skin is on fire with that sound. It moves past the skin and fills up his head, his chest. It halves him.

Here is something none of them know:

How long they can bear to stand here, like this, before anyone moves.

We are not meant to stay in moments like these, all that hate hung in the air. It is why we watch horror movies. We want something to leap out and split the dread open, so fast it couldn't be real, its teeth longer than in life, our bodies releasing more blood than any body has. We need it. We need it. Life without it is intolerable.

The rebel closes his eyes. The actress has started to thrash. He is thinking shut up, stay still. Please, just let me think.

He doesn't realize just how long he's taken his eyes off the American actor.

He didn't realize: when the director tossed the machete, he didn't see where it landed.

When he opens his eyes, it's like a swift kick in the brain: the glare on the steel, right there in the mud. He sees the whites of the American actor's knuckles, the American actor's feet moving, his hand sweeping the machete up. Then he looks up and sees his face.

He has never seen a man more scared.

· · ·

The American actor is not you.

You are not the one who swings the machete, hard, into the tendon behind the rebel's knee; the American actor does that. He hears it split with a pop, like a vine breaking, and then the rebel's hands go limp. The rebel drops everything at once, the

rifle, the knife, his grip on the girl. His whole body goes slack, and then he is on the ground.

You could never be the kind of person this American actor is.

Because if you were, why is it so easy to imagine the way the rebel must have felt? The hard punch of the earth as it finds his back. The canopy of leaves, swarming into his sight line like insects. You are all so deep in the jungle that there is almost no sky, just trees, air thick as soup, the howl of invisible birds. If you were the man who struck this man down, why can you feel it so clearly: the snap and the grunt and the wet suck of the mud under you, the rush of bloodless fear as the director appears above you, holding the gun.

The American actor doesn't drop the machete. The grip is covered in filthy medical tape and its texture feels strange in his hand. He watches the director aim the rifle, squinting through the sights like he's focusing a lens. The American actor feels the way we all do, when we are witness to things like this and do nothing: like he is two steps outside of his body, waiting for some signal to come back.

The rebel opens his mouth to speak. The director shoots twice: once into his cheekbone, once into the center of his throat.

.   .   .

The actress has her back to the men when the shots come. She holds her palm over the wound and turns to face the sound.

The actor's heart is made of salt. His tongue is made of salt. This isn't happening, he thinks. This couldn't be happening to him.

But then he hears the director, a high sharp sob and a sniff. His voice is quiet, strangled.

How can we bury him? he says. We can't bury him.

The actor stalls, trying to make his tongue work. Ugo—

The mud is too thick.

What are we—

We don't have a shovel. I—we don't.

Is the director crying? The rifle is still in his hands.

Tears are sticky and half dried on the actress' face. She's stepped closer, within two paces of the body, and stuck herself there, staring and clutching her arm.

Who is he? The actor tries.

The director hardens. I shouldn't tell you that.

The actor looks at the actress. She flinches but says nothing.

His mouth is full of salt, but he tries to talk. Maybe he's—

He's no one. The director is furious. His skin is full of a sudden flush of blood, his voice fully his own again. He's no one, okay? It's better for you, if—

He falters.

I am the director, he says, uncertain. I will take care of this. I—

The actress sobs once. The director looks at her, his face full of a look like jealousy.

. . .

Later, the actor will lie in his hotel room and ask himself questions. Years later, in another room, he will admit to himself what he has done, and that it *was* him who did it. He will try to understand what he did next.

He gets down on his knees. He uses both his hands. He hauls the mud out.

The director says the actor's name, a question.

The actor coughs. What?

The actress says the actor's name, a statement.

We have to try, he says. We can't just leave him here.

The director steps forward. But we can't just bury him, he says.

Why?

The director swallows. Because he's a human being. He's someone to somebody, he must be.

The actor's tongue works without him telling it to: But is he someone anyone will *miss*?

·　·　·

In the film, Richard leaves after midnight and brings a machete.

He goes alone. He walks off the trail, and leaves the electric lamp switched off.

He doesn't know that Gayle is following him with a directional mic, the cameraman Joe tentative and stumbling ten paces behind her. Their lamps are switched off, too. She walks fast. The darkness is like mud and the mud is like darkness. You can just see the gray shape of her shirt ducking under a branch, her boots laced tightly to her ankles and struggling over stumps.

Joe, she whispers, get closer, there's no light back there, but he yells back, Jesus, Gayle, there's no light anywhere. Why are we even—

She stops. Hushes. She points straight ahead.

A thumbprint of firelight is bright in the distance, and Richard's silhouette is haloed by it, standing so still.

Gayle breathes: Look, Richard thinks the girl is still alive. Okay? Veronica. He thinks she's in that hut.

Joe whispers: Then why the fuck is he going there alone? We could *all* help—

The side of her hand scissors through the air behind her and swats him on the shoulder.

Jesus, *Gayle,* he says, but then Gayle hisses back, desperate: It's not a rescue mission anymore, Joe. Not for Richard.

He tries to ask more, but then Gayle is walking fast, and so Joe has to move, too.

The camera bucks as he jogs. The trees convulse. As they get closer to Richard, the fire grows and reddens.

Joe calls after her in a breathless stage whisper: If it's not a rescue mission anymore, then what the fuck are we doing?

Gayle swats a strangler vine out of her way, and it strikes at the camera like a snake.

Gayle, you have to stop right now and tell me what—

But then Gayle stops, claps a hand over her mouth. The camera aims to the place she is staring, through the vertex of two trees: a sagging hut to the left of the flames, mud and leaves and rain forest wood, and Richard standing eerily still, right outside the doorway.

Gayle changes her course and jogs right, stays low, keeps moving.

The camera ducks, too. They circle behind, slowing. They are forty paces behind Richard now, staring straight through the fire and into his back.

Richard is staring straight into the doorway, at a man who has just appeared in it.

Gayle stops, throws an arm like a bar across Joe's chest, and breathes.

Richard still hasn't heard them. They're close enough to see the color of his shirt, a faded plaid red, long-sleeved and too hot for this country. They can only see the tops of his shoulders over the flames, the uneven cut of his hair over his neck. Gayle did it herself just this morning with a pocketknife and canteen

water. There was a quick take of it, one scene before this: she nicked him behind the ear and he spat into his palm, slapped the wound and smiled up at her. This is how you know I trust you, babe.

Is he smiling now? She cannot see his face.

But she can see the Indian who appears in the doorway, now; she can see his face, and she uses it as a mirror. He is stony-eyed and on alert. He reaches both hands to his temples and shrugs his headdress off, supplicant. He keeps eye contact with Richard until the headdress is resting on his belly, and then he lowers his brow in what looks like prayer.

The machete strike comes fast and clean and sudden, Richard's elbow swinging through the firelight.

It is not the same: to strike hard through the neckbone and hear the prop head thump, to strike hard through the knee tendon and know that the snap and the crumple and the blood are all real.

It is not the same: to kill and to kill, to perform and to act.

But it gets down in the cells, still. The things you do. Even when you are pretending. No matter who you do it for. There was never any Richard, or if there was, he has no hands and no mouth. He is the place you put the things you wish you hadn't done. He is a weight that settles as you stand up out of the mud, your knees creaking, the rebel's blood thick under your nails.

You are not Richard, but admit it: you will be the one who does the things in this film. You will step over the body of the Indian you just killed and into the hut. You will see the missing daughter, Veronica, on her sickbed, malarial, the sweat over her breastbone gleaming in the dark.

You are the one who sees the rebel at the edge of the pit you've just dug, the yellows of his eyes and the bleed where his voice once came.

You will grab both of them by the ankles and drag.

The camera doesn't see you do it, either time.

You push the rebel's body down into the hole.

You will haul the girl's body out of the dark and into the firelight.

The rebel keeps his eyes open as the earth comes over them.

The girl twists onto her stomach and finds the strength somehow to stand, to run.

VELLUTO: Signor Procuratore, I'd like to present to you my cast. Alive and well.

PROCURATORE: Thank you, Signor Velluto. Thank you for ending this charade.

VELLUTO: This is Irena Brizzolari, our principal actress. Irena, please wave.

[Whereupon Velluto indicates witness.]

VELLUTO: Teo Avati, actor. Teo?

[Whereupon witness steps forward.]

VELLUTO: And our American, Mr. Adrian White.

RICHARD

Ovidio

In the last week of filming, the village of Ovidio has its first telephone installed.

For reasons you can't fathom, the president of Colombia himself will fly in for the occasion. Trees throughout the jungle have been repurposed as telephone poles, acres of wire arching between the leaves. The men who erected it sleep in the same hotel as you, come out to the meal tent at night to drink and tell stories.

You don't join them. You hear it secondhand: how they camped on felt pallets for months and took turns looking out for prey cats through the night, how they hauled out the elephant gun to show to whole the crew. It's unclear, from the gossip, why the president even wanted a phone all the way down here—whether he thought Ovidio was important somehow, or if someone in his office simply saw a PR opportunity in building it, a distraction from the violence of the cartels. Our noble Colombian countrymen, fearless and bold, venturing into the jungle to connect our nation's wildest reaches with our fair capital! Our grand president, architect of our country's future! An above-the-fold image, the president in a white bow tie, one elbow looped around an Indian's shoulders.

You think of something Ugo said: That's an image they'll print.

You think of Ugo's voice, buckling with the effort of swinging his machete through the bush: It's hard to photograph so many dead.

The telephone will be installed in the hotel's main office. There's really nowhere else it could go. There will be a ceremony, and the president himself will make the first call to say good afternoon to his wife over her lunch in Bogotá. Production has halted for the morning while all the residents of Ovidio pitch in to help clean up for his arrival.

In your hotel room, you lie on your bed with the lights out and watch as a maid in a blue dress squints at a smear on your window. She pokes her thumb against a soaking rag, rubs hard to erase the mark. She doesn't bother to look through the plastic. She doesn't see you there, one arm slung halfway over your eyes, staring at her like a television with the volume turned down lower than you can hear.

When she walks away, a muggy wind pushes the back of her skirt against her body, articulating her shape.

You close your eyes and repeat your own phone number in New York to yourself, over and over again, like a code you can't decipher.

· · ·

In the afternoon, the work is done, and the river guides are ready to row you out to set again. You study the guide's back as he paddles, his shoulder blades shifting like landmasses under the ocean of his blue shirt.

It has been five weeks. You know there can't be much of the film left yet to shoot. You've already shot the arrival of

the crew in the jungle, and the scene where they glimpse the Yanomomö for the first time, splitting open the brains of live monkeys with stone knives, sucking the warm gray matter straight from the skullcap. You've filmed the scene where you, Richard, ordered the cameraman to shoot arrows at the villagers from behind a fence of pikes speared through shrunken heads to simulate a tribal war. You've filmed the scene where you, Richard, ordered the ritual execution of a pregnant woman.

Last week, they took the three of you out at night and shot a confusing scene in total darkness, a hut by a campfire, an Indian dressed up as a kind of shaman that you feel certain his tribe doesn't really have. You killed this man and stomped into his hut, dragged a naked extra out by her ankles into the firelight, and faked being startled when she stood up and ran away. Teo and Irena sprinted in from nowhere, holding cameras and microphones, screaming Richard, what did you do? You stood still, the heat of the fire warming exactly half of you. You didn't answer; no one had told you how to answer. One of the producers mentioned that the extra playing Veronica was only a stand-in; they'd probably recast by the climax.

You were fairly sure you hadn't filmed the climax.

The next day, the props crew built two bodies out of animal bones wrapped in thick cuts of bacon to simulate human muscle. They threw them in a little gully where the rain had washed out the earth under a tree, in front of the exposed root system and whatever animal had made its stinking nest inside it. The extras crouched and ate, jawing at the fat, plunging their wrists deep into body cavities, a cameraman barking at them to do it bigger, exaggerate the movements.

Who are they? you asked Teo, meaning the Indians.

Gayle and Joe, he said, meaning the bodies.

You looked at him.

Retaliation, he said. For what the three of you did to Veronica after you found her in the hut.

What did we do to Veronica?

You'll see.

Did Ugo give you a script? Show it to me.

I can't.

But I don't understand.

What's there to understand, Richard? You die later.

At the end of the final take, the Indians stood up, bloated and dragging their feet. The props crew kicked the bodies into the river. They washed up the next day, the bones sucked clean by nocturnal scavengers.

· · ·

You do not allow yourself to think: *That was what happened to the rebel, after we put him in the ground.*

You do not touch the tendon at the back of your knee at night, as you try to will yourself to sleep.

They have not filmed the scene where Richard Trent is killed.

They shot the deaths out of order; first the bodies were eaten, then the bodies were murdered, and you still haven't shot the scene that instigated the revenge. Joe was beheaded and castrated in a long handheld shot, with a few short lengths of thin rubber hose to fake the sinews in his genitals. Gayle was gang-raped and bludgeoned with rocks.

It was Irena's best work; you watched it from the beach. You were far off, but you could see her lips part and wince as the natives hoisted her up by her elbows. You could see her chin fall to her chest under the force of the rock, and the thick bone

at the top of her spine that appeared when her hair parted and fell over her shoulders.

She went back home to Italy the day after her death scene. They'd rushed it forward in production to send her home as fast as they could. No one on the crew asked why. No one on the crew told you. There is no one next to you on the boat now; there was no one in her hotel room, the last time you looked, the window polished free of her fingerprints, sheets pulled taut over a long shoal of heaped pillows.

Here is something you don't know:

How much silence there will be in this movie. They won't be able to find convincing voice doubles for all of you, and without the ability to reshoot for continuity, they'll go abstract. There will be scenes of Irena, pointing her sound recorder at nothing. There will be scenes of Irena, smiling at you across a campfire, but you won't film these with her.

.   .   .

Here is something else that you don't know:

How to die convincingly on camera.

Your death will not be filmed today, but when it is, you decide to try the Stanislavski method. You will try to locate some part of you that has died, in some small way, before, to summon up some remembered sensation of passing from this world. But you can't think of anything like that. Or, at least, you can't call up a memory you can face. The woman from the props crew will flick pig's blood over you, standing above and out of frame. You will lie staring on your side as the villagers bring their clubs down over your body over and over. The stones are Styrofoam and they will not hurt, but you'll thrash and flinch as if they are crushing the breath out of you. You will keep your eyes open

and trained straight on the camera, lying where you dropped it in the mud after your arm was lopped off by a villager's machete.

You will try to show that last flash of consciousness. After considering all the ways to do it, pacing the beach before the take, you settle on a tremble: localized in the eyelids and along the upper lip. No final breath in the ribs. No gasp. You will die with your eyes open.

Here is something you don't know:

Ugo will decide to cut your last moments in postproduction. In the last scene of the movie, the camera runs out of film just as the shadow of a raised weapon begins to spread along your cheekbone. Your mouth opens, and your scream starts, and then there are a dozen frames of quick black scribbles racing over a cell of solid white.

A voice-over: *I wonder who the real cannibals are.*

Credits.

. . .

But that will be filmed later this afternoon. Ugo has one more take he wants first.

Since what happened when you shot the love scene, he's decided that there isn't enough sex in the film. The audience will already hate the film crew for what they've done, but a rape—a rape will make them want to cheer when they die. A rape will make the film infamous. Or at least that is the reason Ugo gave Fabi after the third time he got sick on set while they filmed a kill shot, the third time he yelled cut suddenly and stormed off into the trees without explanation. You never followed Ugo, but you saw it in his face the next time you shot: the quick wince when the prop gun fired, the terror in his eyes when the prop blood gushed. Everyone thought he was being

overdramatic, the usual Ugo, but you watched the trees for his return. He was pale and shaken and walking slowly. He wiped vomit off his lower lip, and then he got himself together, and stepped out amongst the crew.

He made an announcement: I've made some decisions about the climactic scene.

Richard will do it. He will chase Veronica away from the fire when she runs. She will run all the way to the black river and Joe and Gayle will film it. Richard won't let her get away, and when he catches her it will be too dark to see what he does. The audience will hear it: a quick Gotcha, a splashing thunk, a scream, a zipper. Stay down. A mud squelch. Hey—

Then a quick cut: daylight, the next morning. In the background, the same river, licking at the muddy shoreline. A girl impaled on a pike, stuck ten feet off the ground, the pike run straight from the space between her shoulder blades to the space between her breasts.

Eyes wide with faked terror, Richard will pretend that he is not the one who did this. He will tell the better story: he will stand next to the pike as the camera travels in a wide circle—no wires, no tricks—taking in the perverse arch of her back, the blood dripping off the ends of her hair. Richard will wonder: This must be some kind of hideous Yanomamö sexual rite. How could these savages do such a thing to an American citizen?

Then a close shot of the blood on your shoes.

Ugo won't be the one who films the bloody parts. No one will ask why. He'll get Fabi to supervise these shots while he goes out to get long stills of the river, while he climbs trees and films the flying birds.

It will be Fabi who stands with the naked teenage girl, while the props crew slathers her body with fake blood, Fabi who tells the girl jokes in Italian while the costumers rat up her hair.

The girl is one of the maids, but you don't know this. Her name is Anahi, and Teo has been harassing her every night since he got here, and so she understands Fabi's Italian at least a little when he talks to her, at least laughs into the back of her right hand while the other arm covers her chest. The pike is a actually a log staked to the ground with a back support nailed on top and painted the color of her skin, the tip of the pike puttied onto her chest with some kind of effects magic so it looks like the whole thing's gone straight through her. The stunt is actually agonizing for the girl, her neck and the small of her back craned for half an hour, but she never complains.

She'll use the money Ugo pays her for this scene to bribe the last of the M-19 to take her along when they flee the area, in response to the murder of two compañeros by the cartel. Her father is in this cartel, and he will not look for her, but of course you don't know that.

You will stand in your position, waiting for Fabi to call Action. You'll stare at what you've done: a girl on a pike with her eyes wide open. You'll feel vomit well up in your throat, the planet tipping forward to release it. But you'll make yourself hold it in. You'll make your face contort into an expression that is the opposite of what you feel. You'll tell yourself: I did this.

· · ·

But still: that is later. That is how the scene will end. The rape scene comes first.

You can't rush past this part, however much you want to. The part where Anahi takes off her clothes. The part, now, when Fabi yells, Va'! and she sprints naked through the reeds, quick enough that before you catch up, you can see only her calves flashing through the slatted green and the dark. You know that

the only way to get this scene right is to feel it—the aggression, the brutality, whatever it is that consumes a man as he violates another person like this. You have to admit that all this is in you, somewhere, that there are many monsters secreted deep inside, and acting is simply about giving them an aperture to slip through and show themselves. You have to be devoured by it: to let Richard Trent swallow and digest you, to become a part of *his* skin.

The grass flickers. She runs. Your breath clatters in your ears.

That's it; that's been the problem all along. There has been a thin shell between you and your character until this moment, and you need to crack it apart. One machete swing straight to it. You will let Richard dissolve you from the inside like an acid. You know that acting is a kind of cannibalism, and you indulge in it: you will be eaten, and you will eat your own. You need to find it in you, somehow, to cackle as you lunge at the girl, yanking open your belt buckle already. You need to hold her down at the elbows. You need to push her body deep into the mud as she struggles, until the mud coats you both so thickly that it will harden into a thin shell, later, in the light.

You need to deny yourself any reminders. This has to be real.

You need to convince yourself: that no one will yell Cut. No one will put you back on a plane at the end of this, and that plane will not land in a thunderstorm, the armrests bucking in your grip and lightning creasing the square foot of sky outside your window. You will not haul that same little suitcase through the terminal and then the rain.

If your goal is to become Richard, then you can't make it home alive. If you become Richard, then you can't be Adrian White anymore: a shitty actor in size ten and a half shoes, soaked and slouching toward the taxi line in some other universe.

Adrian White is the one who will sign the contract that says that he will disappear for a full year after the film opens. That he will go by a different name and avoid crowded places where anyone who's seen the movie might recognize him and raise a pointed finger and remark. That in the eyes of the world, he will be the disappeared journalist Richard Trent, whose fateful last assignment is screening now in theaters near you under the title *Jungle Bloodbath*. That in the eyes of the world, he will be dead—until Ugo gives up and announces eleven months later that it was all a hoax.

You will not be the one who opens the door to your old apartment and find Kay gone, and all her things gone, and a note under a paperweight on the kitchen table that says she's paid the rent through the end of the month, this time it was just too much for her, and please don't try to find her again.

You will never see Irena again. The Italian courts will not demand your presence at trial eleven months later, where Ugo Velluto will stand accused of murdering his actors on film in the name of some perverse verisimilitude. You will not glimpse her slouching posture in the witness booth: Irena, her hair washed clean of river mud and gathered tightly at the neck. You will not file into the booth next to her and sit, straight-backed and still, as if the bench were a canoe whose balance you could upset. After an hour of testimony, she will not lean over and whisper, Richard, fucking relax; it was all pretend.

You are Richard.

You will not look at the scar on her forearm, whiter than the rest of her skin and shiny as a beetle.

You are Richard.

You are Richard.

You are Richard.

You will never think of the guerilla you killed again.

You will not dream of black mud falling into a man's open eyes.

Maybe Adrian will try, but you certainly will not search the international news for mentions of a mysterious disappearance of a young Colombian man in the Amazon, and find nothing. Maybe Adrian will wonder, but you will not try to imagine what he was fighting for, or why he was there. This might be Adrian's burden: whoever the hell Adrian becomes after this. But it will not be Richard's. Not yours. You will not scan the news for years for mentions of Colombia, or Brazil, or Peru, wondering which army he belonged to. You will not find more violence than you can process: so many photographs of people disappeared, of guerillas dead on the red marble floors of the Senate, of paramilitaries setting fires to coffee farms, of black American planes stuck like pushpins in white skies.

You will not read about the town of Ovidio, raided by the DEA and Colombian special forces, Hank Vance absconded to parts unknown, but the town still doing a brisk tourism business, especially among American vacationers.

What you did here will not stay with you for the rest of your life.

In an Italian courtroom, eleven months from now, you will not stand next to Irena and Teo on the witness stand and declare, in turn, that it was all fake, that each of you is who you are and you are, in fact, alive.

And you will not buy the tape that proves it otherwise: the tape that you have to give a stranger in a basement apartment in Queens sixty dollars for, and even then, it will be unlabeled, wrapped in brown paper, handed over with a warning: don't tell INTERPOL where you got this.

You will not watch it, because how can you watch a tape of your own death? It is a logical paradox. Your body cannot

sit in an armchair in Woodside when it is also curled on its side on the ground in the jungle three thousand miles away. It's impossible to see when your eyes are so full of blood. The scene is silent beneath the soundtrack, but how could it be? The stones must be so loud, striking at your ribs. The stones must be so loud, striking through the skull, scattering your brain. Your brain can't process what you're watching: the weak tremor across your eyelids, and the hand, someone's hand, a stranger's hand gripped around a rock that is attached to an arm that is joined to a body out of frame with a face you can't remember, no matter how hard you stare into the eye of the TV, some native you did not bother to meet, some Colombian or Brazilian or Huberto or Benyamin or Laura whose name you did not learn, whose face you did not memorize and whose voice you could not understand, whose hand is rising over you, whose mouth is lowering over you, whose teeth are in your brain now—

A cameraman is in the sky somewhere, yelling Roll film, come on, andiamo! He's fine!

Mud is in your mouth. Blood is in your mouth.

Who are you? Your voice says, battling the music. Why are you doing this?

Your voice screams, and you listen.

The VCR whirs, and you listen.

Your skull opens wider.

The cannibal takes a part of you up in his mouth, and then he opens his teeth wide, to show that it is gone.

Author's Note

This is a work of fiction, and its characters and events are the product of my imagination. In its creation, I have drawn inspiration from many histories, memoirs, oral histories and works of fiction about Colombia's drug trade and armed conflicts, US–South American relations and the complexities of filmmaking in this area. I owe a special debt to Ruggero Deodato's amazing film, *Cannibal Holocaust*, and the aftermath of its release, which provided a starting point for my imaginings.

Acknowledgments

I owe my highest gratitude to three women: my extraordinary editor, Kathryn Belden; my tireless and inspiring agent, Jin Auh; and my mentor and teacher, Kathryn Davis, who has read *We Eat Our Own* more times and encouraged me in more ways than anyone else—without all you have given me, this book would not exist.

Thank you to the entire MFA program at Washington University in St. Louis and especially my teachers there: Marshall Klimasewiski, who was the first person to tell me this project could be my first book, and Danielle Dutton, for crucial guidance.

Thank you to Kris Kleindienst, Jarek Steele, and the entire staff of Left Bank Books for friendship, home, support of so many kinds, and creating an irreplaceable space for readers and writers.

Thank you to the many writers in the MFA program who read and offered essential feedback on versions of this book, in addition to their friendship: Ross Rader, Dolly Laninga, Maria Xia and Gwyneth Merner; Catherine Chiodo, Avery Gallinat, Rav Grewal-Kök, Jordan Jacks, Rickey Laurentiis, Ariel Lewis, Katie McGinnis, Caitlyn Tyler, and Phillip B. Williams.

Thank you to J. Robert Lennon and Sarah Shun-Lien Bynum, who read and offered essential critique on the chapters "Andres/El Puño" and "Irena," respectively.

Thank you to Brody Klotzman, for her best guess on how a special effects team would have built an edible prop body in the jungle in the late '70s.

Thank you to the entire team at Scribner, especially David Lamb, for helping me find my title and for essential insight in the book's final stages.

Thank you to the entire team at the Wylie Agency, especially Jessica Friedman.

Thank you to my friends and family, for their love and support.

Thank you to my partner, Chris Bowman, for everything.

About the Author

Kea **Wilson** received her MFA from Washington University in St. Louis, where she lives and works as a bookseller. *We Eat Our Own* is her first novel.